I PROMISE YOU PAIN

CORDON FINN VENGEANCE SERIES Book One

Bart Baker

WARNING: As the title of the book notes, I PROMISE YOU PAIN contains violence. Some of it brutal. The novel has graphic language. It also has sex, some consensual, some not. The story is dark and gritty, bloody, raw, and sometimes shocking. There are trans and gay characters in this novel as well. If any of these things trigger you or are not something you like to read, this is not the book for you.

This is not your daddy's Jack Reacher. Cordon Finn is a different breed, battling his own demons, with his own skill set, and own damaged point of view. Enjoy the ride.

I PROMISE YOU PAIN

THE BRUTAL START

Splatters of blood co-mingle with the sweat that beads up on Cordon's forehead, trickling down from his hairline, pausing in the deep, well-earned crevices before continuing their journey down towards his gray eyes. Blinking blood and perspiration out of his eyes, he uses the sleeve of the white jumpsuit to wipe off his face.

The sweat is his. The blood is not.

Drawing a deep, agitated breath, he tightens the blood-soaked wraps around his bruised knuckles, flexing his thick hands to regain circulation. As he steps towards Innis Parker, Innis' teeth, which dot the concrete floor, crunch under Cordon's feet. Grabbing Innis by the hair and lifting his face to stare into his eyes, Cordon's gaze remains polar, lethal. Blood crisscrosses Innis' face like a trail in a maze, his skin beaten raw, the blood pooling on his shirt in a harsh brownish stain. Bound to the metal chair, intricate knots cutting off the circulation to his wrists and ankles, there is nothing Innis can do.

"I've done this to men with much more to live for than you," Cordon states slowly, his voice harsh and gravelly, his accent thickly Chicago. "It ends one of two ways. I get the information I need, or I cause you so much pain, you beg me to die."

Dragging the protective goggles down over his hooded eyes, any sympathy that Innis might look for in Cordon's gaze is now masked. Not that there was any. Cordon knows what's required. He's done this for years. In many places around the globe. He's good at it. An expert, some would say. As he punches Innis in the head again, Cordon focuses on his goal.

Information. Truth.

Turning Innis' face back towards him, his fist pulls back again. Somewhere deep in Cordon's dulled and battered soul, he despises this; witnessing the 'damned-if-I do, damned-if-I-don't' terror in the eyes of the person upon whom he's inflicting pain. But experience tells Cordon when someone refuses to be forthcoming. Licking his lips, Cordon swings again, jacking Innis' head so hard, Innis passes out.

It's the job.

A job he'd perfected in Afghanistan, extracting information from enemy combatants during the war, where the locals knew him as 'The Mountain'. Cordon's six-foot-four, gnarled and muscled frame, close-cropped hair, and gray eyes terrified villagers every time he appeared, needing to "have a conversation" with a local. When they knew he was in their village, the locals wouldn't say a word; they would just lick their lips as they passed each other. Because it was Cordon's "tell"- licking his thick lips when he was coming to gather information. A tick he had developed to remain focused and stay calm while he inflicted maximum damage in his effort to obtain the information he needed.

Information that often saved many lives...and just as often took one.

Grabbing a bottle of water, Cordon pours it over Innis' head, slapping him back to consciousness.

"Last time, Innis. Where. Is. The. Girl?" Cordon growls.

Looking up defiantly, Innis' right eye swollen completely shut, he mumbles something obscene, adding, "He'll kill me." Innis tries to smile, but it comes off more like a broken grimace.

Cordon's massive fist plows into Innis' face, opening another cut above his eye, rocking Innis' head back as if it's barely connected to his neck. Punching Innis again with a succession of blows, Cordon then lets Innis' face drop as he moves to a nearby duffle bag.

Opening it, Cordon slowly takes out a container of Morton salt. Then a liter bottle of rubbing alcohol. Next, a glass jar with a clear liquid sloshing inside.

And finally, a can of lighter fluid. Lining them up in front of Innis, Cordon selects the canister of salt.

"You know what salt feels like when it gets into a cut? And look at your face, Innis. If I have to, I'll tear that shitty Kid Rock t-shirt off your body and slice you up and down before I pour it all over you," Cordon purrs like a roused tiger.

"If I still don't have what I need, I pour on alcohol. And when your screams subside, I'll ask again, where's the girl? And if I still don't have the answer I need..." Cordon says, picking up the jar of clear liquid, "hydrofluoric acid. Melts skin off the bone. I'll start on your feet, then your hands. Finally, your face. It's not pretty to watch. The smell coming from your melting skin sticks in your nostrils as you die. And if you still manage to have a heartbeat and I don't have the information I want," Cordon licks his lips as his toe taps the can, "Lighter fluid."

Slipping a silver cigarette lighter from his pocket, he holds it up so Innis can see nothing but the lighter, with the insignia of his military battalion from the Afghan war. Flicking back the lid, Cordon snaps a flame to life. It dances in front of Innis' eyes.

"Each one, a horrendous way to die. And for what? To protect who? We can end this right now, Innis."

Cordon squats down in front of Innis, getting right into his face.

"Last chance before you experience unimaginable pain. Tell me where the girl is."

Innis opens his mouth, blood dribbling out.

"That's it. Tell me or you die here and I toss your body into an industrial shredder and no one will ever know what happened to you."

Innis drops his head away from Cordon, spitting blood to the floor. Cordon stands. Deliberately, he picks up the salt container and opens it, dumping a pile slowly into his hand. Carrying it over to Innis, some of the salt slipping through his fingers, Cordon moves to rub it into Innis' face. Innis screams.

"She's dead! Liam Fogerty! He raped and murdered her! It wasn't me!" he garbles out through broken teeth and blood.

"What was your part in this?"

"I helped get rid of her body. We dumped it in the lake," Innis speaks through coughing sobs and streaming of phlegm and blood.

"Where?"

"About four hundred yards off Stateline beach. Last night. Weighed it down with some cinder blocks."

Cordon lets the rest of the salt drain between his fingers before he pulls up his goggles, his gray eyes staring down at Innis in disgust.

"She was twelve," Cordon rumbles.

"I didn't do it! Liam Fogerty. He's going to kill me when he finds out I told you," Innis blubbers, spitting blood as he does.

"He won't get that chance..." Cordon states, his voice even lower in register than usual as he gets into Innis' face one more time.

"If they find your DNA on that girl, kill yourself before I find you again."

"I didn't touch her. Swear...I swear," Innis sobs.

Cordon returns the items to the duffle bag before cutting Innis free from the chair, his body falling to the concrete, where he lies crying. Cordon strides away without another word, unbinding the wrappings around his hands as he continues towards a secluded space on the other side of the compactor at this recycling plant, the noise so loud it makes it impossible to hear anything else. Even human screams.

Digging into the pocket of the coveralls, Cordon extracts a burner phone, punching in a number.

"Says Liam Fogerty raped and murdered the girl," Cordon says slowly, his voice low, stony as an unpaved road, one ear to the phone, his hand over the other to hear. "Body is about four hundred yards off Stateline Beach. They weighed it down. Says all he did was help dispose of the body."

After he hangs up, Cordon takes a moment, gulping down an atypical moment of emotion before stepping to a garment bag that hangs from a piece of twisted metal. A half-dozen-gallon containers of water and a towel sit on the ground. Cordon unzips the blood-stained coveralls, stepping out of them. Military tattoos decorate his thickly muscled body, along with scars and inked affirmations of hope and anger. He picks up the containers of water, one by one, and pours them over his body, the blood and sweat washing off and draining away on the concrete floor. After drying off, he stuffs the towel, goggles, burner phone, and coveralls into the duffle bag on top of everything else inside.

Unzipping the garment bag, he takes out a pair of charcoal slacks and yanks them up over his naked ass. Pulling out a loose shirt, he flips it over his tattooed back and slides his arms in before buttoning it. He runs his hand through his damp hair before slipping into a pair of loafers. Walking out from between the conveyors which carry garbage to the compactors, he jams the duffle bag into the garment bag and tosses them both onto a conveyor line of waste to be recycled, then listens as it's chewed between the metal teeth, glass breaking, bottles crushing. He fishes out a pair of dark sunglasses from the pants and disappears through the complex, as men on forklifts move bundles of compressed plastic and metal from the facility to waiting semis.

Eyeing his bruised knuckles as they wrap around the steering wheel of his Lexus LC 500, Cordon's mind jumps back to Afghanistan, where he received an education in the various methods of information extraction by the most seasoned sociopaths ever to be employed by the American military. They rejoiced when they lured Cordon into their noxious web. Not only because of his imposing size, which intimidated the most unbreakable and belligerent combatants, and those gray eyes that gave away nothing, most especially sympathy, but because he walked in broken and emotionally scarred. He was not only a coldly direct, no-bullshit man of few words, but everyone sensed that something evil had already consumed his soul, allowing him to manage the psychological tonnage of inflicting torture without cracking under the pressure.

This job tore most men to pieces, annihilating their spirit, often their very will to live.

Cordon did not possess enough of those facets walking into the carnage required of him. To his jaded superiors, he was perfect. A soulless, damaged vessel, calloused and efficient. He couldn't be demolished, either physically or spiritually.

And even better, Cordon always accomplished the goal.

Spotting a vanilla Lincoln Navigator on the street behind St. Hyacinth Basilica, Cordon parks behind it and steps from his car. A man climbs from the Lincoln with a groan of middle age. He is a big man, just not as imposing as Cordon. But from the Van Dyke, the shitty leather jacket, and the tattoos that have faded under the graying hair on his forearms, it is not hard to tell what Frank Lonaman does for a living. Frank is a senior detective with the Chicago Police Department. Old school and proud of it. He gives a nod and a "hey" as Cordon moves towards him, greeting each other with a handshake.

Frank smashes a thick, letter-sized manila envelope into Cordon's barreled chest.

"The city of Chicago thanks you," Frank mumbles as he chews a large wad of Nicorette. "And I'm sure so do her parents. At least they can put her to rest."

"I wanted to find her alive," Cordon says.

"I'm sure you saved another little girl from the same fate," Frank adds. "They already recovered her body. Right where you said. We have Fogerty in custody. He's blaming that slug, Innis Parker. Forensics will tell the tale. My guess, they'll both end up on death row. You hungry? I'm starved."

Cordon shakes his head, stuffing the envelope into the pocket of his slacks. "Watching you eat is like watching somebody mop up a fish factory."

"Fuck you, meathead. I like to eat," Frank spits back, pulling out the wad of gum. "Goddamn cigarette gum. Tastes like a shit burger."

Cordon's smirk, as faint as it is, surprises and elates Frank. He rarely sees Cordon crack a smile of any sort.

"Got plans," Cordon says.

"Always so fucking mysterious. Another time," Frank shrugs before he shifts the conversation. "I'm talking to someone about something..." Frank leads, "...something that could use your expertise."

"Not for the city?" Cordon quizzes.

"Not for the city. This is private," Frank replies, as he gives Cordon a wave, stepping back to his Navigator.

"For who? You know how I feel about surprises."

Frank smiles, half-reassuring, half-fucking with Cordon. "Big payday for an easy-peasy gig. Don't even gotta get your knuckles bloody."

Cordon's face remains placid, his eyes flinty, announcing to Frank that he doesn't appreciate being fucked with.

"What, big guy?" Frank chuckles as he climbs into his Lincoln and starts it. "I'm telling you, it sounds like easy money."

Cordon's eyes narrow. Frank can see that Cordon doesn't believe a word he's saying, and he's going to have to sell it.

"No, man, serious as a heart attack, this one just might be. You're gonna have to trust me. I'll call you when things are set up," Frank says, hoping to end things on a lighter note. Something that isn't always easy with Cordon.

Pulling away from the curb, Frank waves, driving off, leaving Cordon standing in the street, watching him go.

Cordon doesn't move, standing eerily still, ruminating. He swallows a deep breath of stale southside air, a mix of urine, garbage, and decay rising from the sweltering pavement.

If there's money involved, there's no such thing as easy, Cordon muses warily as he strides back towards his car and climbs in.

BROKEN TOYS

With shirt and pants neatly folded on a chair, Sam Smith's falsetto mixes with the pleasured moans and groans of epic sex. Laying back on the bed, eyes closed as he growls in ecstasy, Cordon thrusts into the woman whose thin waist his hands nearly wrap completely around. His feet on the bed, knees bent, she straddles him, her body undulating as she rides him rhythmically, their skin clapping together as they fuck. Cordon's hand slips up between her arched breasts, his fingers spreading across to both nipples, while his other hand squeezes her round ass. Her eyes are dark, her nose rhinoplasty thin, and her lips full, giving her a mysterious Mediterranean, explicitly sexual appeal. Her deep auburn hair cascades down to her mid-back as she throws her head back, screaming with frenzied joy. The tautness of the muscles in her arms and legs gives her the appearance of a former college athlete, which compliments Cordon's battered brawn.

As Cordon comes, he grips her hips tightly, his head rocking back. The beautiful woman rides him more furiously, making sure that Cordon's orgasm is powerful and lengthy, causing Cordon's grateful moans to turn into groaning laughter.

"Okay, okay...I give, I give," he chuckles, his hands stopping the rise and fall of her hips, having nothing more to give.

"That feel good?" Natasha asks as she lifts herself up, allowing Cordon to pull out. "That's how much I love you."

"You love me?" Cordon asks.

"I wouldn't say it if I didn't mean it," Natasha whispers as she leans down and bites his erect nipple.

"Oww!" Cordon protests as Natasha continues toying with his nipple between her front teeth as he winces with pained pleasure.

She settles her chin on his chest, giving him a coy smile. "What's life without a little pain?" Natasha asks before climbing off him and standing. She lifts a short, dark purple silk robe that hugs her curves from the bedpost and wraps it around herself.

Cordon can't hide his mixed feelings at her rhetorical question, opting not to answer as he lays back amid the messy sheets and pillows. Pulling the condom off, he tosses it into a trashcan under a vanity next to the bed in the tight apartment bedroom, decorated in soft lavenders and sky blues that clash more than blend, before watching Natasha cross to the bathroom.

Turning to him before she enters, she smiles, flipping up the back of the robe, displaying her heart-shaped buttocks. "I like when you watch my ass," she giggles.

"It's quite an ass," Cordon answers in as sweet a voice as he can muster as she giggles.

He continues watching Natasha as she steps to the toilet. But instead of leaving the seat down and sitting, she puts it up and stands to pee. As she finishes, it's apparent that she shakes off. As she turns, she ties the robe around her, Cordon getting a brief glimpse of her penis. Trotting back to the bed, Natasha climbs on top of Cordon again, looking down with a satisfied smile. Dragging her painted fingernail across his wide chest, her smile grows.

"God, I love your chest," she utters before kissing him across his torso, her tongue leaving wet spots from the Chinese symbol for 'saint' on his right pec, over to the symbol for 'sinner' on the far side of his left pec. "You're perfect," she purrs.

"No," Cordon croaks definitely, uneasy with compliments. "I'm not. But I think you are. You are fucking beautiful."

Losing herself in the grayness of his eyes, a sad smile covers Natasha's face. She allows her finger to trace his thick lips before leaning over and kissing him with voracious need. Their tongues dart in and out of each other's mouths for a moment before Natasha pulls back, tears welling in her eyes.

"You know I'm not, Cord. I'm a broken toy."

"Nothing broken about you," Cordon counters. "To me, you're the most perfect thing I've ever held."

Her tears fall as Natasha cannot help but be moved by the words of the most gorgeous man she's ever been with. Even with the often menacing aura of pain which radiates from Cordon, Natasha cannot remember any man she's met in her life who holds a candle to Cordon's raw sexual allure. Despite Cordon turning himself into a monument, a stone entity that allows no one but a special few to get below the craggy, gnarled surface, Natasha was drawn in by his eyes, until she felt like she was drowning in the warm, gray, churning waters on a stormy day in the Caribbean. She knew she was one of the few lucky souls who'd ever been allowed to dive into that deep ocean and survive the storm surge.

Leaning up and kissing her lips again, loving her taste and the light aroma of Lake and Skye which she dabs between her breasts, Cordon feels himself stirring again. And Natasha smiles brazenly as she feels him growing beneath her. But her smile wanes as she reaches down and takes him in her hand, stroking him.

"I love that you love a girl like me," Natasha begins. "But I have to tell you something."

The wariness in Cordon's eyes amplifies as he unties her robe, revealing her gorgeous breasts. Cordon's mouth goes to one, taking it.

"Cordon, please," Natasha moans, as she pulls up, wanting to look him in the eyes. She takes a moment to calm herself, needing to say something more than she wants him inside her.

"When I get the money, I'm finishing my transition."

Cordon's body tenses as if a current of electricity is shooting through him. He reaches up and pulls Natasha's hair back. He can't take his eyes off her face.

"Don't."

"Cord, I hate the way I am."

"You're beautiful."

She allows that sad smile onto her lips again.

"To *you*. Not to me. I want to look like the woman I feel I am. I told you, I'm tired of being the broken toy."

Cordon can't hide the pain in his eyes. He slides out from under Natasha, sitting up, his back towards her.

"Why can't you understand how beautiful you are?"

She wraps herself around him from behind, kissing his neck.

"I love you like you are," Cordon continues.

"I can't stay something I'm not. What would that say about me?"

"Not even for a man who loves you?"

Natasha slides her body around Cordon until she's sitting on his lap. She kisses him deeply, wanting nothing more than to pull herself into his arms and stay there forever. But Natasha understands there is something unattainable inside Cordon, a piece of his soul so off-limits that even she, no matter how much he loves her, could never break through. She senses that if it ever did open, if she could ever touch it, a crushing pain would engulf everyone and everything around him, twisting whatever he loved until it was unrecognizable collateral damage.

Letting herself go limp, she slides down his body, her hands slowly dropping from his neck to his chest, down to his stomach, her head sliding to his crotch. She kneels on the floor between his thighs, looking up at Cordon. Natasha again allows herself to be washed into his aching eyes.

"If you really loved me, you'd want me to be me. Or this is all we'll ever have..."

As she takes him in her mouth, Cordon stares across the room. Vacant. Disoriented. Slowly, he allows his body to lie back on the bed, forfeiting his control to Natasha as she continues to pleasure him. Cordon closes his eyes tight, his arm dropping across his eyes, blocking out the world.

***

His ringing cell phone wakes Cordon. Sitting up in his own bed, he checks the phone. It's Frank. And it's early.

"Yeah?" Cordon says, answering.

Frank is in his Navigator, stuck in traffic. "You got time to take a drive this morning?"

"Where?"

"You really don't like surprises, do you?" Frank replies.

"Surprises are how you end up dead."

"Trust me on this," Frank requests.

Cordon stands, stretching his long body, his face scrunching up as he answers, "I got a bad feeling about this."

This makes Frank laugh as he lights a cigarette. Frank became acquainted with Cordon not long after Cordon returned to Chicago upon being discharged. There was a debate whether Cordon quit, was asked to leave, or knew too much for the military brass to keep him in the field. While it might be next to impossible to break Cordon Finn if he were ever taken hostage himself, everything he knew, everything he'd done, everything he witnessed, was a liability both militarily and politically. Returning him to civilian life, though hard on Cordon, allowed the government to surveil him, and if necessary, exploit his skills stateside.

Or kill him.

Cordon kept his head down and lived off the money he'd stashed through the dozen years he'd worked for the government. He said nothing to anyone about what he'd done, the abilities he had. Cordon mostly kept to himself. And knowing they consistently followed him, he knew how to elude the agents assigned. They weren't half as skilled as he was.

And there were things that Cordon didn't want them to know.

Though Cordon's talents were more myth than verified, his reputation became lore within the CPD. Frank, who'd grown frustrated with the legal system, finding it more about city politics than justice with each passing year, was one of the first to voice that if what was whispered about this guy living in their city was even half-true, they could use such an asset. Working outside the constraints of the law, Cordon's training and abilities would be invaluable in obtaining time-sensitive information from those unwilling to offer it up conventionally.

As the myth of Cordon Finn mushroomed in the hushed conversations among detectives and the PD brass, Frank took it upon himself to reach out. Even if this guy was nothing but horseshit, at least he'd know and could crush all the bravado chatter like the smoldering butt of a Lucky Strike. Dubious by nature and twenty-plus years on the force, Frank didn't believe most of what he heard about anything, much less this guy. As far as Frank was concerned, most of the stories that were circulated by those who had purportedly worked with Cordon on secret military missions were nothing more than chest-puffing twaddle from assclown liars. While Chicago prided itself on being a brass tack city, too many cops and wannabes wallowed in their own bloated bullshit. For Christ's sake, most of them were Cubs fan. Enough said.

But Frank needed to know. If this Cordon Finn character existed and was even half as qualified as his legend, he could be an invaluable asset, working outside the confines of the system to aid the system with the most acute offenders. It could shave hours, if not days, off of investigations. Funnel this guy some cash from the secret city funds and let him work his magic. If he came back with information, the cops looked good, kept their hands clean, and solved crimes.

Never being that good at surveillance, Frank liked the more direct approach. He got an address, drove to a row of industrial townhomes not far from the water, smoked a Newport to relax, and then knocked on the door.

When Cordon answered, his shoulders filling the doorway, Frank, who was a big man himself, felt physically intimidated. Something that seldom happened to him.

"Can I talk to you?" Frank asked as he flashed his badge, offering no frame of reference as to exactly what he wanted to talk about.

Cordon turned and padded away from the door, saying, "I wondered when one of you guys would show up."

Frank didn't know whether to walk into Cordon's place, but the big guy left him standing at the open door. That was enough of an invitation for Frank. Still, Frank had enough apprehension to make sure the safety was off on his service revolver before closing the door behind him.

Frank got little personal information from Cordon that day; Cordon refused to confirm or deny any of the anecdotes that Frank shared about Cordon's alleged exploits for the military. But he didn't feel that Cordon hated him either. As he left that day, Frank asked, "If I have a situation where your skill set might mean the difference between life and death for someone, can I call you?"

Condon winced, reluctantly nodding.

"Make sure it's necessary," Cordon rumbled.

"I'll never waste your time or your talents," Frank assured him.

That was two years ago and as close as Frank ever got to Cordon. Not for lack of trying on Frank's part. They'd even shared a few meals together. But Cordon didn't just play his cards close to the vest, he kept his cards locked in a vault. Sharing wasn't one of Cordon's aptitudes. Which, for Frank, was perfectly fine. It allowed him to bitch and moan about his job, his wife, and the women he dated on the side, without judgment or interruption. Something he couldn't do with any other person. Frank viewed Cordon's usual muteness as free therapy.

"Meet me at Overflow Coffee in an hour. You get there before me, order me a large coffee, black," Cordon tells Frank before hanging up, tossing the phone on the nightstand, and walking through his open townhouse, which is one vast room in an industrial building. The few pieces of furniture are sleekly modern, but there's also a heavy bag and racks of weights tucked in one corner. There's no television, and noticeably, not another living thing in the apartment. No dog, no cat, no fish. Not even a fern.

Striding into the bathroom, Cordon climbs into the shower, turning on the cold water. He stands under it, huffing out breaths as he lets the frigid spray bring him back to life. He lets it pour over his body until his breathing regulates, gaining control over himself as if showering is just another exercise in self-discipline.

Waiting in front of the coffee shop as Cordon lopes up from where he parked down the block, Frank holds out the tall cup of coffee.

"Black. Like you asked."

As he takes the coffee, Cordon asks again, "You going to tell me where we're going?"

"Jesus, big man, I beg you, have some patience," Frank asks more than states as he moves around to the driver's side of his large SUV and climbs in.

Cordon remains where he is, taking a sip of the coffee. Frank looks at him from the driver's seat, giving Cordon a 'you coming or not' shrug.

"Fuck..." Cordon mumbles under his breath as, against his better sense, he paces to the passenger side and gets in.

Driving north, with views of Lake Michigan popping out between buildings on Cordon's side of the Lincoln, the Red Hot Chili Peppers pound through the vehicle. Knowing he will not get small talk from Cordon, and tired of talking himself, Frank cranks the music to fill the obvious void between them. Frank can't recall a single conversation they've had that's lasted longer than ten minutes. He knows Cordon has a father he vehemently dislikes, but doesn't know why, and a sister he cares for deeply, but Cordon has never shared her name with Frank. Cordon never talks about women, in general, or specifically. He doesn't even like to talk about sports. Which, in Chicago, is a cardinal sin. If you can't talk about the Blackhawks, Bears, or Cubs, as if they are the Father, Son, and Holy Ghost, there has to be something severely wrong with you. Not that Frank would ever say that to Cordon. Not even as a joke.

Though married for twenty-eight years, Frank and his wife lead separate lives, with Frank dating a succession of other women for the past fifteen of those years. He doesn't discuss his affairs at work, too many Catholics among the ranks of detective, but with Cordon, Frank knows any exploits he crows about will never be repeated.

"Met a new girl," Frank says, turning down the stereo. "Thirty-six. Divorced. No kids, thank God. Hot little thing. Works in commercial real estate."

Cordon says nothing as Frank prattles on about the woman and finally ends his monologue by asking, "So, you seeing anyone?"

His gray eyes narrowing to slits, Cordon fumes. "What kind of shit are you getting me involved in, Frank?"

"What? What do you mean?" asks Frank.

"You never ask me about my life."

"Because you never talk about yourself."

"Exactly. Which leads me to believe you're nervous about where you're taking me and what I'm about to get asked to do."

"I was just trying to have a conversation. Jesus H. Christ, I'm tired of hearing myself talk."

"Then you should have left the music up."

"We're friends. At least I consider you a friend. Maybe you don't consider me one, but I do you. There's nothing nefarious going on, man, I was just trying to get a dialogue going. It's what friends do."

Cordon mulls Frank's words for a moment in silence. He knows Frank is correct. And he does like Frank. At least more than most people.

"I'm in the process of getting dumped."

Having witnessed how women respond when Cordon confidently strides in anywhere, Frank is genuinely surprised at this tidbit of personal information. It isn't just Cordon's height or his massive frame, which causes both men and women to turn whenever Cordon is present. But Cordon possesses what Frank could best describe as primal magnetism. Animalistic. Ancient. Raw. Warrior.

"She's dumping you? Holy shit. What the fuck hope is there for the rest of us mere mortals? This bitch must have some balls," Frank responds.

The irony of Frank's words is not lost on Cordon. But he's not sure whether to wince or chuckle.

"Yeah, she does," he replies flatly.

Not catching Cordon's expressionless sarcasm, Frank nods in solidarity. "Sorry, man. You want to talk about it?"

Cordon's hard glare gives Frank a definitive answer, killing this conversation in its crib.

Frank shakes his head, then breaks up laughing. "Fucker," he mutters. "Well, at least I know you're human."

Aware that this is as much back-and-forth as Cordon is capable of, Frank turns the music back up to quell the silence. But as light as he makes it, Frank cannot help but feel a weird compassion for his friend. He presumes that whatever Cordon endured working for the military, or maybe even in his upbringing, the big man next to him defensively prevents anyone from coddling up to his private life.

But Frank couldn't possibly grasp the depth of the reasons. And Cordon is too wise and too wary to allow anyone he cares about to be poisoned by the toxicity of his sins.

Pulling onto Lake Road, private homes are hidden by enormous walls; the trees, full and green, loom over the lawns, as they have for centuries. Cordon can smell the money. It's old, quiet, and well-hidden behind the walls, doors, and alarms. There is very little new money in Lake Forest. While some is tech, some crypto, some sports and entertainment, most of the money here is generational.

Turning down Frank's music, Cordon gives him a sharp look that begs to know what they are doing in this area.

"Told you. Big payday. Hang tight, we got about another half mile," Frank responds, with Dr. Dre rapping in the background.

Cordon remains silent as they pull up to a gated entrance to one of the largest estates right on Lake Michigan. Frank pushes the intercom as Cordon notes the cameras which cover any vehicle entering from four angles: the entire vehicle, the driver and passenger side, and the license plate on the front.

Thorough.

After Frank announces himself, the gates slide open and the Navigator motors to the front of the intimidatingly stately stone house as a sharply dressed Asian man opens the front door and walks directly to Frank's SUV. Frank steps out and shakes his hand, and the two men exchanging greetings. Cordon examines the house, a place so vast, he couldn't tolerate it as a home. Cordon never likes to enter any building where he can't determine at least three possible exits. Even if it means blowing out a wall.

"Cordon, this is Chen. He's head of security," Frank announces as Cordon steps from the Lincoln.

"Head of security for...?" Cordon asks suspiciously, as he shakes Chen's hand, the anchoring of Chen's grip subtly proclaiming that he is an expert in martial arts.

Ignoring Cordon's question, Chen moves towards the front door, saying, "Follow me, please."

Frank follows right behind Chen, while Cordon trails, again taking in the exit routes from the home. Cordon watches as both men disappear inside, the door still open for him, armed security at the entrance. Cordon can see more security men positioned at various vantage points inside the two-story mansion.

Whoever owns this place is famous, sick-wealthy, and/or incredibly paranoid, Cordon reasons, as he crosses the threshold, quickly making a mental note of where every security man is stationed.

Immense. Showy. Echoey. Even in his soft-soled shoes, Cordon's steps reverberate off the marble floors and bounce back off the plastered walls. With a view from the front door all the way through to the backyard, where a thick, tinted, Plexiglas wall separates the expansive property from Lake Michigan, there is a view of the lake. Though Cordon correctly imagines that the wall is not see-through from the other side. The frosty ostentatiousness of this home must exemplify whoever owns this gargantuan palace, Cordon surmises. It's surely the largest home he's ever been inside, and as far as Cordon is concerned, a reason never to get too rich. Living like this is as warm and inviting as residing in the Hermitage Museum in Saint Petersburg, Russia. Grandiose without a drop of hospitality.

As Cordon follows Frank and Chen, he notes the wide stairway leading to the open U-shaped landing on the second floor with a bank of doors that disappear down the walkways on each side. Cordon assumes each is a bedroom, and that each bedroom has at least a partial view of the lake, with the master in the back facing directly east towards the water and the sunrise. There are also two more men on the upstairs landing, making it a team of ten security men in the house, counting Chen.

Chen opens two carved double doors at the end of a short hallway, which leads into another expansive room with a view of the backyard and lake. Sparsely furnished, Cordon recognizes that it's an office as a heavy wood desk sits almost in the middle of the room, allowing a lot of space behind it. There are vases and pieces of art on pedestals circling the periphery, and a credenza chockful of framed photos, which as Cordon steps in, he sees are all of an Asian man with the rich, powerful, and famous.

Behind Cordon, the man at the door shuts it. By his stance, Cordon knows the man is a former police officer, no military training. Cordon can tell if someone was once military, police, or both by the way they stand, often ascertaining which branch of the military they were by how they hold themselves.

Chen walks up next to a well-tailored man wearing a sizeable cross on the outside of his shirt, making sure that, as he stands, the cross displays prominently on his chest. Cordon catches up with Frank as the robust man, well-coiffed with tailored clothes, comes around the desk, extending his hand to Frank with a smile that he believes puts people at ease around him, but for Cordon, does the opposite.

"Good to meet you, Mr. Lonaman. It's a privilege to meet you in person," he says as he shakes Frank's hand heartily.

"You too, Mr. Fu," Frank responds. "It's an honor."

Fu's eyes then travel up to Cordon, almost stepping back to take him in as if he's viewing an architecturally significant building. Fu pulls his hand away from Frank and extends it to Cordon.

"I'm Daniel Fu. Mr. Lonaman recommends you highly, Mr. Finn," Fu squeezes Cordon's hand as best he can, considering Cordon's hand nearly engulfs his.

"Recommends me for...?"

Fu smiles, turning back to Frank.

"I appreciate you keeping your word, Mr. Lonaman. You did not tell Mr. Finn anything about my situation," Fu states, his smile never wavering, which makes Cordon uneasy.

Taking another slight step back to look at Cordon face-to-face, the difference in height does not allow Fu to look Cordon in the eyes. "I asked Mr. Lonaman not to speak to you about my situation. I wanted to discuss this with you face to face, as it is a personal matter. You might be the best man to help me."

As a man who believes surprises are his kryptonite, Cordon's eyes shift to Frank, narrowing harshly. Frank knows immediately that Cordon is pissed, but

Frank needed Fu to know that he is a man of his word or this opportunity could be lost.

"Can we get to the point? Why am I here?"

"There's a specific task that I need handled and I was referred to Detective Lonaman. He spoke avidly of an individual who worked SOG in Afghanistan and other situations around the world, an expert in extraction and information gathering, who was now residing in Chicago and does favors for the city when necessary."

"I don't do favors."

"Wakarimasu," Fu nods with a smile. "You solve problems. Quickly. Quietly. That is necessary in this situation. I appreciate a man who believes the ends justify the means. It's Biblical."

"I don't put faith in a two-thousand-year-old text filled with talking snakes and resurrections, but I know that the ends justifying the means is not Biblical. Old Testament or New. It's Machiavellian," Cordon corrects him, something that Fu is not used to.

This causes Frank to chuckle. Fu does not. He grabs the cross around his neck, squeezing it tightly as he grows serious, moving to the credenza with the photos, selecting one. He hands it to Cordon. There is a boy in a keikogi, a glowing smile on his face as he wears a first-place medal around his neck.

"My son. Lucas. When he won the National Goju-Ryu Under-12 championship," Fu begins. "But a few years ago, when he turned thirteen, everything about him shifted dramatically."

Fu opens a drawer on the credenza and pulls out another picture. This one unframed, hidden from sight. He hands it to Cordon. The boy in the photo is a few years older, hair longer, tips frosted blonde. He's colorfully and femininely dressed, wearing eye shadow, mascara, and lip gloss.

"You can see the style of dress and makeup. They're obvious. But worse, his behavior...he changed. I first believed he did these things just to hurt me. Teenagers. They rebel. His mother babied him, coddled his whims. All I could do was pray for him," Fu confesses as he nods to Chen.

Chen retrieves an iPad from Fu's desk and punches something up. Chen hands the iPad to Fu, who then hands it to Cordon.

"This photo of my son was taken recently."

Cordon's eyes hold on the iPad. Lucas' back is to the camera. He's only wearing sheer dark hose and red heels, his head craned to face the camera. The makeup is now more arch and feminine; red lipstick glistens as Lucas' lips purse into a kiss, deep purple eye shadow, his hair streaked in a 90's girl rocker cut, the pose kittenish, meant to show off his little, round ass.

Cordon remains stoic, but something flashes in his eyes. Something hostile.

"If he were doing this to test me, I could accept it. But he's not. This is my son now. And I cannot accept this."

His eyes staying on the image of Lucas, Cordon asks, "What am I doing here, Mr. Fu?"

Taking the iPad from Cordon, Fu returns it to his desk as he moves around it, standing on the other side. It's all business now for Fu, and he prefers his position of power.

"My son ran away three months ago. I've discovered he's in Palm Springs, living in the home of Wayne Lansing."

"I know who that is," Frank pipes up. "He got rich developing some app. One the gay guys use to get laid."

"If your son is underage, call the police," Cordon offers as his eyes lock on Fu.

Fu sighs deeply, as if something is crushing his ribs.

"No police. I cannot allow this situation to become any more public than it already is, Mr. Finn. Lucas already displays himself and his escapades all over social media."

Again, Fu picks up the iPad and punches something up. He holds it out to Cordon across the desk. Taking it, Cordon eyes the image on the screen. It's a man of 35 or 40 with an odd, tight face of someone addicted to plastic surgery.

"Wayne Lansing," Fu states. "The man who has my son. He keeps a legion of boys and young men at his home in Palm Springs. Go ahead, scroll, Mr. Finn."

Cordon does. Photo after photo of a Mediterranean-style estate in the hills above Palm Springs. Gates, grounds, a large swimming pool, and hot tub facing west, a superb place to take in the sunsets. And in the background of many of the shots, security.

"Mr. Lansing allows these boys to engage in all manners of debauchery, no doubt joining in as well," Fu adds, again signaling Cordon to keep scrolling. "I hired a private investigator who was able to get these pictures of a party at Mr. Lansing's."

The males in the photos are young, many appearing to be underage. Almost all of them are nude or clad in nothing but tiny swimsuits. From the photos, there are also a lot of drugs, drinking, and plenty of sex happening in and around the pool.

Cordon's eyes never blink as he takes in the images one after the other, finally scrolling to a photo of Lucas in Wayne Lansing's arms. Wayne's hand is slipped down the front of the colorful, barely-there swimsuit Lucas wears low on his hips, his lips locked on Lucas'.

"That last one. That's my son. My *underage* son. In the arms of that pedophile. Lucas, or as he calls himself now, Luscious, is trapped. He has never been a strong boy. Brainwashed now and living his life as a 'social media influencer'. Whatever that is," Fu spits out, signaling Cordon to put the iPad down on the desk.

As Cordon does, Fu picks it up and tries to shut it off. But he can't and the image stays. Trying again, Fu frustrates quickly at the image of his son and Lansing, and he smashes the iPad off the desk until it shatters.

Frank reacts, his eyes going to Cordon. Cordon doesn't move, weighing Fu's actions, debating if he was truly enraged or if the tantrum was for effect.

"I'm sorry," Fu apologizes equally dramatically, plopping down in his chair and dropping his head into his hands for a moment before looking up.

Cordon's now sure this is a performance.

"Mr. Lonaman assures me you are the most dangerous man he knows. That is why I want you. I want you to bring my son home," Fu states before his dark eyes go directly to Cordon's. "But not before causing Mr. Lansing immeasurable suffering for his sins."

Taking a deep breath, Cordon's chest expands, making him appear even larger and more threatening, like a male gorilla ready to defend his troop.

"What Mr. Lonaman should have assured you is that I'm wise enough not to get into a battle between two billionaires who could discreetly work out the return of your son."

"Has Mr. Lonaman told you I'm offering a quarter million dollars for Lucas' return?"

Cordon's eyes narrow, the gray growing darker and ominous. He licks his lips, his anger accelerating as he asks, "Why me?" in a tone that suggests he already knows the answer.

Caught off guard not only by the directness of the question but by Cordon's tone, Fu shakes his head. "I am not understanding," Fu questions.

"Why not this guy?" Cordon asks, pointing at Chen. "He's your head of security. Send him. Or hire an ex-cop, P.I., or military badass in Southern California. There are plenty. I can give you names. Anyone of them could grab your boy and give Lansing a quarter-million-dollar ass whipping."

Fu stands. Usually when he does, it gives him more of an appearance of power. But not with Cordon standing across the desk from him, glowering down.

"I'm more comfortable with someone from here. And Chen is my head of security, so I am---"

"Bullshitting me," Cordon cuts off Fu with a growl.

Fu shifts uncomfortably. He takes a long moment, breathing in and out to calm himself before he grimaces.

"You want me to say it?"

Fu looks directly into Cordon's eyes. It's as if all the air has been sucked out of the room. Cordon's body is completely still, waiting for an answer.

"Because I know who you are. You are like my son. A deviant," Fu barks out, his face tight in defiance. But his voice shooting up an octave, gives away his fear.

Frank's eyes widen and he steps up next to Cordon as if he's about to referee a fight. "Whoa! Maybe we all need to take a step back here. Deviant, that's a big word."

Cordon remains motionless, his focus never leaving Fu. Frank doesn't know where to look, his eyes bouncing to Cordon, to Fu, and then to Chen, who steps up next to Fu, ready to take a hit if Cordon comes over the desk.

"What the fuck is going on?" Frank asks. "We all need to chill."

Ignoring Frank and Chen, Fu points at Cordon. "Do you think I would offer you a quarter million dollars without knowing everything about you? I am hiring you because I believe my son will respond to you."

Offended for Cordon, hands in front of him, "No, man, no. Seriously, what the fuck!?"

A wisp of a smile slides onto Cordon's lips as he licks them, this smile harsh and overflowing with cynicism. "Yeah," Cordon rumbles from deep in his gut. "Because when I'm breaking Lansing's legs and dragging your son out by his frosted tips, I'm going to whisper in his ear that it's all good because we both like dick."

Stunned, Frank doesn't know who to look at or what to believe.

Aiming his fury in Frank's direction, Cordon simmers. "You should have vetted this rich prick."

"I'm sorry...I didn't..." Frank stammers, caught off-guard by all the information pouring out. "What the fuck? You're gay?"

Without another word, Cordon strides for the doors to the office, leaving everyone else off-balance.

"Mr. Finn! Please! Do not leave," Fu calls after him.

Cordon doesn't even break stride as he reaches the door, responding as he goes, "Your love for your kid is touching. Maybe he's better off where he is."

Pulling open the door to exit, Cordon comes face-to-face with four security men as they step in, blocking his exit. Turning, Chen steps up behind Cordon.

Cordon smiles again, this time with genuine enjoyment at what's happening, and even more at what's about to happen. He rolls his shoulders and licks his lips as they curl into a psychotic snarl.

"This is where you want this to go? I'm game," announces Cordon.

Panic roiling, Frank steps between everyone, his hands out as if sheer trepidation can keep everyone apart. "Wait! Come on, guys! This is—we can negotiate something. Everybody take a big fucking breath."

Fu sniffs the air as if he's smelled something awful, his face screwing up like that of a Pekingese. "Chen," he says solidly, "take Mr. Lonaman and the men into the foyer. Get Mr. Lonaman something to drink."

"But---" Frank tries to interject, not sure who he's more afraid for, himself or Fu if he's left alone with a pissed-off Cordon.

"All of you! Now! Leave!" Fu demands.

Chen moves to Frank to escort him from the office. Moving past Cordon uncomfortably, Frank grits his teeth.

"Sorry, man, I didn't know none of this," he says to Cordon, who offers nothing back. Frank moves through the four men, and they follow him out, Chen exiting too, pulling the door shut behind him.

Fu circles around the desk again, standing before Cordon. Surprising even Cordon, Fu falls to his knees, clasping his hands over his head.

"I beg your forgiveness. I am not a horrible man. Nor am I a terrible parent. You must understand. My faith is my bedrock. It is who I am. My son has trampled it. Wiped his feet on it. Mocked me. Mocked my faith. My words are not always correct, and I get angry. Please..."

While this mea culpa seems genuine, Cordon still can't shake the feeling that this is all a performance to get him to do Fu's bidding. Cordon says nothing, his eyes cast down on Fu.

"Understand, Mr. Finn, I'd be happy if Lucas stayed in the desert, living whatever life he's chosen. I'm that angry. And embarrassed by him. He has shamed me. Shamed our family."

His eyes burning again with fury, Cordon remains completely still, not responding.

"His mother," Fu continues. "This has made her sick. She's so frightened for him. He's so young. He doesn't understand what he's doing. What's he done to us. She wants him home. She begs me to bring him home. He's just a boy.

Maybe there's still hope for him. Please. Bring him back to his family. We love him."

With tears in his eyes, Fu stares up at Cordon. He recognizes Cordon hasn't moved a muscle other than slowly licking his lips like a hungry wolf.

"And do as much damage as you can to the pervert who is holding him," Fu finishes, wiping the tears from his eyes, still on his knees.

His mind processing, Cordon allows his wrath and disgust to diminish slightly. There are two things Cordon is acutely aware of as he stands over Fu, fighting the urge to put his shoe through Fu's head. The first is that he implicitly doesn't trust Fu. The second is he must get this kid out of that compound in Palm Springs.

***

Waiting just outside the front door, a Newport hanging from his lip, the butts of three others squashed out at his feet, Frank shifts his weight from foot to foot nervously. As the door opens, Frank turns, ready for fists to fly, if necessary, but it's Cordon who strides out, right past him and down the steps, aiming straight for Frank's Navigator.

"What the fuck happened in there?" Frank quizzes as he follows Cordon down the steps.

Both men climb in the SUV, and Frank starts it, spinning it around the courtyard fountain toward the gate. He waits for an answer.

"Jesus H. Christ, Cordon, don't stonewall me. I didn't know what the motherfucker wanted to talk about, not exactly. I just knew there was a big fucking wad of cash involved. And I certainly didn't know about your situation. I mean, how would I know? You're, like, the *last* person I know who I'd ever expect to be, you know," Frank rambles.

"Gay? That the word you're looking for?" Cordon snarls.

"Yeah, gay. I'm not afraid to say it. I don't care. Gay. There, you happy?"

Cordon finally turns to look right at Frank, amused and disappointed at the same time.

"How sure are you that I'm gay?" Cordon asks flatly.

Completely confused, Frank shakes his head. "Then what the fuck are you? I know you're not a lesbian, so which one of those other L...QBGT letter are you?"

Cordon goes coldly silent for a moment before mumbling, "You sound like an idiot," wanting this conversation to end.

As the gate opens and Frank drives out, he again glances at Cordon, who stares straight ahead.

"Whatever you are, how would I know? We've had dinner a few times, but it's not like you dazzle me with conversation. How the fuck did Fu find out about you when I don't even know?" Frank continues. "Not like I give much of a shit, but you could have told me."

"Why would I tell you? You're not someone I want to have sex with," Cordon counters.

"Well, that's good. I mean...wait, is that an insult? Not that I want to have sex with you, either. You look like you'd hurt me. But...what's the matter with me?" Frank groans, not sure he should be insulted, but is. "I'm just saying I don't care what you're doing, who you're doing, or why you're doing 'em. Okay? Now, onto what the fuck just happened in there. You're doing the job?"

Cordon's stillness feels like a positive to Frank.

"I hope to fuck you negotiated a better deal. That cocksucker...sorry, sorry. I'll watch what I say. That prick invaded your privacy. You should get something for that. Hell, I want something for it since I looked like an idiot not knowing you were gay. So, you're going after his kid?"

No response from Cordon.

"How much is the fee?"

Again, Cordon doesn't answer.

Frank smiles. "More than double what he offered?"

A sliver of a smirk falls across Cordon's lips. Frank raises his hand to high-five Cordon, who does not participate. Realizing it's futile, Frank returns his hand to the steering wheel.

"This'll be easy money," Frank assures Cordon.

And though Cordon's face gives away nothing, he knows the opposite to be true. Besides having an itch he couldn't reach when it came to Fu, and the man's despicable feelings for his child, Cordon knows Fu would not have agreed to the exorbitant price he attached to this job unless there was something harder, bigger, more desperate, at stake.

For twenty percent of the fee, Fu is Frank's problem. Frank set this operation in motion and Cordon wants him to remain the middleman, allowing Cordon to focus on grabbing the kid. Cordon is perfectly okay never seeing Fu again.

But once he has the kid, the boy is his problem. Cordon has never kidnapped anyone unless he needed to extract information. This job was a "virgin," a term Cordon's military team used when faced with a new target or new location. The unknown inevitably spawned danger. And instinctively, Cordon sensed that information about this job was being held back. Working for the government and, more specifically, for the military, taught him to expect half the truth. There was never a job where all of the vital information necessary was shared. Plausible denial was more important for the brass than human life.

The epic payday that came with nabbing this kid only made Cordon feel that whatever he wasn't told was not only dangerous but insidious.

As they drive back towards the city, Cordon promises himself that once he's pocketed the money and put Fu and family in his rearview mirror, he intends to break bread with Frank again, only this time to have a detailed pow-wow about how they handle these private ops in the future. Cordon wants no more surprises, especially coming into a situation. Because they always lead to more down the line.

And it was his ass on that line.

BLOOD LINES

Driving his Lexus towards the Lower East Side, Cordon reaches into his pants pocket and pulls out a crumpled photo. Unfolding it, it is the photo of Lucas Fu, in the dark hose, coquettishly posed, blowing a kiss at the camera over his shoulder. Setting it on the passenger seat, Cordon tries to straighten out the folds, his finger running down Lucas' leg to the red heels.

Red heels. Cordon couldn't help but continue to glance at them. As he continued to drive, images popped in and out of his head. A little boy. Wearing nothing but his tighty-whities, scampering from the alcove where he slept on a mattress on the floor of a trashy apartment. There are articles of clothing, men's and women's strewn across the living room. The little boy finds red heels shoved under the coffee table.

Crawling under, the eight-year-old pulls out the heels and sets them up, his feet sliding into the first one, wobbling as he stands tall. Once he has his balance, the little boy's foot slides into the next red heel. With a smile on his face, he sashays across the room, heels clicking. As he spins in the heels, nearly toppling over, he catches himself and clatters across the stained wood floors in the other direction.

"What the fuck are you doing?!"

The little boy hears the voice before he can react. He's yanked off his feet, the heels flying off as he's thrown viscously into a wall. Smashing into it, the little boy slides to the floor, the wind knocked out of him, blood flowing from his nose as tears wash into his eyes. Cowering, he turns to see his father, Nelson, coming at him. Nelson's face is screwed up into a wrinkled, hungover horror show. His bare foot kicks at the boy's side.

"No son of mine is going to be a sissy! I am not raising a little bitch!" Nelson bellows.

A set of hands wrap around Nelson from the back as a woman, her hair tussled around her face, tries to hold him back from the boy. "Stop! Nelson, stop!" Marissa screams, yanking at his t-shirt to pull him away as Nelson's foot connects with the little boy's side again.

A massive man, Nelson elbows his girlfriend off his back as effortlessly as he grabs the boy up again by his neck, strangling him as he holds the eight-year-old off the floor, grotesquely pressing him into the wall.

"You wanna wear women's clothes? I'll peddle your ass on the street and you'll find out what men do to pussies like you!" Nelson barks into his son's face.

Marissa grabs hold of Nelson's arm, twisting herself in front of him. "Stop this! Nelson, stop! Jesus Christ, he's your son!"

"That's right! He's my son! MY son!" he screams at her.

As he gasps for a breath, tears fall from the little boy's eyes. Nelson again smashes his head into the wall.

"You going to cry?! Huh!?"

"Nelson, please, come back to bed. Please..." begs Marissa.

As Marissa tries to tug him away gently, hoping not to enrage him further, Nelson relents, opening his hand and letting the red-faced boy drop back to the floor. He kicks him one more time, making his point.

"I'm not raising a homo," Nelson caws as Marissa pulls him from the boy. Nelson pushes past her and disappears back into the bedroom, allowing Marissa to check on the boy.

"Cordon, honey, don't put on my heels again. He'll kill you," she coos, touching Cordon gently but fearing Nelson too much to offer any real aid.

Marissa picks up the red heels and carries them with her into the bedroom, shutting the door behind her.

His phone ringing snaps Cordon back to reality. Picking it up, he sees AN-NIE. Cordon gulps back a hard breath, his fingers pressing into his eyes before he punches in the call to speaker.

"What's going on?" he asks, as his free hand grabs the photo of Lucas and crumples it.

"Can you come by Dad's?" Annie asks through the phone, a wiry tension in her voice.

Cordon pauses a second, his jaw clenching, knowing when it comes to his father, it's never good.

"Yeah. I'll be there."

Cordon turns off East 83rd onto a side street lined with post-war apartment buildings and small, brick bungalows. He parks and gets out, dropping the photo of Lucas into the street, before walking to an older building and ringing an apartment. The thick glass door buzzes open.

As Cordon steps into the dimly lit apartment, the sound of Family Feud blares from down the hallway. Cordon hugs his younger sister, Annie, whose charmed smile and earthy beauty have been diminished by years of bad choices. Cordon pulls her arms down from around his neck, checking out the bruises on them.

"Dad...had another tantrum," she admits.

Cordon licks his lips, his head shaking.

"It's time we put his ass in a home where they strap him to a bed."

"I promised my mom I wouldn't," Annie replies, eyeing the bruises herself. "I'll tell Aaron I got them down on the dock. I get banged up plenty servicing the boats."

Cordon slips a roll of cash out of his pocket and hands it to Annie. "Here. This should cover things for a few months."

As Annie takes the cash, she grabs Cordon's hand and turns it to reveal his bruised knuckles, her eyes rising to her brother's. Smiling wanly, Cordon touches her face lovingly before pointing down the hallway to the sounds of Family Feud.

"He down there or in the bedroom?"

Annie points to the room at the end of the long hallway before giving her brother another hug. Cordon tromps that way, toward the room at the end.

Stepping in, his eyes can't help but slide to the alcove where he slept on the floor for most of his childhood. Cordon's face hardens, a lump in his throat choking him. The mattress is long since gone, a chair and a dusty side table there now, but for Cordon, it's like visiting the cell in a foreign jail where he was once a hostage.

Slumped into a worn-out recliner is his father, who appears as worn out as the chair. Nelson recognizes the sounds of his son's steps, even over the blaring TV. He sneers over his shoulder at Cordon, Nelson's eyes never leaving the game show on the screen.

"What the fuck are you doing here?" Nelson crows.

"Grab my sister again and---"

"And you'll what? You'll cry, sissy boy?

Nelson laughs so hard that he starts to cough, which turns into a fit of phlegm, turning Nelson's face red, unable to draw a breath.

"I don't need her hovering over me all the goddamn time," Nelson huffs, wiping the spit off his chin.

"If she don't check on you, who will? I'd leave you to rot in your own filth."

Nelson grimaces hard. His eyes, even grayer than Cordon's, are murky, bloodshot, and narrow. Not like a drinker, more like a man who craves a drink and there's nothing in the house.

"Hell, she sleeps here half the time. She tell you that? That piece of shit she married knocks her around. Picked a fucking loser there. Lucky, I don't kick his ass," Nelson offers.

Cordon shakes his head, almost pitying his father. Almost.

"Right, Dad. Let me know when you pull your sorry ass out of that chair."

Fury in his eyes, Nelson wraps his fingers around Cordon's wrist as tightly, but he cannot get his fingers around Cordon's thick arm like he used to.

"I can still make you cry, princess," Nelson laughs harshly, deriding his son. "You can get as big as a mountain, but you'll never be anything but an embarrassing little cocksucker."

As Cordon tries to pull his wrist away, Nelson latches on, still believing he's dominant enough to humiliate his son, his twisted enjoyment captured in a cruel smirk.

Cordon freezes, remembering his face on the hard pavement, his eye almost swollen shut as blood drips from his mouth. Nelson stands over him, his face screwed up with rage.

"Get up! Get up!" Nelson screams at him as the tears in Cordon's eyes keep him from seeing anything but blurred images of all the people screaming, taunting, laughing, and barking advice.

"Goddamn it, get up," he hears his father yap into his ear, yanking him to his feet. Barely into puberty but a large boy, Cordon wobbles until he has his footing, surrounded by a group of men in the middle of the street. A handful of cash is crushed into his hand, and Nelson pops Cordon in the back of the head over and over, screaming, "Stop being a pussy!" until Marissa, again, tries to pull Nelson back while still holding onto Annie's hand, terror in her five-year-old eyes.

Across from Cordon is a young man in his twenties, his shirt off, his taut body muscled, his fists raised, ready to do battle.

"Get your damn hands up!" Nelson demands, kicking his son in the ass which pushes Cordon towards the young man.

"Stop this!" Marissa pleads. "He's a kid!"

But her protests fall on deaf ears as everyone around Cordon and the other fighter cheer. Nelson is ignoring Marissa, focused on the fight.

Cordon wipes the tears from his eyes with his forearms as he wads his fists, ready to get back in the fight, much to the crowd's delight. The young man stalks Cordon, moving in on him quickly with a flurry of punches that again knock Cordon to the concrete.

Nelson's face is immediately in his son's.

"Get up or I'll make you regret the day your mother pushed you out of her overused pussy!" he snarls.

His eyes locking on his father, tears falling, Cordon pleads, "Dad, please...stop!"

Again, Nelson yanks his son up off the hot concrete and plops him back on his feet. He grips Cordon tightly by his neck as Cordon can't help but to sob. Nelson turns to the growing crowd that surrounds them.

"My son's a little cocksucker! Anybody want to take a crack at his pretty, little face? Step up. Come on!"

Disgusted by Nelson's behavior, Marissa turns away, protecting Annie from watching her brother's degradation.

Dragging Cordon over to the young man he's fighting, Nelson gets right in the guy's face. "You got my permission! Beat the shit out of him!" Nelson demands. "Show him how pussies are treated in life! You'll be doing this little bitch a favor."

Shoving his son towards the young man, Cordon's opponent comes up with his fists, readying to swing. But seeing his father's intense enjoyment at his shame, something cracks in Cordon, as if anything good in his soul is squeezed out like dirty water from a rag.

As the other fighter swings at Cordon, Cordon swings faster and connects with the guy's face. Blood shoots all over Cordon from a cut he opens above the other fighter's eye. The fighter's legs quiver. Cordon moves in, swinging as if possessed, wanting to do as much damage as he can.

He pounds the other fighter over and over, until the fighter sinks to his knees, much to the delight of Nelson and the hungry crowd who soak up this violence. Cordon stands over the guy, who can barely hold his bloody face up.

"Jesus Christ, don't be a fucking pussy! Finish the fucker!" Nelson laughs as he grips the money in his hand even tighter.

Cordon comes around with one last brutal blow, sending the guy to the pavement, where his head bounces like an overripe melon, the other fighter unconscious and bleeding.

Ecstatic, Nelson rushes past Cordon to collect the money from those who bet against his son. Cordon staggers through the crowd, his tears mixing with his blood and his sweat. As he turns to leave, he's grabbed by the neck and pulled against Nelson's sweat-stained t-shirt.

"You did it, you little cocksucker. I'm going to make a man out of you yet!" Nelson howls more for everyone's enjoyment than his son's ego.

Balling up his fist again, Cordon comes around with a hard right to Nelson's midsection, doubling over his father as he comes around with a left to Nelson's chin, knocking Nelson on his ass. The cash Nelson collected flutters from his hand.

Nelson's face screws up in frenzied pain. "You fucking bitch! I'll break your ass into pieces," Nelson squawks.

Marissa rushes to Nelson to help him, but he shoves her away, crawling to all fours so he can stand. He yells at Marissa, "What the fuck are you standing around for?! Get the money!"

Doing as ordered, Marissa collects the money off the ground, Annie rushing to help her mother. Nelson spins until he finds Cordon standing at the lip of the crowd. They lock eyes, like two wolves sizing up who will be the alpha. Cordon's face is hard, unflinching as he backs into the crowd until he disappears.

Feeling his father re-grip his fingers around his wrist, Cordon snaps back, easily pulling free from his father.

"Touch Annie again, I'll kill you," Cordon avows with emotionless distance, not willing to waste energy on his father.

As Cordon strides out of the TV room, Nelson battles to his feet. He limps towards the entrance, staring down the hallway, pointing at his son walking away.

"I should have put you out with the garbage when you were nothing but the neighborhood punching bag!" Nelson yells.

Cordon doesn't bother turning back to him. As Nelson continues to bark slurs at Cordon, Cordon moves up to Annie, who comes from the kitchen.

"I don't know why you don't punch him in the face. Like a thousand times," Annie says.

"He's white noise," Cordon replies before adding, "Says you've been sleeping here."

"It's a big surprise I fell for an asshole?"

Touching his sister protectively, Cordon licks his lips, not sure what to say. When he finally opens his mouth to speak, Annie puts her hand on his chest, stopping him.

"I know how to handle Aaron. Truth is, I'm no prize either."

Cordon smiles wanly, brokenhearted. "Part nature, part nurture," he says as he digs into his pocket and pulls out the keys to his apartment.

"I'm flying to the west coast tonight for business. Be gone about a week," he tells her. "Mi casa, su casa."

As Cordon hugs her, Nelson staggers to the door of the TV room, his diatribe being drowned out by the applause from Family Feud.

"Jesus Christ, Dad. Go watch the Feud, will you?" Annie calls to her father.

"Get out! Both of you! I don't need either of you bitches!" Nelson hollers back, his voice cracking, weakened by years of incessant insults.

Shaking her head at the pathetic sight of her father, Annie turns her attention back to her brother. "We are so genetically fucked," she sighs.

Cordon chuckles softly, his thumb running across his sister's chin softly as if he needs to feel her goodness, before kissing her cheek. He stares icily past her at his father once more, feeling nothing but a mix of pity and revulsion before he presses his key into Annie's hand and exits without saying anything more.

Annie's hand wraps around the key as if it's the only thing keeping her afloat in a sea of oily vitriol and fiery sadness, as she lets go with a relieved breath. Looking up, her father is still staring at her from the end of the hall.

"What are you looking at, Dad?" she asks solidly.

Nelson scowls but says nothing. He shuffles back into the TV room, a wounded bear, his body waiting to catch up with his already dead spirit.

Half an hour later, Cordon's Lexus slowly rolls down a residential one-way street lined on both sides with cars. He takes the first parking spot he can find and pulls in. As he gets out and treads back up the block to a narrow, unlit bungalow home, the neighbors across the street share a joint watch on a porch. Cordon bangs on the door until it yanks open and a tall, bare-chested man swings a revolver up into Cordon's face as he stares Cordon almost straight in the eyes.

"Cordon," he says, relieved. "What the fuck are you doing banging on my door this time of night? I work the midnight shift. Annie's not here. She got mad about something and is sleeping---"

Cordon's hand juts forward, grabbing Aaron by the throat, slamming him into the door.

"You beat up my sister?" Cordon snaps. "That why she's sleeping over at my dad's?"

Aaron jams the barrel of the revolver up under Cordon's chin as the neighbors across the street come off their porch and down to the sidewalk to get a better view of the action.

"What happens between me and Annie is our business. Not yours," Aaron responds. "Now get your fucking hand off me or I'll blow your head off."

Cordon lets go of Aaron's throat, allowing Aaron to relax slightly, falling back on his heels. But as he does, Cordon jackhammers him in the face, grabbing the gun and twisting Aaron's hand until he releases it, driving Aaron back into a wall inside the house.

Turning to the neighbors, Cordon growls, "Show's over, get the fuck out of here." He kicks the door shut before putting a fist into Aaron's nose, spinning him around, and shoving him into the other wall, holding Aaron on his tiptoes, with his forearm across Aaron's windpipe.

"Listen to me, you knucklefuck, piece of shit. You and Annie fall in love, that's your business. You hurt her, that's mine."

Cordon releases him, swiftly grabbing Aaron by the back of the neck and smashing him face-first into the slender hall table, sending everything on it flying.

"You ever treat my sister less than a queen, there will be blood. Lots and lots of blood," he warns.

Cordon cracks Aaron in the back of the head with the gun before snapping open the chamber, letting the bullets bounce to the floor, and then dropping the gun.

"I know you know what I am and what I can do," Cordon states.

"You're a fucking faggot, that's what I know," Aaron chortles, wincing.

"Who can kill you a dozen different ways, each with their own unique but unbearable pain," Cordon replies, throwing Aaron to the floor. "Now clean up this mess."

Cordon opens the door to leave. As he does, Aaron's hand quickly grabs the revolver and fires at Cordon. The gun just clicks as Cordon's foot slams down onto Aaron's hand, causing Aaron to scream, releasing the revolver.

"I made sure there wasn't a bullet in the chamber, knucklefuck."

Cordon kicks the gun back into the darkness and walks out, shutting the door behind him. As the neighbors see him coming down the walk, they rush back into their porch.

"Night," Cordon nods in their direction, continuing down the block toward his car.

***

Standing in the hallway outside Natasha's apartment door, Cordon knocks. He waits, hearing nothing for a moment, then knocks again.

"Just leave the food at the door! Thanks..." Natasha calls from the other side of the door.

"It's me. Cordon."

There's silence for a moment. "Oh..." Natasha nervously answers from inside her apartment. "Hang on one second..."

After a moment, Natasha answers, holding her tiny robe closed around her.

"Hi," she says surprised, standing in the doorway, which is only half open. "Why didn't you call?"

"I did," Cordon responds. "It went to voicemail."

"Oh...right. I have my phone on Do Not Disturb."

Behind Natasha, a half-dressed man crosses the apartment quickly, catching Cordon's eye. Natasha glances at the man and then steps out into the hallway with Cordon, shame on her face.

"Sorry. I didn't know you were coming by. You know I work."

"I didn't mean to bother you," he says, handing her a letter-sized envelope. "I want you to be happy, Natasha."

Looking in the envelope, she finds it stuffed with cash. As her mouth falls open, her eyes go to Cordon.

"Should be enough for you to finish what you want to get done."

Natasha shakes her head, unable to form words for a moment.

"Cordon... but...what about you? What about what you want?"

"When it comes to happiness, pick your own."

She opens her mouth to respond, but Cordon cuts her off by repeating, "Pick your own."

The apartment door swings open behind Natasha, her client slipping out and rushing towards the stairwell with an "excuse me" to Cordon.

Natasha feels caught, her feelings for Cordon and her sense of self tangle into a knot. Cordon recognizes that his generosity, while not unwelcomed, is ill-timed.

Kissing Natasha on the cheek, he steps back, not wanting to prolong his exit.

As he turns to go, Natasha finds the words she's been searching for. "This is the end of us...isn't it?"

The pitiful look set in Cordon's eyes gives her the answer. Natasha bursts into tears, holding the envelope filled with cash to her stomach.

"I love you, Cordon. I want you to love me...after..."

Leaning in, he kisses her on the lips. The kiss blossoms with intensity and passion. Cordon accepts that this will be the last time he ever kisses her lips, and he's not willing to hide his desire for her. She reaches out to pull him into the apartment, but to stop his heart from aching, Cordon pulls away. He steps backward down the hallway, his eyes never leaving her as he goes. At the door to the stairwell, he gives Natasha one last wave.

DRY HEAT

Cordon sleeps all the way to Los Angeles. There's a Mercedes convertible waiting for him, with the concierge at the AC Hotel near the airport, for his drive to Palm Springs.

Top down, Cordon enjoys the heat of the afternoon as he puts Los Angeles in his rearview mirror. And though there's more traffic than he would like on the 10 Freeway, it was worse just leaving the airport and getting to the 10. Chicago traffic is bad, but it doesn't hold a candle to what the drivers of Los Angeles face daily.

The desert appeals to Cordon. There's a sense of unpredictability, a placidity that hides a hostile environment. For Cordon, it's a level he can relate to as there is still something untamed about the desert, even as built up as it's become from Los Angeles to Palm Springs. Cordon feels that the afternoon shadows only enhance its capriciousness as storm clouds build near the mountains. It's seldom that Cordon feels free, but driving through the desert, even on the freeway, offers him a bit of solace.

But about five miles from where Cordon gets off the 10 freeway and onto the 111, which leads him into Palm Springs, the traffic slows to a crawl, then a stop.

At this time of the morning? Cordon muses, looking at the trail of taillights ahead of him and then at his phone for the time. 3:48 am. "What the hell," he says to himself as he inches up to another convertible with four twenty-some-things in the car. With their dance music pounding out into the night sky, Cordon looks over at the guy in the passenger seat.

"What's with all the traffic?" he shouts over the music.

The four guys trade looks, laughing, as the guy in the passenger seat eyes Cordon like a medium-rare T-Bone. "It's Pride, sweetheart."

"It's what?" Cordon quizzes, confused.

"Pride Week...gay pride."

"You gotta be kidding me..." Cordon mutters, his words not heard over the dance music. He immediately knows that he's going to have to realign his plan of operation in a town packed to the gills with gay men. Realizing that, while this changes everything, it could offer Cordon an advantage. More anonymity. As he wraps his fingers around the steering wheel over and over and licks his lips while recalibrating his plans, the young guy in the car next to him waves to get his attention.

As Cordon turns, the young guy smiles, and all the young men in the convertible peer in Cordon's direction.

"Just so you know," the young guy purrs at Cordon, "my legs automatically go into the air and my Andrew Christians fall right off for a muscle daddy!" The young man swings his legs up into the air in the front seat and spreads them to the delight of his cackling friends. All but the driver follow suit, throwing their legs in the air for Cordon.

Cordon can't help but grin awkwardly. *Gonna be an interesting few days*, he speculates silently, realizing these guys will be right next to him for the next couple of miles, so he might as well make the best of it.

An hour and a half later, Cordon turns down the long drive of the Ritz Carlton, as the western sky glows with the first hint of daybreak. Parking in front, Cordon hands the valet the keys before pulling out his suitcase and shoulder bag from the small backseat and walking into the hotel. Once in his suite, Cordon reaches into the shoulder bag and pulls out a large manila envelope, dumping the contents on the bed: a copy of Lucas' birth certificate, Lucas' school I.D., drone photos of the Lansing's estate which give Cordon an idea of the layout, a certified letter which states Fu has hired Cordon to collect his underage son and bring him home, two burner phones, a credit card and twenty thousand dollars in cash. Cordon collects the cash and slides it into a secret pocket in the shoulder bag before slipping the credit card into his wallet. Picking up one of the burner phones, he makes a call.

"Hey Frank. It's me... What? The view?" Cordon moves over to the window and pulls the curtain back. He has a view right down the front drive leading up to the hotel. "I prefer poolside, but I'm not on vacation... Frank, shut the fuck up about the view. I don't care. Did you get a number for Fu's P.I.?"

Grabbing a pen off the desk, Cordon scribbles down the number on a pad.

"Thanks," Cordon says then listens as Frank speaks on the other end of the line. "My plan...? Find the kid, grab the kid, get home with the kid."

Cordon pulls off his shirt, falling on the bed next to the contents of the manila envelope. "I need to get a few hours of shuteye before I start my recon. Call me if anything comes up," he adds, sliding out of his pants and laying them on the end of the bed neatly.

Cordon hangs up, tossing the phone next to the pillows. Opening his suitcase, he digs under his clothes, extracting a .45. Settling it right next to him, Cordon lays his arm over his eyes, taking deep breaths, allowing his body to calm, his mind drifting.

***

The light behind him brightly outlining his ominous frame, Cordon steps into the building in his dress uniform. As the door closes, the serene décor and large table with fresh flowers gives away that he's in a funeral home. Spotting the viewing room he needs to find, Cordon walks toward it. Even from the distance, he can see Marissa in the open casket. As Cordon is about to step into the room, Nelson spots him and quickly stops Cordon in the hallway just outside the room.

"Came all this way to pay your respects, war hero?" Nelson remarks, reaching into his jacket pocket, sliding out a flask and taking a drink.

"We're not at war," Cordon responds, looking past his father, spotting Annie, now in her early twenties, in her black dress, talking to mourners up near the casket.

Nelson holds his flask out to his son, but Cordon waves it away.

"If we're not at war, what are you still doing over there?" Nelson asks.

Cordon remains silent, not willing to talk about anything he does with his father, much less what he does for the military. This only pisses off Nelson, who quickly swings another gulp of the whiskey, leveling a cold smirk at his son.

"Sissy boy is now a badass. Who'd believe it? At least you gave me one reason not to be embarrassed by you," Nelson grumbles.

Annie spies Cordon trapped by their father, so she smiles in his direction, rolling her eyes. Cordon smiles back as he says, "Good to hear, Dad," pushing around Nelson to get to his sister.

Grasping his son's arm, Nelson stops him again. Cordon's body tenses. His gray eyes burn into his father.

"My wife is dead. I want you to have a drink with me," demands Nelson, shoving the flask into his son's chest and holding it there.

Looking down at the flask, Cordon smiles at his father, a smile that Nelson can't figure out.

"It's a surprise that it took you this long to kill Marissa. But she was a stronger person than my mom."

"Your mother was fucking crazy. That's why she killed herself. Had nothing to do with me," Nelson spits out.

"Tell yourself whatever lies you need to get you through your shitty life, Dad," Cordon sniffs, done with this conversation. "I didn't come back here for you," he adds, stepping around his father.

Maneuvering through the small crowd to Annie, Cordon engulfs her in his embrace, letting her cry into his chest as Nelson watches from the lobby, squeezing his flask as if he'd like to crush it.

***

Cordon's eyes pop open. Glancing at his phone, he realizes he's slept for a few hours. Though it was hardly restful, it means he won't fall back asleep. Pulling himself from the bed, Cordon ambles into the bathroom and turns on the shower. One thing he always enjoys is being a stranger. Anonymity equals freedom. Even though his size causes him to stand out regardless, no one knowing anything about him allows Cordon some comfort. He can relax, something that doesn't come natural to him.

He can be the person he wants, which happens so rarely for Cordon, he's not even sure who that person is.

Walking down Palm Canyon amid the throng of Pride Week partiers, young guys part like the Red Sea as Cordon strolls through, all either staring or glancing as he passes. Clad in a t-shirt and jeans, even among the many bodybuilders and gym rats, Cordon commands attention. The tattoos up his thick forearms only exaggerate his overt, iconic sexuality with this crowd. A flamboyant young man rushes up to Cordon and sidles next to him, snapping a selfie with him. Cordon laughs, but then leans over to the young twenty-something and whispers, "Delete that pic, man," in his ear. Looking up into Cordon's eyes, the young man realizes Cordon is coldly serious and does as requested. Cordon gives him a smile just before nodding at a club doorman who isn't about to stop a guy Cordon's size from passing into the club, sensing that this is not someone he wants to hassle.

Allowing his eyes to adapt to the dim, purple haze, and his ears to adjust to the thumping music engulfing the dance floor, Cordon pushes through the fetish club, packed well beyond the P.S. Fire Marshall's wishes with partiers. Cordon weaves around the hands continuing to reach out and touch his body, something not uncommon in clubs but still foreign to Cordon, who avoids clubs in Chicago. On his way to the bar, a half-dozen shirtless men, many of them large and muscled, wearing leather harnesses or vests, lean up to Cordon, speaking in his ear. He smiles but shakes his head, continuing to the bar.

Working this end of the bar, Luka, the bartender-slash-model-slash escort, who is nearly as tall as Cordon, wearing only a leather jockstrap and chaps, gives Cordon the up-and-down as Cordon shoulders his way to the front. Luka's angular handsomeness and gym body keep his tip jar overflowing. And Luka knows how to make a big tipper feel he's got a chance. Or, if not a chance, that Luka has a price.

Which he does.

And while Cordon isn't Luka's type, guys his size or bigger intimidate Luka because he likes to be in charge, it's insulting to Luka being overlooked by any man. But Cordon doesn't notice Luka; his gaze is locked on a group of trans women, each one more beautiful than the next at the apex of the bar. Hair and makeup done. Tight dresses showing off their gorgeous curves. Realizing he's licking his lips, Cordon turns away, signaling Luka.

"Jack. Double," Cordon says as Luka leans over the bar to hear him and Cordon places a twenty in front of him. Luka nods, pouring Cordon a generous double of whiskey.

As Cordon downs it, Luka holds up the bottle and nods toward Cordon's glass. Cordon takes out a wad of cash, peeling off another twenty, and sets it on the bar. Luka pours again and Cordon downs it just as quickly, letting the heat of the whiskey rush down his throat into his belly. Waving off another drink, Luka pours Cordon another double.

"On me," Luka announces, vying for Cordon's attention, Luka's accent vaguely Eastern European tempered by too many years in California.

Feeling obligated, Cordon downs his third double, his head immediately getting foggy from the whiskey that burns in his belly, which slashes Cordon's natural distance and inhibitions. He smiles, nodding at Luka, pulling out the large wad of cash again and tipping Luka before turning toward the gorgeous trans women at the far end of the bar. As Luka moves closer to the group of women refreshing their drinks, one woman notes Cordon's attention. She gives him an unabashed smile, slipping off her seat at the bar as she says something to her girlfriends, and then sashays through the crowd until she's next to Cordon.

"It's hard not to notice a man your size staring," Sonya states flatly, her accent softer but also Easter European.

"I am?" he retorts.

"A man like you can't hide."

"Can I get you a drink...?" Cordon asks, leaving the question open, trying to get her name.

"A drink?" Sonya laughs. "That's not what I want from a big man."

Sticking her fingernail into Cordon's chest, Sonya bites her lower lip flirtatiously. "You know, I have a sixth sense about men."

"You do?"

"I do. I know what they want without them saying a single word."

"That is a gift," Cordon jokes, the liquor allowing him a genuine smile.

"I'm a gifted woman. I can sense who is good for me. And who is not," Sonya adds.

"Interesting. What's my vibe?" Cordon asks, his buzz killing any of his natural reservations. He is far more lighthearted than he ever would be without it.

"Your vibe is telling me you are going to leave here."

"It is?" Cordon smiles, playing along. "What if I don't want to leave?"

"You are going to leave here and walk down three businesses to the Rose Club. The back rooms," she says, taking his hand and placing something inside. She holds his hand closed. "If it doesn't fit, don't bother joining me."

As Sonya walks away, heading for the exit of the club, Cordon opens his hand wide enough to see what she placed in it. An extra-large condom. He closes his fingers around it and turns, seeing that Luka is watching him with a sly, almost puerile grin, nodding.

With his better judgment impaired, Cordon licks his lips as he struts through the bar, ignoring everyone trying to get his attention, and exits through a side exit door.

Slipping through the curtains into the back rooms of the Rose Club, the sounds of sex, some sensual, others rougher, lap over each other in a cacophony of groans and moans. Cordon's wide shoulders barely fit the narrow hallway and now tipsy, he sways just enough for his shoulder to bump the walls on both sides. Down near the end of the hallway, Sonya waits with a leer. She glides into a room, disappearing as Cordon follows her into the tight room.

Their lips lock. Cordon is drunk enough to want this badly, needing to replace the memories of Natasha. He reaches down and slides up Sonya's short dress. Feeling her cock, he strokes her as his other hand grasps the top of her dress and pulls it down, revealing her large man-made breasts. His mouth goes to them needily.

"You like?" Sonya says.

A growling laugh lifts from her cleavage as he smiles. "I like," he says, spinning her around so she's facing the wall. Cordon unhooks his pants and pulls them down, biting open the condom and unfurling it over his hard penis, the tightness of the condom only turning him on more. Sonya lubricates herself, and Cordon slowly works himself into her as Sonya grips the door knob, Cordon's size taking her breath away.

As he rides her hard, one hand on her breasts, the other on her penis, his face buried into her neck, the barrel of the gun slams into Cordon's temple, making his already unsteady stance even more so.

"Stupid, stupid, piece of shit tourist," a fetish-masked gunman snaps, as Cordon pushes away from Sonya. He quickly yanks his underwear up, as Sonya pulls her dress down and covers her breasts.

Cordon faces the gunman, whose eyes and height he immediately recognizes as the bartender. Luka holds a .38 up to Cordon's face. "Big man thinks he can nail whoever he wants, wherever he wants. This shit costs, man. Give me that wad of cash you were flashing around."

Too slow to respond, Luka taps the barrel of the gun off the middle of Cordon's forehead. "Come on, come on!" he barks, his accent getting thicker the faster he speaks.

Sobering immediately, Cordon slips the roll of money from his pocket. Sonya's eyes widen.

"You are an extra-large..." she murmurs, grabbing for the cash.

Cordon holds the cash over his head, out of her reach. Pissed, Luka jams the barrel of the gun under Cordon's chin, getting right in his face. "Bad fucking move, cowboy. I'll fuck you with this gun. Now hand her the money!"

Cordon slowly drops his hand toward Sonya, and she reaches for the wad of bills. As she wraps her hand around it, Luka's eyes glance in that direction. At that moment, Cordon swings his knee up into Luka's side as the back of Cordon's hand sharply slaps the gun from under his chin. Luka falls into Sonya as Cordon punches Luka in the face three times quickly before wresting the gun from Luka's hand. He grabs the latex mask and yanks it off Luka's head before punching Luka again in the face, breaking his nose and splitting his lip.

Sonya screams, blood spraying across her, as Cordon shoves them against the wall, his forearm going into Luka's neck.

"My dress! Fuck! This is silk!" she caws.

Luka gives Cordon a blood-covered smile. "I call my friends, we hunt you down. We take turns on you."

"You're not my type," Cordon responds, cracking Luka across the jaw, knocking him unconscious.

Fighting back his self-loathing fury, Cordon steps back, letting him slump to the floor.

"His *face*. Shit! That's how he makes his money! You fucking dick!"

Cordon peels off five one-hundred-dollar bills from the roll of cash, letting them flutter down on top of the unconscious Luka. "Get his nose set," Cordon says before pushing his way out of the sex stall.

Sonya quickly bends over and grabs the cash off Luka and stuffs it down between her cleavage. Then she shakes Luka back to reality, helping him to his feet. "We have to get you to the hospital," she whines, "and get this blood out of my dress."

Cordon is furious with himself for getting buzzed and allowing his craving for touch, for sex, to draw him into something so obvious. Any other time, he would have caught the vibe between the bartender and the woman. He would not have walked down to a sex club and stumbled into the back, wanting to get laid. Angry, he balls up his fist, storming down the sidewalk, a frigid scowl cemented on his face. The thick crowd of partiers witnessing this large man blowing down the block, clear out of his way as if they are witnessing a growing tsunami rolling towards shore. *I should have never come out. What was I thinking?* He doesn't make mistakes like this. And now he's worried that too many people have noticed him. Even more so than usual.

Other than the gym, where there is often another guy that rivals Cordon in size and muscularity, people notice him. Since puberty, when he sprouted up six painful inches between twelve and thirteen, and another three the next year, people see Cordon. He doesn't want the attention. Hasn't earned it. It is always just there. But Cordon knows he could have avoided this idiotic clusterfuck. And should have.

"What's wrong with me?" Cordon grumbles to himself as he passes a large group of young partiers. A baby-faced partier passing by, as Cordon mumbles, turns towards Cordon, yelling loudly, "You're fucking hot, that's what's wrong with you!", snapping Cordon out of this negative head space. As the young men fall all over themselves laughing, Cordon doesn't break stride. He needs to escape the crowds, the young partiers' laughter echoing in his head.

Cordon turns and stares at the group of young guys, obviously all friends, celebrating Pride together, which startles them. Cordon knows being as big as he is, his presence can intimidate. He's made a career out of it. As they hightail it down the block, Cordon glances around.

Everywhere he looks, there are groups of guys, groups of women, same-sex couples holding hands, kissing, most are playful, filled with the joyous freedom that comes with being in Palm Springs during Pride. Stopping in his tracks at the corner, Cordon absorbs the crowd he is in the midst of. But instead of soaking in their festive liberty, what he sees aches his soul.

This should have been him. It could have been, if he hadn't had it beaten out of him at such an early age. If his mother hadn't given up and taken her life. If his father had an ounce of humanity. If he had anyone who supported him, instead of filling Cordon with oppressive deposits of worthlessness, maybe he would have stood a chance. But that never happened. He never found the savior he needed. So he transformed into a calloused, wounded goliath, a ruthless monstrosity of humiliation and pain. He buried any goodness, allowing his self-loathing to rule his soul.

He quickly paws away a rim of tears, his stomach churning from whiskey and longing to belong, longing to be comfortable in his own skin. But even the times he opened himself up to who he was and what he wanted, each time his world caught fire, scarring him with burns that would never heal.

A man like him could never be a man like him.

He knew the words and phrases. Trans-attracted. Transamorous. Tranny-chaser. Tranny-hawk. Ceterosexual. Skoliosexual. Cordon had studied the scientific and not-so-scientific terms, wrestling with them in his head, wishing he wasn't who he was, wishing he wasn't attracted to what he was attracted to. Gynandromorphophilic. That's what he was; that's what turned him on. He craved pre-op trans women who hadn't or wouldn't finish the surgery. Their breasts, their hair, their lips. And their penis.

If he was attracted to a trans woman who had completed her transition, no one would bat an eye because no one would know. Maybe if they found out she used to be a man they would care, but on a macro scale, Cordon believed he wouldn't have to hide. Even if he were with another guy, a big guy like himself, things would enormously less complicated. Society had grown blasé about gay relationships. And those who did have a problem were never brave enough to come at two hulking men.

But being with a woman who hadn't finished her transition, and wanting her to stay like that, seemed to alienate even free-thinkers. Cordon was an enormous man, but he wasn't big enough or strong enough to handle that. And he hadn't met a trans woman who didn't want to complete her transition if she could. Cordon's desire to have them stay that way only seemed to pique their desire to finish their change. His attention to their body parts, especially the ones they wanted gone, only exasperate any self-loathing they had, making him feel guilty and more of a freak.

While Cordon desires them, they crave to be the person they have always wanted to be. There is no reconciling the two.

As he slides into his car and shuts the door, muting the outside noise, he reminds himself that he is in Palm Springs to do a job. To take care of business and get the hell out. Even more than Chicago, there is too much temptation in Palm Springs. Especially this week when the sexual energy of the town is on steroids, figuratively and literally. The amplification is beyond anything Cordon can cope with.

He drives away from the partiers, putting the revelry behind him, and finds a dark street and parks. He knows that in some of the other cars parked up and down this street, there are couples having sex. But Cordon is here to break down where no one can see him. To release, at least for a moment, the deep eddy of pain that he just can't conquer. He steps from his car almost silently and places his hand on the roof, breathing almost metrically. Looking at his reflection in the driver's side window, a darkness overtakes Cordon. Again, he balls up his fist. He tries to reason with himself, but he can't. Closing his eyes tightly, he smashes his fist through the car window, shattering it.

He isn't the man everyone thinks he is.

His greatest, unspoken fear is, he never will be the man he wishes he was.

TRUST COSTS

The morning was bearable, but Cordon knew it wouldn't be later in the day. The sun that broils Palm Springs almost daily can be brutal, allowing the denizens of the city to wander out only after sundown. "It's a dry heat," they tell you. But heat is heat. And 110 is just fucking hot.

After exchanging the car with the smashed window at the rental service, Cordon tools through Palm Springs in a similar Lexus convertible, the top down. He wouldn't think of owning a convertible in Chicago where it could only have the top down half the year, and a soft top is an invitation to steal your car. But in a town like Palm Springs, if you're driving with a modicum of speed, the dry, warm air of the morning, while not refreshing, is a step up from the same temperature congealed with the brutal humidity in the Midwest.

Pulling up to the Tropicale Restaurant, Cordon parks and steps out in slacks and a shirt, pulling on a suit jacket. Again, it's a misjudgment, believing he's keeping things businesslike; all it does is make him stand out more in this land of t-shirts and shorts. Everyone Cordon passes can't help but peek at this well-dressed paragon, wondering who he is, as he strolls across the restaurant patio, finally spotting a tanned woman in her forties, clad in a sleeveless shirt, shorts, and sunglasses. And like everyone else, she can't miss Cordon. Knowing he's the guy she's meeting, giving him a wave.

As he walks toward Jackie Pruitt, she pulls down her sunglasses, giving Cordon the clear once over, smiling.

"Jackie?" Cordon asks as he steps up.

"Jesus, gym much? I didn't know they grew them so big in Chicago."

As he slips into a chair opposite her, Cordon responds, "We get sun and water there too."

"It's Pride Week here. Where's the tight tank top and loose shorts showing off your favorite pair of designer underwear?"

"I didn't get the brochure."

"Clearly," Jackie jokes. "You look like a bouncer that some D-list YouTube starlet has to fuck to get into the club de jour in Hollywood."

Getting the attention of a server, Jackie calls, "Valerie, coffee for my bodyguard."

"Black," Cordon adds as he glances around, realizing almost everyone on the patio is surreptitiously sneaking glances at him. He masks his self-consciousness, wishing he could just fit in somewhere.

"So, you're the P.I. that Fu sent to grab his kid and haul his skinny, flawless ass home?" Jackie quizzes.

"I'm not a P.I."

Jackie sits back in her chair and looks across the table at Cordon. If he could see her eyes behind her dark glasses, he would see the perplexity she's feeling.

"Then what do you do?" Jackie then asks.

"I'm a jack of many trades," Cordon cryptically responds.

"I bet you are. But you're who he sent. And there must be a reason for that," Jackie offers, prying for more information about Cordon.

"It's bad enough I'm sitting here in a suit jacket, thinking I would blend in with the other folks who were up for a morning business meeting. But apparently, those folks don't eat here. Look, I don't really talk about myself. Fu hired me to bring his son home. That's why I'm here. You got onto Lansing's property. I saw your photos from the party. What can you tell me about the property that I don't already know?" Cordon asks as Valerie brings his coffee, Jackie signaling her to fill her coffee as well before she goes.

"I'll say this, I didn't see anybody not having a good time. Lots of sex, drugs, and terrible fucking dance music. I miss good, old-fashioned, rock 'n roll, you know? Anyway, these are all young, some very young, gay men. At Lansing's, they can be themselves and do what young gay, bi, and trans men do. Quite uninhibitedly, I might add. Fu's son was a willing participant in the action. I don't think he's going to go quietly into the night with you."

"I didn't think he would. He ran away for a reason. Meeting his father, it's not hard to understand why," Cordon states.

"Yeah. I get it. He does come off as a cartoon villain. That big cross he wears...I mean, really, we get it, you're religious. He's not without his sympathies, nevertheless, not the warmest and fuzziest man I've ever met. But the checks cleared."

"Good to know," Cordon responds. "Any chance I could get you to drive me up to Lansing's estate and have you help me get a lay of the land?"

"I'm sure a guy like you has laid a lot of land," Jackie responds, grimacing at her quip.

Cordon doesn't react at all.

Jackie sighs. "I suspected I would get pulled into this further. I don't do things gratis."

Cordon pulls off two hundred dollars and sets them on the table. "I'm asking for about an hour of your time."

Jackie waves at the server again. "Hey Valerie, could we have these coffees to go?"

Driving up into the mountains just outside of Palm Springs, with Jackie in the driver's seat, Cordon relaxes slightly. The frenetic pace and over-charged sexual vibe of Palm Springs throughout Pride Week is not what he envisioned, or needed, coming here. Having never been to this city, he'd heard it was laid back and mellow, a retirement town for gays and straights. Lots of golf and tennis. An oasis of green in the middle of the desert. But it wasn't just green now. It was rainbows. Lots of them. And bodies, most shirtless, most taut, muscled, and tanned. The cruisy energy, everyone on alert to get laid, adds a layer of discomfort for Cordon, having vowed to stay focused on the task at hand.

"You're not an easy read," Jackie says out of nowhere as she drives the winding road. Cordon wishes she wouldn't keep glancing at him and keep her eyes ahead. "Can't tell which team you play for."

"My own," Cordon drawls out into a deep growl. "If it's common knowledge that some of the kids at Lansing's are underage, why haven't the cops stepped in?"

"Lansing's no fool. He takes care of any problems with a lump sum payment and a confidentiality agreement."

"To the kids he has sex with, or the police?" Cordon asks.

"Both. This is Southern California. Everything has a price. Especially young ass," Jackie lays out with blasé factuality. "He uses off-duty cops as security and pays them very, very well to keep their mouths shut as well as protect him. He also donates handsomely to local politicians."

Unsurprised, Cordon responds, "Palm Springs is just Chicago with better weather."

Continuing up the winding road that narrows to where oncoming cars would have to wait until the other driver passed, Jackie comes to a stop up against the craggy mountain wall on the passenger side.

"Just so you get an idea of how large his property is, this is where Lansing's property starts," she informs Cordon, who makes a mental note, also noting that you can't see the actual house, which means it is built below the view line from the street.

Jackie slowly winds around the road, climbing the mountain, the property below behind a high metal fence. They drive nearly half a mile before Jackie stops again.

"And this is where it ends," she says.

"Quite a piece of property," Cordon answers.

"Yeah. If you look right back there, you can see just a hint of the roofline of the main house," she tells Cordon as she turns and points.

Cordon can see a small ridge of Spanish tile, again, making a note of where the house is located on the expansive property.

"This gate up here, the only way in and the only way out," adds Jackie.

"Dangerous in a fire."

"Lansing keeps a helicopter on the property. And I'm sure he has a few other ways down the mountain, but from this road, this is it. So, if you're driving in from the road, you'll have to come through here. And if cars are parked on this road, which they are when he has his parties, it's one way only, and people block each other in constantly up here, coming and going. You really have to *want* to come to one of his parties. Maybe that's the old me talking because it doesn't seem to matter to all the boys in Palm Springs, and extending to Los Angeles and San Diego. They show up. There's liquor and drugs and all sorts of other young ass for them to enjoy," she tells him.

"They ever get tired of it?" Cordon dryly asks.

"There are parties going on up here all the time. Especially this week. Invitation only. Not that the invitations aren't spread through social media like a social disease," she says, driving until they are just outside the gate. "This driveway winds down to the estate. It's crazy huge. Tons of bedrooms. Which makes sense since there's a harem of boys that stay here. He's carved out a backyard that goes on forever until it falls off the mountain. Wouldn't be surprised if there's a body or two down there, forever lost. On a clear winter day, you have a perfect view of the snow-capped San Bernardino's from the infinity pool."

A security guard putters up the driveway in a cart and parks at the gate, staring at Jackie and Cordon. Jackie's eyes shift to Cordon as she smiles. "Cameras everywhere. I'm sure they watched us drive the perimeter of the property. Billionaire problems. But can you blame him?"

"Especially with what he's got going on, on the other side of this fence," Cordon nods in agreement. "How did you get in and get those pictures?"

With a smirk, Jackie grabs her breasts. "Gay men admire tits more than straight men."

Cordon can't help but chuckle as Jackie laughs.

"Seriously, it's a thing..." she says as the security guard steps from the cart and moves to the fence.

"Can I help you?" the security guard asks.

"Just doing the sights," Jackie says, throwing her convertible in gear as she swings her car right at the gate, backs out, and spins the car to head back down the mountain.

In the parking lot of the Tropicale Restaurant, Cordon pulls his jacket from the backseat, where he placed it neatly folded, as the brunch crowd turns into the lunch crowd and the sun beats down. He rolls up his sleeves.

"Thanks for the tour," he tells Jackie, as he leans into the open passenger window.

"No problem. There will be parties up there every night this week. But you're not going to muscle your way into that house and throw Lucious over your shoulder and shoot your way out. That may be how you're used to doing things, but it's not going to work up there."

Cordon nods in agreement, arms crossed, now resting on the window.

"And you certainly aren't going to pass as some skinny twink who can twerk his way into a Lansing party."

Again, Cordon says nothing, his mind flipping through his options on how he's going to get onto the property and get Fu's kid out of that fortress.

"No offense, but I am not sure what Fu was thinking, sending a goon like you to pull his kid out of there."

His eyes narrowing until they are slits of gray, Cordon answers, "Makes me wonder too."

"This isn't exactly Fu's wheelhouse. But he picked you for some reason."

Cordon's eyes narrow again.

"You know anything else about any of the other boys living there?" he quizzes Jackie.

Shaking her head, she finds a pack of cigarettes in her bag. Using her lips, she snags one from the pack.

"I'm trying to quit. But..." Jackie says, trailing off as she lights the cigarette. "Most are boys hoping to be famous and believe Lansing and the men he invites to his parties are their ticket. All competing for Insta and TikTok followers. That's why Lansing loves the sleek, shiny, little girly-boys. They all believe they deserve fame and fortune, with no discernable skills except having a tight, fuckable ass. And that includes Lucious."

She takes another drag off the cigarette as she says, "Gimme your phone."

Taking his phone from his pants pocket, he hands it to her.

"This a burner Fu got you or your own? I want yours," she says. "I'm sure it's better than this piece of shit."

Cordon pulls out his iPhone and hands it to her. Jackie quickly punches in her number and calls herself and hangs up when it rings.

"I'll send you anything else I got," she says, handing him back his phone, before adding "Ciao," and driving off.

As she goes, he drops both phones back into his pocket, eyeing the groups of guys rushing to get their names in for a table, a line forming out the door.

Pangs of longing strike Cordon again. He needs to get out of there, his mind locking on the friends he never had. Most certainly not gay friends. He knew plenty of men, especially while working for the military, as there were far more men working in the prisons and holding arenas. Guards. Information Specialist. Extraction Experts. But like himself, Cordon found every one of them intensely fucked up. Often more so than he was. At least that's what he would tell himself. Gitmo. Abu Ghraib. Mexico City. Dahuk. Cordon knew he was different from the men he met there. Men who worked in pain and mind games all day and spent their off time getting drunk or high, searching out prostitutes who they paid to endure their peccadillos and damaged souls for a night.

But chumming around with other men is elusive for Cordon. Friendships with gay men, any sort of bonding, seem out of his reach. As Cordon watches these young men in line, their comradery, the way they interact, touching, kissing, coyly pushing and pulling, is completely alien. And it leaves a gaping pit in his stomach. Climbing into the new Lexus, the leather seats already hot from the sun, and driving away quickly, Cordon tries not to focus on the groups of men hanging around together, but he can't avoid his conflicting feelings.

Back in his hotel room, Cordon strips out of his clothes, vowing never again to dress like he would in Chicago while in Palm Springs. He has to stop standing out. There are plenty of gay muscle heads here, and he needs to find the uniform that will allow him to blend as just another big man looking to get laid. Especially since he had to go fishing for a young guy who could help him slip onto Lansing's property. Dumping the clothes he'd wear to a Chicago gym, baggy sweatpants and an xxxl sweatshirt, Cordon opts instead for a tight yellow tank top and thigh-length spandex underwear with a pair of loose shorts over them. While he loathed using his body as bait, time left few options.

Pulling into a space far away from the entrance to the gym, Cordon parades across the lot, using his hulking body as a bird whistle. His confident stride hides his awkwardness, feeling he's dressed like a porn star. Entering the gym, Cordon peacocks through the place to the usual glances and stares, until he spies a dance class in progress in a glassed-in room, off the weight area. Half the males moving across the dance floor are young; some appearing *very* young. They are taut and thin, somewhat boyish, somewhat girlish.

Cordon knows his mark had to be in there.

Tossing his towel onto a bench, Cordon grabs a pair of sixty-pound dumb-bells and plops himself down, facing the dance room so whoever is in the class can get an eyeful. And it doesn't take but a moment for the flurry of sweaty young men in lycra to catch sight of him as they try to keep up with the lithe instructor.

He performs dumbbell flies, stretching his massive chest in the small tank top, his legs wide. Hiding his self-consciousness and masking his self-loathing, Cordon forces himself to embrace the weird exhilaration of being ogled.

Even better, he knows it's working.

Especially when a young, pretty boy in short-shorts and a half shirt that shows off his tiny waist, eyes Cordon lasciviously. Unsure of the kid's age, Cordon estimates that while he is older than he appears, the kid still Peter-Pans somewhere in his teens, his tight gym shorts displaying one of his selling points.

Making eye contact with this kid, Cordon watches him dance, putting in even more effort to preen for Cordon; his hips gyrating, an extra thrust for added viewing pleasure. Cordon can't help but chuckle. The kid fires Cordon another suggestive glance and raises his arm, trying to coax him into flexing.

Knowing he has the kid hooked, Cordon obliges, flexing a bicep. The kid provocatively smirks, throwing Cordon a kiss.

Not to overplay, Cordon settles himself back on the bench and goes through another set of chest flies.

"That your thing? You into the little dancing fairies?" a handsome guy with chic stubble and a gym body quizzes as he gives Cordon a wistful smile. "They gravitate towards money. I know. I used to be one. But alas, I'm not young anymore. Now I gotta spend hours in here getting pumped to have any hope of landing a rich Palm Springs daddy."

The handsome guy laughs at his own semi-joke. Cordon doesn't, which causes the guy to feel weird about being so open.

"Not that you have that problem, getting what you want. Guys like you never do. Don't even give guys like me a second look. You either want another steroid freak or a sweet, little thing to hang from your bicep. Happy Pride," the handsome guy huffs as he flops back on the bench to start another set.

It isn't lost on Cordon that when a guy as young and good-looking as the one next to him is already bitter about being past his prime, the collective sin of the gay culture, the desire for youth and beauty, even in a town like Palm Springs that caters to older gay men, where they should feel at home and past that pressure, still wreaks havoc on those who aren't who they once were. How do you compete against something you aren't part of any longer? Reinvention is hard, especially in the gay culture. Some are capable, others only wallow in what they once were, their past always being the best days of their lives.

Flipping the weights up onto his shoulder, Cordon's eyes return to the young dancer. As he's about to lay back on the bench and stretch out another set of chest flies, the kid zeroes in again with a kittenish glare as he pushes through the group he dances with, aiming himself directly at Cordon on the other side of the glass. His hips sway, his legs dig into the floor, toe first, one in front of the other, arms whipping behind him, in some Palm Springs version of a Fosse routine. Cordon grins, trying his best to appear accessible instead of threatening. Falling back and pressing the weights together over his face, Cordon licks his lips, hoping he's reeling the kid in and that this guy can get him into where he needs to go.

Gulping down a protein drink at the juice bar, Cordon waits until the slew of sweaty dancers escapes the steamy dance room. The young dancer steps out with a group of other young man/boys but peels off with good-byes and trots towards the exit while the others herd toward the showers.

Cordon quickly downs the rest of his drink and follows.

Once outside, Cordon sticks his thumb under his shirt and lifts it off over his head, strutting shirtless across the parking lot to his car, the sheen of sweat enhancing his immense, frame, catching everyone's attention.

Glancing side to side behind his sunglasses, Cordon can't find the young man anywhere. *Dammit, where the hell did he go?* Cordon asks himself, furious he didn't get up the instant the kid turned in the direction of the exit. His head spins back and forth, but Cordon can't spy the dancing queen anywhere. Cussing at himself, Cordon grits his teeth. He's wasted an afternoon, his plan now shot to hell.

Arriving at his car, Cordon puts down the top and tosses his bag in before opening the door to climb in, when he hears, "We're even," from behind him.

Turning, he finds the young guy, smiling cheekily, standing behind him.

"Even?" Cordon asks, unsure.

"You enjoyed the show I put on for you inside, I enjoyed the show you put on for me as you sashayed across the parking lot," the kid says.

"I don't sashay. And I didn't take off my shirt for you."

The kid giggles, rolling his eyes dramatically as he says, "Liar. That's the only reason you took off your shirt. Hoping I'd notice and coming running up to you."

"And here you are."

The kid's face squishes up like he's eaten rotten lemons.

"I'm a sucker for a muscle daddy. And you certainly got size. Hopefully, in the places I can't see."

"How old are you?" Cordon asks, ignoring the kid's comment.

"Twenty-two."

"Now who's the liar?"

The kid smirks mischievously, hand on hip. "Nineteen. Five-ten. Twenty-eight-inch waist. My name is Gio. Want to know my cock size?"

Cordon doesn't answer, which causes Gio to grin mischievously.

"Come on, I saw you looking at it. Though I imagine being a giant, yours is bigger. But for my frame, mine is super-sized," he laughs.

"This bullshit work?"

"Work how?"

"On other guys. Talking about your dick like it's a 78-inch flat screen."

"Just the ones who I think are interested," Gio laughs, then suddenly gets more direct as he adds, "or have the money to pay."

Cordon nods, understanding more clearly Gio's game. "Which one do you think I am?" Cordon asks.

"You're driving a really nice car, so you got the money. But I don't think you have to pay men to have sex with you, unless you do it for the control, or you're married, which I wouldn't doubt, and you hope money will keep your trick's mouth shut. Either way, I know you're interested. I always know."

"You party up at Lansing's?" Cordon asks, tiring of the conversation.

Again, Gio's smile fades, his head turning slightly as if looking at the Cordon from a different angle might jog his memory. "Did we meet up there?" Gio asks more to himself than Cordon. "No. I'd remember. Lansing would never invite a guy like you. All his little boys would flit around you like butterflies to bougainvillea, and he doesn't allow anyone to steal his thunder. You a cop?"

"No."

"You know if I ask, you have to tell me," Gio inserts.

"That's bullshit. But I'm not."

Gio takes Cordon in silently for a moment. And even though he knows he shouldn't say too much to the statuesque man he doesn't know, Gio is not adept at shutting up, even when it's in his best interest.

"Sure, I party up at Lansing's. Never lived there, though. Those guys think Lansing's the answer to their prayers. Please. He has a revolving bedroom door with guys going in all young, dewy-eyed, and hopeful, and coming out all used up and sad. The man's an emotional vampire. Sucks the life out of everybody. They all think that he's going to help make them a star, or they'll meet some other old queen through Lansing that will. And they all end up going back home, broke, hungry, and completely jaded, or they end up selling it to pay the rent. Hell, even when you're up there, all that's there are other fairies just like them or some dried-up, old, coke addict trying to get his Viagra dick up your ass. Don't know anybody Lansing's actually helped. Ever."

"You don't hold back, do you?"

"Just so I know who just insulted me, what's your name?"

"Cordon."

"Cordon from where?"

"Chicago."

"You're a long way from home, aren't you, Dorothy? Are you here for Pride Week? I mean, I don't get that vibe from you, that you're down here to party with the boys. But you could be one of those sad, married men who told your wife back in Chicago that you're going on a golfing trip or a hunting trip or something equally lame. And you're here because you really like dick but you're Catholic or worse, Evangelical, like my parents, and your guilt is off the charts because you married some pretty blonde, church-going girl, you have two kids, but all you think about when you're fucking her is guys like me."

"You hungry?" Cordon asks, ignoring Gio's smart-ass comment.

"If you're paying and I get to pick the restaurant," Gio quickly tacks on.

Cordon lets a half-smile slip on his lip at Gio's young, alpha nonsense.

"Get in," Cordon says.

"Can I drive?"

"No," Cordon responds, sliding into the driver's seat.

Gio sighs with boyish drama as he moves around to the passenger side and jumps over the door into the passenger seat.

"Do *not* ask me to blow you while you're driving. That's not happening. And don't for a minute think I'm intimidated by you just because you're a giant muscle daddy. All you muscle heads turn into screaming, little bottom bitches in bed. And you're not allowed to parade me around like I'm your boy toy unless I get paid," Gio lists off.

"You done?" Cordon asks as he backs out of the parking spot and points the convertible away from the gym, which frustrates Gio, hoping he could cajole a little more than lunch out of Cordon.

Except for asking for directions, Cordon doesn't say another word to Gio as he drives to the restaurant Gio selected. But that doesn't stop Gio from yammering nonstop, about how his parents threw him out at fifteen when they caught him "balls deep" in the assistant pastor of their church back in Nebraska, about his "fabulous yet grimy" life in Palm Springs, how desirable he is and how men are always coming onto him, about how he "monetized" his appeal because he's first and foremost an entrepreneur, and even though he's had offers, he hasn't latched onto a rich guy yet. Cordon didn't even have to ask a question, which for a man whose skill is information extraction, leaves Cordon bored. But he believes that this kid could be very helpful in getting onto Lansing's property, even though by the time they arrive at the restaurant, Cordon wishes he would shut up.

Diving into two grilled chicken breasts and black beans, Cordon glances up as Gio picks at a club sandwich and ketchup-covered French fries on the nearly empty back patio.

"I thought you'd pick somewhere more expensive," Cordon offers, almost wishing he didn't have to make conversation with this kid, and enjoying the brief bits of silence that seem to annoy Gio.

"You didn't look like you could afford it," Gio pops back which makes Cordon smile.

"Why did you want to sit out here?" asks Cordon.

"I like the heat. That's why I picked Palm Springs. That and all the old guys here love the young hot guys like me and have the money to pay for it. But I don't get why everyone here gets their panties in a bunch about the weather. Yes, it's hot, it's the fucking desert. What did they think it was going to be?" Gio responds, holding up a French fry on his fork which he uses to point at Cordon. "So, what do you want with me? If I haven't been clear, I charge for my time."

Cordon opens his bag and pulls out the photo of Lucas in the heels. "You know this kid?"

"So, this isn't about sucking my dick?" quizzes Gio, glancing at the photo as Cordon slides it across the table towards him. "That's Lucious."

Gio's eyes narrow as he nibbles on the French fry. "That's why you were asking if I party up at Lansing's. Lansing loves young Asian ass. Why are you looking for Lucious?"

"You ever hook up with him?"

"*Her*," Gio snaps, sitting back in the chair, shaking his head as if he disapproves of the question. "Call me shallow, but no fems, no fatties, no fakes. Unless they're paying. But if you're asking, I prefer big-muscle daddies who like big dicks. Hint, hint..."

Cordon's expression doesn't change. Not getting the reaction he wanted, Gio rolls his eyes at Cordon, huffing in disappointment as he says, "You don't know what you're missing."

"When you get out of high school, look me up," Cordon answers.

"I told you, I'm nineteen."

Cordon holds up Gio's wallet. "You're seventeen. Barely," Cordon says as Gio digs into his bag, realizing his wallet is gone. Cordon tosses it across the table to him.

"How did you---?!?! Cunt!" Gio barks, standing, indignant.

"Do your parents know where you are?" Cordon asks.

"Do you *listen*?" Gio snaps back. "Some of us were pushed out of the nest prematurely so our parents could go to church on Sunday and feel better about themselves, even though that same church is where I had my first sexual experience. You're an asshole. Going through my stuff! My life is what I tell you it is, not what you find out. And what do you care anyway? You said you weren't a cop, but I can tell you're something like that. But whatever you are, fuck you, I don't want any part of it."

Gio turns to leave when Cordon says, "Get me to Lucious and I'll put ten grand in your pocket."

Pausing for effect, Gio finally turns back to Cordon, staring down at him. "Cash. No check, no gift cards, no Venmo, none of that PayPal bullshit."

Cordon nods. "Sit down and finish your meal. You shouldn't have ordered it if you weren't going to eat it. I don't like wasting time, food, or money."

Gio's lip curls into a snarl. "Oh, okay, Jeff Bezos."

Pulling out his chair, Gio plops back down as Cordon adds, "Just so I'm clear, I don't pay unless I get what I want."

"Fuck you. You will. And don't threaten me again or you won't get shit from me," Gio says, sticking another French fry in his mouth and chomping on it to make a point.

"For ten grand, I need you to get Lucious alone. And if you can get Lansing and make it a threesome, you're worth your money," Cordon tells Gio.

"I'm worth ten grand. Lucious has always had a thing for me. I have what she likes. And if Lansing knows we're going upstairs in his house so I can fuck Lucious, he'll want to join. But I will not fuck Lansing. That's off the table."

"You're sure you can get both of them alone?"

"As long as Lucious isn't on the outs with Lansing. And last time I was up there, which was a couple weeks ago for a party, she seemed to be Lansing's number one."

"I asked you before, have you ever hooked up with Lansing? I need an answer."

"Please. He wants to, but I know he's not going to do anything for me, so why bother having sex with another old man I have to pretend I'm enjoying? I'm a business. I have my own place and I have a car. There's enough other money in Palm Springs that I don't need Lansing's. Though I do love his parties. I can hook up with guys my own age for some fun," he tells Cordon.

"Tell me about these parties," Cordon asks.

"What's to tell? There's a lot of young dick and some old guys, Lansing's friends, or maybe some entertainment execs he's trying to impress. I avoid them because I don't give it away for free. There's always music, usually a DJ. And food. He always has a long table filled with tons of food, which for guys like me who are on a budget, is fucking awesome. We all sneak food to take home at the end of the night. Mostly guys hang out in the pool or the hot tub. There's always drugs floating around. Lansing always has coke and party drugs. When these guys get high, it makes them hornier. So, there's lots of naked boys doing what naked boys do."

"Anything else?"

"Fireworks. I don't know how he gets away with it, but he always has a fireworks display. But when you've seen it once…eh, who cares?" Gio says, then asks, "So when do I get paid?"

"After I get Lucas."

"Lucious," Gio corrects. "And that's what I thought, which sucks."

"This is business too, kid."

"Thanks for the update," laments Gio as he pushes his half-eaten meal away. "We got a lot of time to kill. Why don't we go back to whatever cheap hotel you're staying in and let me crawl up and down your muscles? Be like climbing a mountain or something. No charge."

Cordon casts his eyes down on Gio, who coyly curls up in the chair. Cordon wants nothing more than to smack the shit out of this chatterbox, but at the same time, admires Gio's bravado. If he had it at the same age, the trajectory of his life would have been different.

Taking Cordon's silence as a 'no', Gio grabs both his legs and lifts them straight up in the chair, taunting Cordon, but still gets no response.

"God, you are *no* fun," Gio mutters, setting his feet back on the ground. "And you were going to get it for free. Are you going to hold me hostage until we go to the party, or am I allowed to go?"

Cordon signals that Gio can leave, responding, "I'll call you an Uber. Just tell me where I'm picking you up tonight and what time."

"An Uber," Gio sighs, gratefully. "Thank God. The driver has to be more interesting than you."

Borrowing a pen and a slip of paper from the waiter, who Gio can't help but flirt with just to irk Cordon, Gio writes his address and phone number before standing and shoving it against Cordon's chest. "Pick me up at eleven. Lansing's parties don't really get started until then. Call me when you're out front. And make sure you have my cash with you. I'm not going back to your place to get it at the end of the night. I know that trick. I'll be tired then, and this was a once-in-a-lifetime offer that doesn't extend into the wee hours of tomorrow."

Gio struts into the restaurant from the patio and disappears. Cordon takes a deep breath once he's gone, exhausted by the kid's weary attitude and incessant chatter. Cordon knows he should call Frank and check in but needs the quiet. And what is Frank going to do at this point? Cordon doesn't need a pep talk. Once he has the kid, he'll call. Frank can then make arrangements with Fu to pick up the fee before Cordon delivers Lucas back to his family.

This has got to go smoothly, Cordon tells himself, though he's preparing for the opposite. Never has a 'snatch' gone as planned. Some have come close, but there's always a hitch somewhere that dissolves the plan into chaos. Sometimes momentarily, sometimes through the entire grab. And this grab already has too many variables that Cordon feels unprepared for.

Cordon is still dubious about the reasons Fu hired him. What does under-standing your target's sexuality have to do with this sort of work? The more Cordon ponders it, the more he sees the holes in the reasoning. A man his size is skilled at stunning a 'grab' and muscling them from a house into a waiting van. But slipping into an estate unnoticed? Cordon can't even walk down the block without eyes being on him, much less crash a party loaded with twinks less than half his age, and worse, half his size. There's just too much he doesn't know about Lansing. About the estate. And even about Lucas.

Adding this overly chatty youngster into the mix only inflates the chances of something going sideways. Working alone or in tandem with other professionals cuts out the noise, keeps things simple. Cordon accepts that using a high-strung, jaded, seventeen-year-old to get onto Lansing's property is not a calculated risk. He's used to those. But this is a tremendous gamble that could lead to a messy extraction. It makes Cordon's skin itch as if he's allergic to complications and volatile personalities. And he suspects Lucas is going to be just as dramatic, making an escape with that kid doubly hard. No one in an extraction goes willingly. But in those situations, Cordon can choke them out, knock them out, put a gun to their head. And if the target dies, if you die, it's all factored into the gamble. Cordon is not in a position to wager with Lucas' life. Cordon is hoping he doesn't have to get violent with the kid to get him off the property and back to Chicago. But if he has to put the kid to sleep for a few hours, so be it. He just doesn't want to hurt him.

That he wants to save for Lansing.

Cordon came to do a job. A high-paying job. And he intended to get it done.

Finishing his meal, Cordon sits back in his chair, his mind ticking through the litany of moving pieces he must arrange. "I'm too old for fairies or fairy tales," he says aloud, the server turning as he hears Cordon's words.

"Sorry," Cordon apologizes to the server. "I'm thinking out loud."

"About your...friend? These kids come out here, running away from one thing, looking for another. I was one of them. Maybe not as young as him, but I was young."

"What saved you?" Cordon asks.

The server smiles. "I gave up hoping someone else would and found a job. Managed to stay employed for the last decade here. Guess I should consider myself lucky. What saved you?"

Cordon thinks for a moment. "Who says I'm saved?" he responds without a hint of sarcasm.

The server nods, giving Cordon an understanding smile as he places his check on the table. "Pay up front."

(UN)DRESSED FOR THE PARTY

After a speedy trip to a big box hardware store, Cordon drives up the mountain toward Lansing's home. Stopping about a half mile below the Lansing estate, Cordon parks behind some high evergreens, his car hidden. Hiking over the craggy hillside with the items he purchased, he sends up a few prayers not to run into a rattlesnake. He finds the service road that leads up to Lansing's mansion, and jogging up the road, he finds what he's looking for: the concrete platform Lansing had built for his fireworks displays. After a quick survey to make sure he's not being watched and cutting the feed to the cameras, Cordon attaches a remote ignition to the larger rockets which have already been set up for the evening's display. He then connects all the other fireworks together so they are on one fuse string, with a remote ignition.

Arriving back at the hotel, Cordon bribes one of the maintenance crew to help him remove the backseat of his rented Lexus and store it in a maintenance closet. Cordon attaches a thin black sheet of gardening material across the back of the car, making an area underneath where he not only can conceal the handguns he's taped to the back of the seats, but could also reasonably hide a 6'4", 245-pound man, if he's limber enough to lay flat on the floor, knees bent, arms tight at his torso.

As Cordon showers, his demeanor shifts. His already severe persona hulks out until he's totally in a zone, focused only on what he needs to accomplish. Changing into a black t-shirt and black pants, he exits the hotel with a dark duffle bag over his shoulder, using the back service elevator to return to the garage. In most places, people would look at Cordon and think he was about to rob a home, but anywhere near a coast or major city, he resembles a club bouncer about to go to work.

Phoning Gio from out front of his apartment building, the location stupefies Cordon. The narrow three-story building with a long, slender parking garage behind it, is sandwiched between a fetish bar and a sex shop. Pride revelers crowd the street, most in leather or kinky attire. Music pounds from the club out into the street and right into Gio's apartment building next door.

As Gio ambles down the apartment's walkway, costumed in a tight tank top and even tighter shorts that prominently display the outline of his penis, the men in line for the neighboring club cheer as he struts past. Enjoying the attention and always ready to put on a show, Gio adds a little extra sway into every step as he makes his way to the waiting Lexus convertible.

Climbing in with a big grin, Gio comes eye-to-eye with Cordon's glower. Sighing emphatically, Gio complains, "God, you're a buzzkill," before adding with equal drama, "You don't make money being shy."

"You fuck this up, I will wreck you."

The lack of sarcasm or even a hint of humor in Cordon's voice shivers Gio. "Jesus. I'll do what I said. Fuck. Lighten up a little, will you please? I'm doing you a favor," Gio yaps harshly.

"You're doing a job," Cordon reminds him.

"I know what I'm doing. Do you? And you'd better have brought the cash."

Pulling back onto the street, through the bodies crossing back and forth, Cordon takes a deep breath, shaking his head as he finally makes his way to the stoplight. "How do you live down here?"

"It's not always like this. I mean, it gets crazy most weekends, but not like this."

"You live next door to a club."

"And a sex store!" Gio giggles. "I like it. The music from the club is sorta the soundtrack of my life," he reasons. "Some people live near airports, some near trains, some have loud neighbors. I have music. And I never have to go far to drum up business and can always meet a potential client right next door and decide if I'm comfortable enough to take him home. If not, I can skip out and be locked inside my place in half a minute."

"What about when you want to sleep?"

"Earplugs," Gio says, as he puts Air Pods in his ears and starts bouncing in the passenger seat.

Cordon accepts Gio's silence as a blessing. Needing to keep his mind un-cluttered and focused on what needs to be done, Gio's continual babbling as they drive up to Lansing's would only enrage Cordon and potentially throw him off his game. When extracting someone from a location, Cordon needed a clear head. He had to be ready to change an operation instantaneously, and most importantly, not mess around. The longer an operation went on, the more the chance for something to fuck up. Even though this wasn't Afghanistan or Eastern Europe, Cordon has approached each job since being stateside with a similar application and fervor. He never attached the word 'professional' to what did. It bristled him to think there was anything professional about what he did. Even when he was working for the government. But it required a certain skill set to be good at the job. And despite what this job often entailed, Cordon prided himself on being good.

As they get within a few miles of Lansing's estate, Cordon signals Gio to take the Air Pods out of his ears. Calmly explaining again what he expects from Gio, Cordon reminds him that if he wants to get paid, he needs to treat this seriously. He can't afford any fuck-ups. They could both go to jail. Or worse. Gio nods almost absently as if he's being droned to by his junior high school English teacher, but when Cordon taps Gio on the forehead saying, "And the most important thing. Stay alive. If this goes sideways, get the fuck out. Don't wait for me, don't ask for help, you get your ass out of there."

The seriousness on Cordon's face brings it back to reality for Gio.

"You think it will?"

Shrugging, Cordon adds, "I'm flying blind here. I usually know more about what I'm heading into. I don't know the layout other than what I've seen in photos. Don't even know what sort of security team he has in place, but I'm sure they're solid."

"He has guys. At least when I've been there. I thought maybe they were just for parties. Sometimes guys get in fights, and there's always a guy, or five, who slept with someone's boyfriend or banged someone and never called them again, and they run into each other. I swear, they need a film crew to come in and film all the gay drama."

"I'm not worried about all that shit. In fact, if some of that happens tonight, it'll make excellent cover. But Lansing's a billionaire. His team is permanent. Maybe they hire more crew for parties, but he has full-time security," Cordon relays. "But they'll be just as surprised by me if things get hairy. I'm sure they're more used to throwing out the drunks and boys who don't behave than some-one like me."

"If things go bad, when do I get my money?"

"You'll get it," Cordon responds as he applies black camouflage to his face. "You know too much about me. So, it's either I pay you or I kill you."

Gio reacts sharply, eyes widening.

Finally, Cordon smiles. "I've decided to pay you. Just remember, if things go bad, don't wait to get paid. Get out. We'll settle up later."

"You're *that* big of a badass you can take on an entire security detail?" Gio asks.

Without changing infliction, Cordon says, "I hope we don't have to find out tonight."

Pulling off a few miles down the mountain from Lansing's estate, Cordon slips his body onto the floor where the backseats were and pulls the black cover over himself. With the top up, it's hard to see anything in the back of the car, but just in case, Cordon pulls a handgun from where he's taped it to the back of a seat.

"Let's go," Gio hears Cordon say from where he's hiding. Before he gets into the driver's seat, Gio shimmies out of his shorts, revealing a tiny, sheer, swimsuit that leaves nothing to the imagination. Stripping out of the swimsuit, Gio slides the shorts back on over his bare ass, squeezing the swimsuit tightly in his hand.

He climbs in and revs the engine, spitting rocks as he drives back onto the road, continuing up the mountain.

A half mile up the road, the line of cars heading towards Lansing's stops dead.

"Why are we stopping?" Cordon asks.

"We're in line. This party is huge. Lots of cars…"

Cordon debates whether this benefits him. It allows him more cover, more mayhem if necessary, but also adds more potential witnesses.

They don't exchange another word as Gio inches up to the security check that stops each car. A security guard flashes his light through the car quickly as Gio flashes him a coy smile.

"Is there a secret password or do I just show you these?" he asks, holding out his tiny swim trunks on one finger.

The guard smiles, waving him through the gate, directing Gio where to park with his flashlight.

"We're through," Gio says as he follows the car ahead of him onto the property where they're parking on the lawn.

Cordon pulls open the black sheet he is hiding under, sitting up. His eyes adjust, getting a better layout of the front of the estate.

"Park up there," he points to a berm amid the cars, slightly away from the other cars, halfway between the house and the gates, with a direct path to the driveway.

Gio parks near a tree, so no one can park next to him on the driver's side. Cordon slips out the passenger side, a black satchel over one shoulder. No one other than Gio is able to see him.

"Got any idea where Lansing's bedroom is?"

Gio smiles, pointing to the middle of the second floor of the long two-story mansion. "Directly in the middle. It overlooks the pool and the mountains. Has the huge balcony. It's the only room upstairs with double doors."

"How do you know this?"

"Had a friend who was one of Lansing's boys," Gio explains. "He finally figured out that he was only there for Lansing to pull out of the harem and fuck when he felt like it. Lansing got tired of him and he got kicked out. Stayed with me a few weeks before he gave up on Palm Springs and moved back home."

"Maybe that was best for him," offers Cordon.

"He killed himself."

Cordon's eyes lock with Gio, recognizing that Gio had feelings for this friend.

"Sorry," Cordon replies.

Gio shrugs, tempering his pain with defiance. "Not everybody has parents who will send some video game mercenary to save them," Gio states. "I told you, Lansing sucks the life out of people and then trashes them. He leaves them with nothing except an STD and a damaged psyche."

Cordon doesn't respond. There's nothing he can say. Anything would just make light of Gio's feelings or bolster his faux indifference. Neither of which Cordon wants to do. He simply sticks out his fist to Gio, which Gio bumps.

"How long do you think you'll need to get Lucas upstairs?" Cordon asks.

"She goes by Lucious now. It's like pronouns. Learn them," Gio schools Cordon before adding, "Give me half an hour. I'm going in horny and letting her know it."

"And you're sure Lansing will follow?"

Gio shrugs again, hedging what he was sure of earlier. "If Lucious is still his number one, yes. If not, I'm going to play the big dick card and get him to follow," Gio smirks. "He'll at least want to watch. Probably expect to join in. Which isn't happening, so get in there fast. I don't want that scab of a man touching me."

"You get him into his bedroom, I'll be there."

"I can do that."

"I like your confidence," Cordon bolsters.

Gio sneers at Cordon. "You may be big, but I'm the one whose got mad skills."

"What you got," Cordon reminds him, "is ten grand coming if you can make this happen."

Understanding his worth, Gio's hand settles on his hips as he glares at Cordon. "What I got is an awesome body, a pretty face, youth, and a big, fat cock

I'm stuffing into four inches of swimsuit. I'll handle my part, you handle the Quentin Tarantino, rock 'em sock 'em stuff. I mean, have you even thought of how you're going to get out of here once you get Lucious? Crash through those metal gates in this little car? You better think again…"

"The car's a rental. It breaks, it breaks," Cordon shrugs, shoving his finger at Gio's face. "Same goes for your dick, kid, if you screw this up or screw me over."

Indignant, Gio straights up as tall as he can. "Why are you always threatening me?! I get it! So, fuck you. You want me to help you or not? If you do, stop with the insults and the slights. You may be all G.I. Joe or whatever you are, but I'm a professional too. Let's hope you're half as good at what you do as I am at what I do."

Cordon opts not to continue the conversation as his eyes follow a group of young men heading around the house towards the rear where the loud party is in full swing.

"Go to work," Cordon says, tucking a small bag under his arm before dashing into the shadows toward the far side of the house. Gio watches as Cordon weaves his way through cars, moving behind bushes and then a tree until he disappears into the inkiness of the night. An uneasy look washes onto Gio's face as he walks toward another group of young guys. Joining them, Gio pulls off his shirt, his preening smiles and little swimsuit are all he wears. He joins the silly conversation as they excitedly trot in the music's direction.

Cordon licks his lips just before he takes a run at the house, leaping and grabbing the spindle of an upstairs balcony railing on the side of the hacienda-inspired mansion. Muscling himself up and flipping his long legs over, Cordon moves against the wall, peeking into the bedroom attached to the balcony. Spying no one inside, Cordon notes the placement of a camera in the corner near the door. Not seeing wires leading into the walls, Cordon takes a relieved breath. This is through the wifi and Cordon quickly fishes a handheld device out of his bag.

Knowing this will also jam the signal of anyone at the party on social media, Cordon works quickly. Once he switches the jammer on, he smashes in a pane of glass on the door, opens it, and pulls a can of black spray paint out of the bag. He sprays the lens of the security camera and then reconnects the signal before the partiers, or worse, security, realize there's anything wrong more than a dropped signal.

Opening the door from the bedroom, which leads into the hallway, Cordon studies the upstairs of the house. There are two sides, with a set of double doors in the middle, Lansing's bedroom, which takes up over half of the back of the house, where the view of the pool and mountains is the best. On either end is a winding staircase that leads down to the two-story foyer. Cordon counts nine bedrooms, including Lansing's.

Cordon can see packs of young men milling through the foyer, most in awe of the massive home as if they've made it to the Promised Land. With these swimsuit-clad kids bouncing up and down the stairs, slipping into bedrooms, taking selfies on the stairwells or up on the upstairs landing, Cordon can't possibly get to the doors of Lansing's room, pick the lock and slip in without a dozen witnesses, including the security men who shoo some of the party guests out of the upstairs.

Cordon disappears back onto the balcony and pulls himself up onto the mansion's Spanish-tile roof. He clambers up to the crest of the house, glancing over at the body-filled pool deck, the pulsing music blasting into the star-filled night. He eyes the plethora of young men, some wearing tiny swimsuits, some wearing absolutely nothing, wrestling and horse-playing in the pool. Cordon watches older men, apparent friends of Lansing's, snorting lines of coke off a young man stretched out on a table. There's a large bowl of what Cordon can only guess is Oxy on a table as well.

A couple dozen young men and boys play in the hot tub, swimsuits getting pulled down. Some have coupled-off, some talk on their phone, while others film themselves for their social media. The number of young men with their phones out, shooting pics or filming themselves makes Cordon nervous since the only way into Lansing's bedroom is to lower himself onto the balcony that stretches over the back of the house and go in through the balcony doors, without even one of the hundred or so mostly naked men catching a glimpse of him. If there were at least a few other musclebound guys strutting around, he could blend in.

From his perch on the roof, Cordon searches for Lucas, wanting to get a look at his quarry. Before he finds Lucas, he spots Gio scanning the party for him as well. Then Cordon's eyes land directly on Lansing. Lansing fondles the parade of young men who have lined up to say hello and thank him for the party. Groping each kid as if it's the price of entry, Lansing eyes each boy up and down, talking to some closely, his hands sliding over their lean bodies, kissing a few, gauging their willingness.

Despite his blood boiling at Lansing for taking advantage of these kids, Cordon again searches for Lucas, not sure he wouldn't leap off the roof, throw the kid over his shoulder and make a run for it. But first stopping in front of Lansing and putting a boot to his kneecap to snap his leg. And after Lansing hit the concrete screaming, boot him in the head so hard his skull would crack.

Knowing what it's like to be used as a kid, watching Lansing takes advantage of these boys, many of them runaways, throwaways, or simply lost, desperate, and needy, roils Cordon. He recognizes that many of these young guys will party all night, eating the food, doing the drugs, and getting laid, but in the morning, the party will be over, and they will be back to living hand-to-mouth, too many of them tricking for cash or a place to stay, with whatever innocence they still possess, being leeched out of them.

Just as it had Gio.

About the only thing Cordon is sure he's going to take pleasure in tonight is beating the shit out of Lansing.

Pulling out a small remote, Cordon aims it past the pool toward the north end of the property.

Suddenly, fireworks explode from the ridge below the house. They fire in different directions, the sky lighting up in a messy, colorful mishmash, startling everyone at the party. As a cadre of security men race down the hill to find out what's happened, with everyone's attention drawn toward the fizzle of fireworks, Cordon throws himself over the eaves of the roof and down onto the balcony of Lansing's bedroom below. Staying low, he jams the camera signal again, unlocks the balcony door, and rolls across the floor, coming up with the paint can. He covers the lenses of the four cameras and then unjams the feed, the cameras coming back on.

Standing, he takes in the vast bedroom. For its size, it is sparsely furnished. The room is dominated by an incredibly massive bed, quadruple the size of anything that Cordon has ever seen, placed in the middle of the room rather than against the wall. It could easily sleep ten. There are posts attached to the floor, four on every side, each with harnesses and bindings, making the bed more of a sex pit than a comfy place where you curl up with a good book at the end of a hard day. Surveying the rest of the room, Cordon finds the bathroom, Lansing's wall-to-wall closet, and a door that leads behind an interior bedroom wall. Finding it locked, Cordon is about to kick it in but stops himself. He pulls a kit from the backpack, and with little effort, picks the lock, entering.

***

After the fireworks fiasco comes to its inevitable and smoky conclusion, the sky goes silent. Lansing raises his hand with a forced smile. "Obviously, that was not supposed to happen," he announces to the chuckles of his guests. "I'm sorry. And while the fireworks at my parties are always a fun addition to the evening, they aren't a party. You all are! Enjoy yourself, eat, drink, play, have fun, do what young men do. This party is just getting started!"

Everyone cheers and applauds, returning to their conversation, food, drugs, and debauchery.

Except Gio. Purposefully moving through the gaggle of young men, he skips any conversation other than hellos and quick hugs, his eyes scanning the area, not finding Lucious.

"Dammit," Gio says under his breath, knowing that Cordon won't hand him a nickel if he can't deliver Lucious.

As a small pack of young men rushes past Gio to jump in the pool, Gio grabs one of the guys. "Denny! Where's Lucious? I have something for her."

"That crazy bitch? She and Lansing got into it this afternoon. Gurl! Nothing like an old queen and a new queen screaming at each other at the top of their lungs to make the whole house shake," Denny relays before jumping into the pool with his friends.

Sighing at his horrible luck, Gio's eyes turn again to Lansing, surrounded by a group of men, young and old, making introductions and holding court. If Lucious and Lansing are on the outs, this complicates things. And he has no way of getting hold of Cordon to tell him. Gio needs that ten grand at the end of the rainbow, knowing that sum pays his rent for the rest of the year. And for Gio, that makes it easier to turn down some of the less-desirable tricks that want to pay for his services.

Noticing Lansing's eyes continually snapping toward the enormous hot tub at the far end of the deck, placed back in the shadows for privacy, Gio strolls around the pool to get a better angle on what is piquing Lansing's interest.

Sure enough, Lucious is in the hot tub with a group of guys, all of whom Gio can tell are drunk, high, or both. One young man is naked, facing the waterfall that pours into the hot tub. Water cascades down his nude backside as the other boys pose on either side of him, snapping pictures as they kiss this guy's ass. Lucious swims over and joins the fun, her tongue circling around one of the wet butt cheeks as one of the other young men captures it for social media. Lucious then takes her turn under the waterfall, pulling down her tiny suit, revealing her tight, round ass as the other guys kiss, lick, and slap it, all of which makes Lucious giggle playfully for the camera, knowing her social media followers will eat it up.

"Make sure you tag me!" Lucious howls at the kid with the iPhone, filming the scene.

Gio notes that Lansing is trying to bury his ire at Lucious' antics as he talks with the men surrounding him. It's also equally clear that Lansing's subdued rage spurs Lucious' behavior. The last thing Gio needs is whatever happened earlier bubbling over into tonight and ruining his chance with Lucious and Lansing. Believing that their tiff will make it easier for him to reel in Lucious, if, for no other reason than to piss off Lansing, Gio slips into the pool, soaking himself, and his tiny swimsuit, which now wet, hides nothing. Flipping his hair back, Gio struts towards the hot tub, making sure his manhood is generously on display, a devilish smile on his lips.

Moving up to the waterfall, Gio makes sure Lucious has an eyeful of every inch he's packing. He then splashes some water with his foot at Lucious, getting her attention.

"I always knew you were a size queen," Gio calls to Lucious playfully.

"One of my many sins! Get in!" Lucious says, reaching out to help Gio into the hot tub without ever taking her eyes off Gio's bulge.

Taking Lucious' hand, Gio slips into the hot tub. Lucious quickly claims Gio as her own, making sure none of the other guys sweep in. "I didn't know you were coming!" Lucious coos, giving Gio a warm kiss on the lips. "I haven't seen you in forever."

"Busy, you know. How you been?"

"Just hanging out around here, doing my TikToks. Boring most of the time. Same old stuff. But it's cool. It's good to see you! I'm glad you came," Lucious prattles eagerly, her hands going around the back of Gio's neck, pulling him closer. "Someone get this on camera for my Insta!"

One friend snaps a few quick shots with his iPhone, Lucious sticking her tongue into Gio's ear. Gio turns his head and slides his tongue into Lucious' mouth as the surrounding friends use their phones to record them making out for a moment before Lucious pats her chest as if she's having palpitations.

"Oh my God, I've wanted this guy for so long!" Lucious exclaims to the cameras.

"He knows you're horny and you're high!" one of Lucious' crew laughs.

"I am! But have you seen the size of this guy!?! My prayers have been answered!" Lucious caws, grabbing the ledge of the waterfall over her head and pulling herself up, then throwing her legs up and spreading them, to the amusement of all around.

Gio laughs, his hands grabbing Lucious' ass, then slipping up to her waist, drawing Lucious into his arms. They make out again, Gio pulling back with a smile.

"You wanna get out of here and go upstairs?" Gio requests seductively, his lips pressing against Lucious' ear.

"For sure!" Lucious cackles, her mind hazy from the party drugs she took earlier and her desire for Gio, as she pauses, asking, "Why are you so into me now? I've tried to jump on you before and you wouldn't have a thing to do with me."

Gio again leans into Lucious' ear. "You look totally fuckable tonight. I've wanted you for a while, but everybody knows you're Lansing's."

"I don't belong to anyone!" Lucious counters. "Especially that shriveled grape of a man."

"You live here," Gio says, trying to gauge how easy it will be to lure Lansing upstairs as well.

"I don't belong to him. No one owns me. Yes, I'm his favorite. But I still do what I want."

"Well, I'm super horny," Gio says, shifting Lucious' hand down to the swell in his swimsuit. "But I don't want to cause any drama for you. I mean, if he wants to come up and watch..." Gio shrugs, signaling he doesn't care. "You know I like an audience."

Lucious giggles. "I can ask. It'll make him so jealous. What if he wants to join in?"

Gio forces a smile and another shrug. The thought makes him nauseous, but the payday for getting both of them upstairs tempers his recoil.

Pulling Lucious from the hot tub, Gio wraps his arm around her, keeping Lucious on her feet, steering her towards Lansing. Gio's smile grows. The subterfuge excites him more than he expected. Gio grinds his hips against Lucious' ass, letting Lucious experience what's going on in his swimsuit, making the conundrum Lucious feels even more complicated. Lucious glares at Lansing as they move in his direction. Leaning up to Lucious' ear, one more time, knowing he can't let Lucious blow this, Gio whispers, "Ask him. I want to do it in his bed."

Giving Lucious a little shove, Gio hopes that, in her uninhibited condition and her eagerness to hook up, Lucious can convince Lansing to allow them into his bedroom. Gio believes that if Lansing thinks he might join in, he'll be more than willing.

Lucious sidles up to Lansing, her hand sliding across Lansing's chest playfully as she speaks closely with him. Lansing's eyes bounce towards Gio; he's offered Gio a room at the mansion multiple times since Gio arrived on the Palm Springs scene two years ago, which Gio always declined. Lucious kisses Lansing on the lips before she hustles back to Gio.

"He said okay!" Lucious giggles. "But he said he wants to join us."

Gio's eyes go to Lansing, who is waiting for a response. Gio smiles at him. "I'm up for it," he tells Lucious. "Let's go."

As Lucious takes his hand, they move toward Lansing, who excuses himself from the group he's speaking with and crosses to them.

"So, you know about my bed," Lansing states, his loose-fitting madras pants and open shirt making him look more like he belongs in Palm Beach rather than Palm Springs.

"It's legendary," Gio exclaims, trying to seal the deal.

"Legendary, huh? Well, that's interesting to know," chuckles Lansing.

"Are there cameras in your room?" Gio wants to know.

Lansing smiles, eyeing Gio's body up and down, but stopping on Gio's portentous bulge. "For my viewing pleasure only. I promise."

"You getting viewing pleasure from what you're staring at right now?" Gio asks, calling Lansing on his overt glare.

Lansing's eyes never leave Gio's crotch as he answers, "We're going to have a lot of fun."

Taking a remote from his robe pocket, Lansing points it up at his bedroom on the second floor, pressing the button. "Door's unlocked. Go up, get comfortable. I'll join you in a minute," orders Lansing.

As Lucious pulls him into the house and toward one of the two staircases, Gio hopes that Cordon is where he says he's going to be and ready to act. He wants his money and to be on his way home before Lansing strips out of his clothes and hops into that gigantic bed with him and Lucious.

TIGHTENED SCREWS

A knock brings Natasha to her front door. She slips on the chain and opens it with a smile.

"Are you David?"

The man in the hallway nods. "Yes," he responds, an anxious edge in his voice.

"You don't have to be nervous. You're handsome," she says, closing the door and pulling off the chain to open the door wider, standing there in her robe, her breasts pushed up.

"You look exactly like your picture," the man states, relaxing.

"I don't like surprises. I don't want my clients to be surprised either," Natasha answers, stepping back and allowing the man in the door. "Come in, sweetie."

As he comes in, the man's right hand goes back and he punches Natasha across the face. Staggered by the blow, Natasha loses her balance in her heels and slams onto the floor hard.

The man standing over her is Chen, Fu's head of security. As Natasha tries to crawl away, Chen closes the door, locking it.

BLOODY HELL

The doors to Lansing's room burst open and Lucious charges in, racing over and leaping on the massive bed in the middle of the room. "Ta-da!" Lucious giggles as she jumps on the bed, and Gio laughs as he moves toward it as well.

Gio climbs onto the bed, his eyes wide at the gargantuan size of it as he joins Lucious jumping like it's a trampoline.

"This is huge!!" Gio cackles.

Lucious falls back and looks up at Gio standing over him. She reaches up and cups Gio's penis. "It is!!" she snickers.

Gio falls to his knees on the bed, Lucious underneath him. Gio crawls on top of her, pinning her down and Lucious smiles up. Just as Gio leans down to kiss Lucious, Lansing enters the room, somewhat staggered by the drugs he's ingested, shutting and locking the door behind him.

"Did you boys start without me?" Lansing slurs as he pads across his bedroom towards the bathroom. "Condoms are in the drawer under the bed with the lube and party favors."

Lansing enters the vast walk-in closet and strips out of his clothes, dropping them on the floor. Flipping on a silk robe, he walks out, crosses the bedroom to the hidden room behind the wall, and unlocks its door.

Walking into the long, rectangular room that runs the length of the bedroom, Lansing steps over to a cabinet, opening it. Four television monitors display the bed from various angles. Lansing presses record on the remote as he watches as Gio's lips go to Lucious', Lucious' arms still pinned over her head, crotch to crotch, grinding. He steps to a sound system, flipping it on. Club music thumps through the walls coming from the speakers in the bedroom. Lowering the lights enough to give the room a mood without making it too murky for filming, Lansing checks the monitors to make sure he can see the action in the bed.

Pulling out a vile of coke from the robe pocket, Lansing taps some onto the side of his hand, snorting it before checking himself out in a full-length mirror. He smiles at his reflection. Coke always gives Lansing the illusion that he's younger and better-looking than reality could ever provide him. He would happily give all the money he has to be thirty years younger, to look like those beautiful teens making out on his bed. Even stoned, Lansing isn't jaded enough to believe that these young guys allow him to take part for any other reason than he supplies them with shelter, clothing, food, and drugs. For that, he gets to forget his age, forget what he looks like, and feels like one of the boys for a night. He's aware that it's more of a pity fuck or a thank-you fuck, but as far as Lansing is concerned, getting laid by a beautiful, young man is worth whatever it costs him. Even his own self-respect.

When his eyes return to his sad image in the mirror, Lansing's mood turns more dour. Even in his youth, the hot guys he desired looked past him; there was always someone better looking, more interesting, hotter. Lansing knows he could never seduce one of the boys who comes to his parties. He was chubby, his eyes were too close, nose too long, front teeth slightly crossed in the front, his brown hair wiry, untamable, and thinning early, acne scars cratered his back and neck.

After his first million, an excellent cosmetic surgeon and an even better dentist repaired the physical flaws. With each subsequent success, Lansing recreated himself. Even at the young age of thirty, there was hardly anything about Lansing that was original. Except the emotional scars. But he found a way to profit from them as well. His desire to be someone that young men wanted pushed him to make more and more money. Lansing promised himself that by the time he was thirty-five, any problem he had, he would be able to solve with money.

He achieved it.

The two kids in his bed proved it.

Drug-confident, Lansing starts to turn away from the mirror, already getting hard at the thought of having sex with two young hotties in his bed. But Cordon's looming frame, just feet behind him, stops Lansing in his tracks. Shocked, Lansing opens his mouth to scream. As he spins toward Cordon, Cordon's gloved hand grabs Lansing by the face and smashes his head into the mirror. Blood spatters, Lansing wobbles. Cordon flings him to the tiled floor before turning and ripping the recording devices and monitors from the cabinet.

As Lansing crawls toward the door leading back into the bedroom, blood trickles into his eyes and Lansing rises to his knees, lunging forward to grab the doorknob. Cordon yanks the last of the recorders from the cabinet and flings it at Lansing. It smacks him hard in the middle of his back, dropping him to the tile floor again right in front of the door.

Grabbing hold of a small cabinet near the door, Lansing wrenches open a drawer, his hand scrambling in. His fingers wrap around the butt of a .44. As he twists to fire, Cordon is on him. Before Lansing can pull the trigger, Cordon grasps his hand and snaps it, breaking Lansing's wrist, the gun clattering to the Spanish tile. As Lansing opens his mouth to scream again, Cordon snaps up the gun from the floor and jams the barrel into Lansing's mouth, gagging him. Cordon grabs Lansing by the hair, Lansing's eyes wide with fear.

"Please don't hurt me, please…" Lansing garbles almost indistinguishable, the gun holding his mouth open. Tears rim his eyelids and he tries to blink them back as they wash into the blood trickling down his forehead.

"How old are those boys in your bed? Huh? Fucking pedophile. Taking advantage of needy kids, boys who have been tossed out of their homes. Only to have you ruin their fucking lives," Cordon growls like a hungry wolf as he pulls Lansing up by the hair.

As Gio rolls Lucious onto her stomach, wondering where the hell Cordon is, the door to the backroom explodes open and Lansing's body flies out, sprawling to the bedroom floor, his face covered in blood.

He staggers to his knees, trying to get to the bedroom door, crying for help as he does. The .44 flies out of the backroom and cracks Lansing in the back of the head viciously, dropping him face-first to the floor, his teeth cracking against the tile.

Shocked, Lucious sits up, her screams drowned out by the thumping music echoing through the room. Gio's hand wraps around one of the poles, steadying himself, terrified, completely unprepared for the violence in front of him.

"*What the fuck, what the fuck, what the fuck?!?!?!*" Lucious screams as Cordon stalks out of the backroom while Lansing slides himself across the floor, his hand stretching out towards the gun.

But as he gets it, Cordon has him by the hair again, smashing his face into the floor.

As Lucious screams again, Cordon spins toward her. "Shut the fuck up!" Cordon orders.

Immediately going silent, a panicked Lucious grabs hold of Gio, unsure of what to do as Cordon balls up his fist, beating Lansing in the face mercilessly.

Horrified, Gio pleads, "Jesus Christ! Stop!!!"

His head snapping towards Gio, Cordon can see in his and Lucious' eyes that they are disgusted by what Cordon considers normal operating procedure. Releasing his grip on Lansing, he lets the bloody and battered man slump into a pile on the floor.

"Both of you, get up!" Cordon demands, waving Gio and Lucious in his direction. "Let's go!"

But Lucious is too shocked to even move. Cordon storms over, yanking her off the bed. "Goddamn it, I said move!"

Behind him, Lansing opens one of his swollen eyes. Just ahead of him is the gun. His shaking arm reaches out, his fingers bringing it to him. As he gets his finger on the trigger, he brings it up at Cordon's back. Without even turning, Cordon's foot comes around, connecting with Lansing's head, jacking him hard. The gun flies from his hand, skittering across the floor, and Lansing's body slumps, not moving.

"You killed him!" Lucious screams at Cordon.

Cordon glances over, diffident, noting that Lansing is still breathing before turning his attention back to Lucious. "He'll live. But you won't if you don't do what I tell you. Am I clear?"

Lucious nods, off-balance and unsure what is happening.

"Find some clothes. We're going on a trip."

Shoving Lucious toward Lansing's dresser, Lucious digs in and pulls out a pair of sweatpants and a tank top. "What about him?" Lucious asks, pointing at Gio.

"He's good undressed. It's how he'll find a ride home," Cordon responds, pulling out a roll of cash and handing it to Gio.

His eyes lighting up, Gio takes the thick wad of cash and holds it up next to the outline of his penis in the swimsuit.

"Mine's bigger."

"Disappear, kid," Cordon commands Gio, "before someone figures out you're the one that got me in here."

Lucious aims her contempt at Gio. "He *paid* you to hook up with me?!"

"Sorry," Gio offers with an innocent shrug. "I didn't know he was going to Hulk out like this. He just told me he needed to get to you, and this was easier than putting out for a bunch of old tricks for the next few months."

Giving Lucious another apologetic nod, Gio slips out the door. Cordon watches him as Gio scampers down the stairs, the two security men, paying him little attention.

"I can get money," Lucious says. "Whatever you're getting paid for whatever you're doing, I can get you more."

"Shut up," Cordon demands, pushing Lucious behind him as he peeks through the opening in the door, plotting their escape route. But he's snapped out of it when he hears from behind him, "I'm at Wayne's! This fucking lunatic is kidnapping me! He about killed Way---"

Cordon whips around to find Lucious with her cell phone to her ear. Yanking it from Lucious' hand, Cordon smashes it against the wall. Dropping the pieces to the floor, Cordon stomps on them.

"What the hell!? That's a brand-new iPhone!"

"Hear me and hear me good. If you yammer as much as that other kid, I will rip that little swimsuit off your ass and shove it down your throat. You talk, you die. You keep your mouth shut, do as I say, you'll come out of this alive," Cordon warns in a harsh whisper.

"Why are you kidnapping me?"

Ignoring the question, Cordon's finger gets right in Lucious' face. "We're going down those stairs together, our arms around each other, and right out the front door. You try to alert anyone, I will punch you in the head so hard you'll wake up in the hospital if you wake up at all. Am I clear? I want a response."

Lucious defiantly nods. As Cordon turns back to the door, Lucious seizes the moment and grabs Cordon's hand, putting a lock on Cordon's thumb, slamming her elbow into a pressure point in Cordon's neck. More startled than injured, Cordon's free hand comes up fast, right into Lucious' solar plexus, the air blasting from Lucious' lungs.

Staggering back, Lucious recovers quickly, jumping into the air and surprising Cordon with a kick to his head. Cordon wobbles a step, his fist coming up defensively. Lucious strikes, pummeling Cordon with kicks and punches, her skill as a fighter remarkable but not unexpected. Cordon knew the kid was a champion and prepared himself for Lucious to fight back.

Blocking Lucious' attack, Cordon finds his back against the wall. He drops to the floor and sweeps out Lucious' legs. Lucious hits the floor hard but startling Cordon, Lucious kips back to her feet, ducks under Cordon's meaty swing, pile-drives a few punches into Cordon's ribs, and screams for help, hoping someone can hear her over the overwhelming music.

Cordon shoves Lucious back into the dresser, but Lucious comes back swinging. Cordon continues to block most of Lucious' blows as Lucious continues to scream for help with each swing or kick, but the music drowns out her pleas.

"I. Should. Be. The. One. Calling. For. Help!" Cordon barks, as he blocks the flurry of Lucious' punches from doing any damage.

Needing to batter Cordon back long enough to escape, Lucious leaps in the air, her hips jerking hard as she comes around with a furious spin kick to

Cordon's head. But Cordon catches Lucious by the calf and slams her leg into the wall, holding her there, the leg up around Lucious' face as the barrel of Cordon's gun jams into Lucious' crotch.

"Hit me again, I'll open you up like a can of fish," Cordon snarls into Lucious' face.

Slowly letting Lucious' leg drop, Cordon grabs ahold of the dozens of necklaces Lucious wears, many appearing homemade, dangling with a charm or amulet, tightening his grip until the necklaces dig into Lucious' skin, choking her.

"Turn around," Cordon orders, spinning Lucious toward the wall.

In the small black bag over his shoulder, Cordon pulls out two zip ties. "I didn't want to do this," Cordon says as he binds Lucious' hands together with zip ties, and then grabs the necklaces again to maintain complete control over the kid. Yanking Lucious' body against his, Cordon holds her tightly, sliding the gun barrel up to Lucious' cheek. "This is how serious I am. I want to get out of here. And unless you want half of your pretty face blown off, you're going to do what I say. I feel you so much as tense a muscle, I'm going to send you home to your family in a plastic trash bag."

"My father would like that."

"Let's not find out, Bruce Lee."

After nudging Lucious out into the hallway, Cordon locks Lansing's bedroom doors behind him. Still holding Lucious by the necklaces, Cordon pushes her ahead, like a dog on a leash, the gun digging into Lucious' back. As a security guard rushes up the stairs, Cordon slams Lucious against the wall and puts his lips right up to Lucious', their bodies tight against one another.

"Scream, and I cripple your skinny ass," whispers Cordon, tightening his grip on the necklaces.

They stay lip to lip as the guard passes, rushing to Lansing's bedroom door and checking it. Finding it locked, the guard bangs on the door, calling Lansing's name.

Seizing the moment, Cordon spins Lucious towards the stairwell as Lucious gasps, "My father won't pay a ransom. He hates me."

"Your father is the one who sent me to pull your candy-ass out of this harem and get you home."

As Cordon shoves Lucious down the stairs, a pained sneer washes onto Lucious' lips, tears rimming her eyes. "Hope you already got your money, Big 'N Dumb. Because I'm not going home."

Controlling Lucious as they descend the stairs, Cordon talks into her ear. "Sorry to disappoint you, kid, but that's exactly where you're going. Your parents' decision, not yours. When you're eighteen, you can make your own decisions. Until then, they call the shots."

"I AM eighteen," Lucious snipes, "you muscled bitch!"

"You're fifteen. I have your birth certificate," Cordon says as he hears Lansing's bedroom doors being smashed in.

"You might have a birth certificate, but it's not mine. I'm an adult! This is kidnapping!"

Cordon's eyes register the icy possibility he's been played. But the alarms suddenly echoing through the house snaps him out of it. Everyone freezes immediately, unsure of what's going on, except for Cordon, who drives Lucious down the last few stairs and turns for the front doors to make his escape.

But the front door swings wide and security men flood into the expansive foyer. Turning, Cordon sees more coming into the house from the back patio. Not wanting to take on an entire security detail, Cordon hoists Lucious onto his shoulder, dips his head, and dashes towards the door.

"Help! He's kidnapping me!" Lucious bellows, kicking and squirming, trying to swing her body off Cordon's shoulder. "Help me! I live here! He's taking me!"

As the security men move toward Cordon, he drops Lucious to her feet and holds her in front of him as a shield. "Bad move, kid," Cordon growls into Lucious' ear as Cordon focuses on the group of confused security men. "This kid's high. Lansing threw him out. I'm taking him home."

"He is not! He's kidnapping me!! Help me, dammit!"

The security detail isn't sure what's going on as Cordon grabs the necklaces again, twisting them to shut Lucious up. As two of the security team reach for their weapons, Cordon's free hand reaches around his back. If they want a gunfight, Cordon's more than ready for that too, but the first one dead will be Lucious.

But just then, the security guard upstairs leans over the railing and calls down to the others. "Up here! Mr. Lansing's been hurt!"

The security detail rushes past, bounding up the stairs. Cordon spins Lucious towards him, looking her in the eyes. "You've pissed me off enough, kid," Cordon snarls just before slamming his thick forehead off Lucious'. Lucious' body slumps, wavering into unconsciousness. Cordon scoops her up in his arms like a sack of laundry.

Witnessing this, a beefy security man stops on the stairs and pulls his revolver. "Put him down!" he calls to Cordon, pointing his gun. "You're not going anywhere. We are on lockdown. No one in, no one out. Police are on their way. Now put that kid down!"

"With all these naked and high underage kids at Lansing's party, you called in the cops? That's genius. Lansing will end up on the cover of Newsweek with the headline The Gay Jeffrey Epstein. Advice brother, call them back and tell them it's a false alarm."

Another member of the security team moves up and puts his hand on Cordon's forearm. "Put the kid down. Who are you, and how did you get in here?"

"Here's my ID," Cordon responds as he reaches behind him and comes around blindingly fast with his gun, cracking the security guard across the head, dropping him, Cordon's aim going to the beefier security man on the steps.

"Toss your gun and your Taser down here. Sit your big ass down on the stairs."

The security guard does as ordered as everyone else backs away, terrified. Cordon kicks the weapons across the floor. Two more members of the security team blow through the front door and, before they can react, Cordon races past, carrying Lucious in his arms.

Once outside, Cordon fires a couple shots into the air, sending young men and boys scattering everywhere in fear as he jogs for the Lexus, still hauling Lucious. Opening a door, Cordon dumps Lucious into the car and flips himself over the hood, getting in the driver's side. Another security guard tries to stop him, but Cordon grabs him by the back of the head and slams his face into the side of the car. The guard slides down the car to the ground, out cold.

Starting the car, Cordon spins the Lexus from the berm where it's parked and punches it toward the gates, which are closing. Cordon buries his foot into the gas pedal, the car speeding at the closing gates as the security crew step in his path, drawing their weapons.

"Come on, come on, come on..." Cordon says aloud, one hand pressing Lucious down in the seat to protect her as he aims for the exit, where there's a line of cars on the other side waiting to get in.

As Cordon closes in on the front entrance to the property, his foot flooring the gas pedal, the security guards dive out of the way, one firing at the car. The Lexus rams through the narrow opening, directly in the middle. The Lexus embeds on the gates, only the nose of the car getting through as the airbags deploy.

Quickly unsheathing a knife strapped to his leg, Cordon slices through the airbags. As the security detail surrounds the car, Cordon realizes he cannot get out. Jamming the knife up into the convertible roof, he cuts it open like a surgeon and rises through the top like a chick hatching, his gun raised.

"You motherfuckers want to die for the twenty bucks-an-hour you're paid, mess with me. Otherwise, toss your weapons into the grass and back the fuck off," Cordon states calmly before firing one shot, which blows the revolver out of the hand of the security man furthest from the car.

Point made. The other security men toss their guns over in the grass and back away.

"Wise move," Cordon says thankfully as he grabs hold of Lucious and pulls her through the cut convertible roof. Lucious' eyes flutter open. Groggy, she realizes where she is and what's happening, her body jolting upright as if she's juiced with sixty thousand volts.

Seeing the confusion, the car jammed up against the gate and the slim opening, Lucious wrestles free of Cordon and throws herself down the crushed windshield. Up on her feet quickly, she maneuvers her thin body through the narrow opening in the gate and jumps to the ground on the other side.

Futilely, Cordon tries to push his thick chest through the slender opening in the gates, but no matter how he contorts his body, he's not sliding through that narrow of an opening. Grabbing both gates, he tries to Hercules them open. But the gates don't budge but a few inches.

Seeing Cordon trapped on the other side of the gate, Lucious backs away. Still dazed, she staggers as she walks backward, laughing at her former captor.

"Next time go a little easier on the protein shakes, Big N' Dumb!" Lucious calls to Cordon. "And tell my piece-of-shit father his fabulous daughter says 'suck my dick'."

As Lucious turns, her hands still zip-tied together, she flips off Cordon. Staggering a few more feet forward, Lucious smiles just a bullet eats the ground at her feet. She freezes in place.

"Next shot is into your ass. You really want to fuck up your best asset?" Cordon calls to her.

Lucious turns to face him, scowling.

"Don't think you're going to outrun a bullet, Kung Fu," Cordon says as he grabs the top of the gate and vaults over onto the hood of the first car into the line waiting to enter the property. Standing there, he aims the weapon right at Lucious again, wishing Lucious would run so he could put a bullet in her ass.

Lucious can see the fury locked in Cordon's eyes. It matches her own disdain. But she's certainly not about to challenge a guy this pissed off with a gun in his hand.

"You're a piece of shit like my father," Lucious barks as Cordon walks over the car, never taking his bead off Lucious. He jumps down off the car and stalks up to Lucious, grabbing her roughly.

"You got no idea, kid," Cordon says as he slams Lucious into an SUV waiting in line. Cordon swings open the door of the SUV and unbuckles the driver, who doesn't look over sixteen.

"Do your parents know where you are?" Cordon snaps at the kid as he yanks him from the SUV. Cordon points the gun at another baby-faced kid, this one in the passenger seat.

"What are you not getting, little boy? Out!"

The kid jumps out and Cordon shoves Lucious in, just as the first cry of police sirens drifts their way up the mountain. Pushing Lucious over into the passenger seat, Cordon climbs in. He takes out one of the small remotes again, and flips it on, jamming phone signals for fifty yards in every direction before throwing the SUV into drive, smashing it into the car in front of him, giving him enough space to spin the SUV out of the line of traffic and aiming it back down the mountain. Cordon tosses the remote into a clump of weeds growing out of the rocky ground, keeping all the signals jammed, and speeds the SUV down the mountain road, only stopping once to let four police cars, their sirens screaming, their lights flashing, pass as they race up the hill.

With the gun sitting on Cordon's lap, pointed in Lucious' direction, Cordon continues down the mountain as fast as the curvy road will allow. Knowing she can't jump out without dying, Lucious lays back in the seat, spent.

"Pull down the visor. I want to look at myself in the mirror," Lucious asks.

Cordon lifts his knife from his thigh sheath and cuts the zip ties from Lucious's wrists. "Don't do anything that will make me tie your ass up again."

"Whatever," Lucious spits out as she snaps down the visor and checks out her bruised forehead.

"Where are you taking me?"

Cordon remains silent, his ire finally back under his control.

"They're going to be looking for us. I'm sure the owner of this SUV who you attacked is telling the police everything as we speak. And it's not like everyone didn't have their phone out recording you taking me. Which means we will be found and you will be arrested, you fucking Neanderthal."

Still no reaction from Cordon, as his eyes watch every direction. Lucious glares at him, then looks out the passenger window.

"If you still think I'm returning to Chicago, think again. I'm an adult. You were tricked into kidnapping me, Big 'N Dumb. I swear. I don't have to do what my father wants, he has no say anymore. I can do what I want."

Again, Cordon remains silent.

"God, do you talk?! You had no problem threatening me before."

Pulling a cell phone from his pocket, Cordon punches in Frank's number.

"I got the kid. Extraction wasn't clean. Call Fu, tell him I need a jet waiting at Cochran Regional Airport. Address?! I don't know, look it up! I'm stopping by the hotel, grabbing my stuff. and heading straight there."

Cordon hangs up. Lucious still has her eyes locked on him.

"You should have killed me back at the mansion," she laments.

"Wasn't the deal."

"So, if my father had asked, you would have? That what you're saying?"

Why do all you kids talk so much? Cordon wonders. But knowing he'd be arguing this until his head exploded, Cordon opts to not to talk.

"What's my father paying you?"

Again, from Cordon, nothing.

"Goddamn it, Big 'N Dumb, it's my life we're talking about! What's it worth to that sick bastard?!"

Cordon growls like a chained dog, wishing this kid would shut the fuck up. "Be happy, snowflake," Cordon snarks. "You're going home. How many of those kids that you've been shacking up with at that mansion have a home to go back to? Your mom wants you safe, Lucas."

Lucious doesn't break her gaze on Cordon as tears well up in her eyes. "Lucious. My name is *Lucious*, asshole. Lucas is the name my father gave me. I'm Lucious!"

Seeing the tears in her eyes, Cordon shakes his head. "You're going to cry over that? Jesus, your entire generation is pathetic."

Lucious swings, smacking Cordon in the face. Screaming, she continues to strike Cordon, who crosses into oncoming traffic, barely missing two cars before he's able to pull the SUV back on his side of the road and get an arm up to prevent Lucious from hitting him.

"What the fuck?! You want to get killed?!"

Lucious snaps the gun from Cordon's waist, pointing it at him. "Let me out!" she demands.

Cordon's foot presses the accelerator, speeding up, weaving through the cars ahead.

"Kill me, you die too," Cordon replies, seeming to enjoy the one-upmanship.

Panicked at the speed and recklessness of Cordon's driving, Lucious hits Cordon in the shoulder with the gun.

"Pull the fuck over! I'm not playing with you, bitch!"

But Cordon smiles, staring straight ahead, his foot lodged on the gas pedal. "I'm just starting to play with you," Cordon mumbles, so softly Lucious isn't sure she heard Cordon correctly.

Cordon swings the SUV into the on-coming lanes again, this time in total control, weaving in and out of the expensive cars that tool down the street in the other direction. Terrified, Lucious turns away, preparing herself for a collision. As Cordon wedges the SUV between two on-coming cars, their horns blaring, their headlights blasting into the cab of the SUV, blinding Cordon and Lucious, Cordon snaps the gun from Lucious' hand, jamming it into her ribs as he whips the SUV back into the correct lanes.

"No more of this bullshit, kid. When you get back home, your mom will have one of the servants draw you a warm bath. You can get cleaned up and put what happened to you at Lansing's behind you," Cordon snarks.

Again triggered, tears rimming her eyes, Lucious closes her eyes tightly.

"What are you crying about now?!" Cordon wants to know.

"My mom died seven years ago, when I was eleven," Lucious howls. "My father doesn't want me home. He wants me dead. You're taking me to my execution."

Keeping his eyes on the road, Cordon listens as Lucious sobs, curling up tightly in the seat. Having spent a swath of his life forcing people to tell him the truth, Cordon hates that he can't tell if this kid is being honest about her mother. One thing Cordon knows for sure is that this kid is not the soft-bellied, prancing, sexually confused, party boy he was led to believe. As Cordon races toward the hotel, he again glances over at Lucious, who stares out the window.

Furious with himself for how this has come down, Cordon knows if something like this had happened overseas, he'd be dead. He vows to never pull another extraction for a civilian party again. No matter how sweet the payday.

Worse, someone's lying to him and it's rare that Cordon can't easily detect who. He assumes Lucious is a consummate liar. A lot of runaways are. They know how to survive, know how to make people believe exactly what they need to get what they want. But Cordon's gnawing fear is that Lucious is being honest. And he's being played by Fu, blinded by the massive amount of cash he's been promised to bring this kid back to Chicago. Glancing again at the distraught teen next to him, Cordon's gut is telling him that something darker is going on, and he blindly walked into it.

And that would mean the kid is telling the truth.

UGLY TRUTH

Zip ties bind Lucious' arms to the legs of the bed, spread eagle. She watches Cordon pace the room, holding a laptop in one arm as he types with the other hand.

"My mother's name was Ai. Capital A, small I," Lucious tells Cordon as Cordon leans up against the desk, facing her, working on the laptop.

Cordon glances over the laptop at Lucious. "Not what I'm searching."

"Sure it is," Lucious states assuredly. "You want to know if I'm telling you the truth. Go ahead, look it up. Look me up, the former Lucas Fu. You should be able to find out how old I really am. Then you'll feel even dumber than you already do, Big 'N Dumb."

Finding an article about Ai Fu's accidental drowning in Lake Michigan, Cordon's eyes again glance over the laptop at Lucious. A quick search of Fu's children gives Cordon their age at the time of her death. Doing a little math, Cordon realizes that what Lucious told him is true.

"Fuck me," Cordon muses, enraged, slamming the computer closed. He is pissed at himself for relying on Frank to handle the due diligence when it came to Fu, and not checking everything himself, especially after negotiating the exorbitant pay. Cordon battles his urge to punch a hole in the wall of the hotel room.

I'm getting soft, he chastises himself, disappointed that he let his emotions conquer his better sense. He allowed Fu to play him. Like he used to let his father play him. Once Fu brought up his sexual proclivities, his buried shame clouded his judgment. He believed that driving up the price for his services was the victory. But actually, it hindered him from doing the necessary homework, accepting that everything Fu told him as gospel and that all the documents he provided about his son were authentic.

Stepping out onto the balcony that overlooks the manicured drive up to the hotel, Cordon grabs the railing and shakes it as hard as he can, pulling it loose from the stucco. The only thing that makes him angrier than being played for a fool is that it happened because he reacted out of disgrace.

"Fuck this," Cordon says aloud, deciding to let Lucious go. He can't bring this kid back to his father. Lucious is an adult. Where she goes and what she does is her business. Fuck her father. He doesn't rule this kid's life. The sooner Cordon lets this kid go and confronts Fu about his lies, the better he'll feel.

Pulling out one of the burner phones, Cordon calls Frank.

"Goddamn it, Frank…" Cordon grumbles in a near-whisper.

"What? What are you upset about?" Frank answers, his brow furrowing at the ferocity oozing in Cordon's voice. "You got the kid? Tell me everything's good," he continues, exiting a South Side restaurant with a young woman, who takes his arm as they walk to Frank's Navigator across the street.

"What did you get me involved in?"

Confusion jumbles across Frank's face. "Involved in? You know what you're involved---What's going on?"

"The kid isn't fifteen. He's eighteen."

"So?" Frank responds, pulling out his keys, opening the SUV by remote. "Where are you, the airport? Just get his ass back here."

"His mother's dead."

As Frank moves around to open the door for his date, he says, "So, Fu stretched the truth a bit. Probably thought you would turn him down if you knew the kid was of age. None of this is a game changer, Cord. It's just a father playing the angles."

"Fu told me the kid's mother is the one who wanted him home."

Frank shakes his head, replying, "Maybe he believes that the kid's mother would want him home. She probably would and he knows it---,"

"Quit talking! QUIT! TALKING!" Cordon demands, stopping Frank in his tracks. Frank's date looks up at him with concern. Frank signals to her that everything is okay as Cordon says, "This kid says his father is going to murder him when he gets back to Chicago."

Frank mouths the word 'sorry' to his date as he opens the door for the woman, assisting her into the Navigator.

"The kid's lying. Wouldn't you? You don't want to go home, you're going to make it sound like the worst thing possible will happen. That's what he's doing. Jesus, man, don't let this kid play---"

As Frank moves to the driver's side of the Lincoln, Cordon watches a Mercedes Sprinter race down the drive toward the front of the hotel. Six men climb out and swiftly move into the hotel as a pack.

"Frank, did you tell Fu I was coming back to the hotel before going to the airstrip?"

Shrugging as he gets into the Navigator, Frank replies, "I dunno. I might have. I mean, I probably did."

Cordon's jaw tightens as he licks his lips.

"I am being set up, Frank."

"What?!" barks Frank, "No, man. Can't be. Where the fuck are you getting this?! Come on Cordon, don't wig out now."

As Frank mouths the word 'sorry' to his date once again, he tries to calm Cordon, saying, "Cordon, eye on the prize. Stay focused."

Pressing the ignition, Frank adds, "Remember, we are about to collect a huge, fucking pay---"

The tremor of the explosion causes Cordon to yank the phone from his ear. He can hear the sound of the explosion rip apart Frank's SUV, windows shattering, glass blasting into the street, raining down onto the concrete.

Every window up and down the block has blown out as the Navigator disappears into a dome of fire, the roof shooting a hundred feet into the air. Frozen, Cordon can hear it hit the ground, not knowing that it almost lands on the first person to stagger from the restaurant across the street. He doesn't need to see it to know that the Lincoln is just a growing tumor of smoke and flames. And that his friend is dead.

Rushing back into the hotel room, Cordon darts up to Lucious and, using his knife, cuts her free. "Your father isn't going to kill you when you get home. He's going to kill you now. Here."

"Now you believe me, Big 'N Dumb? What changed?" Lucious asks, standing, quickly stretching her body, knowing things are going to get very bad, very fast.

Slamming Lucious up against the wall, Cordon's thick finger goes into her face. "Shut the fuck up, you yammering knucklefuck. Pain. It's the one thing I'm good at. If you keep motoring your mouth, you're going to find out how good. Understand?"

Lucious sneers right in Cordon's face. "What-evs..."

Taking a breath to calm himself, Cordon grabs his guns and loads himself up with a small arsenal before opening the hotel room door. Sticking his head out, he surveys the hallway in both directions. Seeing no one, he turns back to Lucious. "Stay with me, do as I say, and remember, they kill me, they kill you."

As furious as Lucious is, being held hostage by Cordon, she knows this is fact.

Cordon steps out, Lucious staying right on his hip. They slide along the wall to the elevator alcove. But as Cordon pushes a button, one of the three elevators dings, the doors sliding open. Mashing Lucious up against the wall, Cordon hunches over her, his body protecting Lucious from being seen, hiding both their faces. Two men uniformly in black, step off, moving past Cordon and Lucious.

One of the men huff as he passes them, "Fags everywhere in this tow---" but stops speaking when he sees the guns lined up in Cordon's waistband.

Cordon spins, the meaty side of his hand brutally catching the man in the Adam's apple, crushing it back into his windpipe. As the man grabs for his throat, the other man reaches for his gun. With one hand, Cordon shoves Lucious behind him again, with the other, he yanks the man grabbing his throat in front of him just as the other man fires. Two shots blast holes into the man's chest. Cordon whips up a gun from his waistband and fires back just as the shooter dives behind the corner. As his gun peeks around the corner again, Lucious snatches one of the guns from Cordon's waistband, firing as just as the man's face appears, putting a bullet right through his eye.

Incredulous, Cordon barks, "You know how to shoot, too?"

"My father really wanted me to be a boy," Lucious responds as the stairwell door opens at the end of the corridor and another gunman steps onto the floor. Lucious fires at him, hitting him from twenty yards, as his partner behind him dives back into the stairwell.

From the other end of the corridor, a pair of gunmen dive into the hallway from that stairwell, taking cover in welled doorways. With a man firing from the stairwell door at one end, and these two firing from the other, Cordon and Lucious are trapped in the elevator alcove. Lucious punches the elevator buttons as Cordon pulls out the last of his guns, one in each hand now, firing in both directions. As one gunman tries to reposition himself down the hallway, Cordon blasts away, hitting him in the side, blood gushing down his shirt and pants as he drops in the middle of the hallway.

An elevator dings its arrival, the doors casually sliding open. Lucious backs in quickly. As hotel guests peek their heads out of their rooms, quickly slamming their doors at the sight of men with guns, Cordon dives into the elevator too.

Alarms sound through the hotel, and the two gunmen race from either end of the hallway as Lucious pokes the CLOSE DOOR button. As the doors slide closed, Lucious takes a calming breath, but an arm juts through the opening, stopping the doors from sealing. In the hand is a Smith & Wesson. 356. Cordon shoves Lucious to the floor as the gun fires over and over, blasting into the elevator, the walls splintering around Cordon. As the door opens, Cordon rips off his shirt and wraps it around the guy's hand and flipping him into the elevator.

It only takes Cordon a second to realize how big of a mistake he's made.

This guy is easily six-foot-eight, his forearms resembling an elephant's trunk, his shoulders nearly filling the entrance to the elevator. Cordon's eyes go to Lucious on the floor of the elevator and he screams, "Out!!"

Pushing herself off the elevator's back wall, Lucious squibs through the big man's legs as he yanks out another gun and tries to shoot Lucious as she crawls under him. Grabbing the guy's arm, Cordon brings his knee up as he drops his weight on his wrist, snapping it. His gun drops to the elevator floor as Lucious rolls out into the alcove.

As the big man roars in pain, Cordon hangs onto the broken arm, swinging his leg up, booting the man in the teeth with one foot, while his other foot comes down on the man's other hand, forcing the other gun from his grip.

The big man's hand, now free, slaps around Cordon's throat, smashing his head into the elevator wall, and holding him off his feet, a lethal position that Cordon has never been on the receiving end of. Cordon swings hard, pounding the man's arm while digging his fingers under the man's grip on his neck, trying to relieve the crushing pressure on his throat, but nothing he does moves the man's hand. The massive man is focused on one thing: killing Cordon.

As the elevator doors close again, Lucious flings her body back through, grabbing the gun the huge man dropped on the floor. As the doors hit Lucious' legs, she rolls over, staring up at the man's crotch. The man's face peers over his bulbous chest and belly, looking down at Lucious underneath. The big man lifts his foot to stomp on Lucious' face.

But Lucious is faster. Jamming the barrel of the gun into the man's crotch, she empties the clip. The enormous man releases his grip on Cordon and grabs his crotch, blood covering his hand. His horrified screams vibrate the elevator walls. As he drops his unsteady foot towards Lucious' face, Cordon grabs the ceiling struts and draws in a life-saving breath. Pulling up his legs, he kicks the big man back, driving his massive body out of the elevator.

Cordon swings himself out of the elevator, landing on top of the injured man as the man swings wildly at Cordon. Taking the incredible blows, Cordon's head jacks back just as he digs his index finger into the big man's neck, pulling out the man's jugular vein. As the big man comes around with his giant fist again, his punch knocking Cordon off, the man's vein still caught on Cordon's finger.

Blood sprays across the alcove, the big man gurgling, one hand trying to cover the gaping wound in his crotch, the other, the blood surging out of his neck. He tries to pull his body up against the wall, his eyes wide, knowing death is seconds away. Somehow the big man staggers to his feet. He kicks at Cordon's head one last time, but Cordon falls back to the floor, the boot flying right over his face, and lodging in the wall right above him. The big man topples, falling on top of Cordon, dead.

"Ohhh, Ugly Betty, that's nasty!" Lucious exclaims, looking at the man's blood-soaked dead body as Cordon crawls out from under it, discharging the two empty clips from his guns and reloading fresh clips from his pants pocket.

Standing, Cordon digs into his other pocket and pulls out the burner phone given to him by Fu. Knowing he's being tracked, Cordon crushes it under his heel before turning to Lucious.

"I thought you'd run," Cordon says.

"I'm safer with you."

"Glad you realize that."

"You're a much bigger target," Lucious adds, sort of joking, but mostly not.

DEATH OF FRIENDS

With her hands bound to the ornate metal work inlaid in the head board and a chain around her neck attached to the wall, Natasha can't wipe away the blood that cakes under her nose. She stares up as two figures loom over her, one standing behind the other.

"You are telling me this is a man," Fu says, sidling up next to Chen. Chen steps up closer to Natasha who struggles against the bindings. He opens her robe, revealing not only her large breasts but her penis and balls as well.

Fu turns away as if he'd witnessed something not only could he not understand, but something also that revolted him.

"Cover it! It's an abomination! Cover it!" he commands Chen, Fu's back turned to her.

Chen leans over Natasha slowly, taking one side of the robe and closing it over one breast, and then does the same to the other side, his hand slipping under the robe and tweaking her nipple roughly before his hand continues down her body to her penis. He then calmly steps back, the wolfish smile never leaving his lips.

Stepping over to Fu, Chen talks closely with him, as Natasha tries to hear what is being said.

"We are moving on the sister and the father," Chen informs Fu.

Nodding, Fu touches Chen's arm lightly. "Let Mr. Finn know you have…this thing…" he says, glancing back at Natasha. "We will trade her for Lucas. Let the bodies of his sister and his father announce to him just how serious I take this."

After making the sign of the cross, Fu glances back at Natasha.

"I'll pray for you," he says.

"Go fuck yourself," Natasha snaps back.

After Fu exits the room, Chen moves back to the edge of the bed. Natasha again battles with the bindings that puts her completely at his mercy. Chen opens her robe again, leaving her naked on the bed.

"I usually like them younger," Chen remarks, his hand wrapping over Natasha's mouth, preventing her from screaming as his other hand unhooks his belt. He crawls onto the bed, sliding his body between her legs and forcing himself onto her. Pulling down his pants past his thighs, Chen spits in his hand and massages his saliva on his penis. He climbs on top of her, his face going to hers.

"This might be the last time you ever get fucked. Lay back and enjoy..." Chen crows softly as he forces himself inside her.

Natasha can only close her eyes and let her body go limp.

***

The intense Palm Springs heat dissipates most nights. Just not enough to make it comfortable. Through the week of Pride, it doesn't matter much, as the men have come to party, don tank tops and shorts, or less, for most of the week, even when eating out.

Lucious and Cordon move through the crowd, hardly unnoticed; the clothes they're wearing are doused with blood, as if they're heading to a Halloween party instead of a Pride rave.

Crossing the street to Our Lady of Solitude Church, away from some of the noise and bodies of celebration, Cordon is on his own cell phone.

"Where are you?" he asks quickly.

As two men weld a hull in dry dock, Annie holds her cell phone to one ear, her hand over the other. "At work," Annie says loudly, making sure she's heard over the noise, trying to find somewhere she can hear without the cacophony drowning out the conversation.

"Listen to me. I need you to leave," Cordon demands, pacing the steps of the church. "Now. Get to my place. Call me when you get there."

"Why? What's going on, Cord?" Annie quizzes, the tension in her brother's voice scaring her.

A Miata rolls up in front of the church and slows to a stop. Gio is behind the wheel.

"Call me when you're at my place. Annie, no bullshit, go now," Cordon says, hanging up, as Lucious bounces down the steps of the church towards the tiny red car.

"Shotgun," Lucious calls out, causing Cordon to grimace.

"My big ass isn't fitting in the back of that thing. You, I could fold up like a postcard. Get in back," Cordon tells Lucious before turning his attention to Gio. "What is this? A lunch box?"

"Cut back on the steroids and maybe you'd fit. You're lucky I'm here at all," counters Gio.

It's then Gio realizes they are both covered with blood, his hands going up, trying to stop them from climbing into his car.

"Holy shit! Is that blood?! Oh no! I do not want blood all over my car. What happened? This is crazy! Oh God, you're going to get blood all over my interior! It better come out or you're paying to have my car cleaned!" Gio chatters in what seems like an endless sentence to Cordon.

His words don't stop Cordon from bending his body into the tight front seat as Lucious climbs into the car and shimmies down into the small space in the back.

"Damn you," Gio huffs out. "Tell me where to drop you off."

"Your place," Cordon states.

His eyes wide, Gio's head jerks in Cordon's direction as he turns off the car. "No! No! Not doing that. Not with you two covered in blood. Whose blood is that?"

"The guys we killed," Lucious states.

Gio spins in Lucious' direction, eyes even wider now, before turning back to Cordon. "*Guys*? As in more than... it's bad enough what you did to Lansing!

Now you murdered someone?! More than one?! Fuck this! Both of you, get out of my car. Call an Uber or something. But I want you both out of my car!"

Simultaneously, both Cordon and Lucious pull out the guns they have, holding them up, the lights from the church to glint off of the chrome barrels.

"You're fucking kidding me?! What, you're kidnapping me now too? I swear, I'm like a magnet for assholes," he mutters, starting the Miata and spinning it around in the street, heading back in the direction he came.

The music from the neighboring club pulsates through the walls of the parking garage. On their walk from Gio's car to his apartment, Cordon counts seven couples having sex in the small garage behind Gio's apartment building. Lucious cheers the couples on, while Gio walks past, totally nonplussed, as if seeing bodies tangled in the shadows of the parking garage is commonplace, which Cordon realizes it probably is.

Having showered and changed into a pair of Gio's shorts and a tank top, Lucious plays in the corner of the small apartment, where Gio has created a video set. There's a wide chair, and a table filled with lubes and sex toys sitting next to it. There are camera lights facing the chair and a stand to hook up an iPhone so Gio can do solo sex acts on camera for his paying customers and fans.

"Can I?" Lucious asks, pointing to the chair.

"Go ahead," Gio responds.

Lucious plops in the chair, examining the sex toys.

"This is so cool!" exclaims Lucious.

"Have you ever watched me?"

Lucious smiles, his shoulders going up around his neck. "Duh! Gio nine-plus-dot-com. We all know who you are. That's why I was so excited when you hit on me. And so hurt when I found out you were just doing it for the money."

"I'm sorry," Gio apologizes. "But come on, Lucious, you know you're fucking hot. Especially now that I've gotten to know you and found out you're kind of a badass and stuff. I'm totally into it. When everything is good again, we definitely gotta hook up."

"Cool! You can use this on me!" Lucious says, picking up a thick dildo and wagging it with a laugh.

"Mine's about that size."

Lucious' eyes widen with an anticipatory smile.

"If you want to do it on camera, I got like six hundred subscribers. They would *love* you and me together," Gio adds.

"You got a date!" Lucious announces, seemingly oblivious to the danger they are in. "I got a TikTok following and a YouTube channel, but that's just me and my friends dressing up and talking about our lives in Palm Springs like we're The Real Gay Housewives..."

"That's cool! I'll come on and play your big-dicked boyfriend," Gio laughs.

Lucious high-fives Gio. "Deal!"

The water from the shower ripples down Cordon's battered, bruised body, stinging all the cuts. But it's necessary. Time to isolate, time to think. He fucked up. Trusted. Didn't do his own due diligence. Relied on Frank. Dead Frank. Frank who told him this would be easy money. And he's stuck with a kid whose father wants him dead and wants Cordon dead as well. Fu knew Cordon wouldn't turn down a million-dollar offer. He studied Cordon's own sexual predilections to know that he would have a connection to his son, either sympathy or attraction, which would compel him to fly out to Palm Springs and retrieve him, a simple enough job on its face. Well, and brutalize Lansing righteously. Which might be the only part of what's come down that Cordon doesn't regret.

And Cordon willingly strolled right into this simple trap blinded by money and his own personal pains.

Hearing the water turn off and the shower door open, Gio and Lucious sneak a peek into the bathroom as Cordon comes out of the shower. They watch Cordon dry off, his hulking, muscled body, his scars and tattoos seen in quick glimpses through the crack in the door. They turn to each other and smile, bonding over their voyeurism.

"Would you?" Gio asks.

Lucious' smile grows. "Fuck yes. He's totally hot. Wouldn't want to marry him, seems way too fucked up, but I'd throw my legs in the air for him. He'd be like going to church," Lucious says, belting out a C note and holding it, making Gio laugh.

Gio concurs, "Give me a weekend in Big Bear with him and if he wasn't gay when we arrived, he'd be when we left."

"You think he's gay?" Lucious asks.

Gio pauses, pondering his answer. "I sure thought so when he picked me up at the gym. I mean, he was not shy about showing off. But he might have been just doing that to get to me because he thought I could get to you, I don't know. But we didn't do anything. Not for my lack of trying. So, I don't know what he is. Look at him, maybe he's one of those guys who works out a lot because he never gets laid."

Lucious can't help but laugh at Gio's observation. "Maybe we can interest him in a three-way," Lucious remarks, sticking up his hand, so Gio high-fives him again.

Gio gives Lucious a long look for a moment. "Did you really kill somebody?"

Lucious' mood shifts. Darker. Uneasy. She nods, nothing more.

But Gio persists.

Hearing this as he grabs the shorts Gio gave him, Cordon glances through the crack in the door at the two younger guys.

"It's not a game," he calls to them as he tries to get his legs into the shorts, but there's no way they are going to fit over his thick thighs much less his ass. He pulls them off and steps out of the bathroom, holding the shorts in front of his genitalia, a roll of steam coming with him. "Each time, it devours a piece of your soul."

"Each time?! How many people have you killed?" Gio asks, a mix of shock and interest in his voice.

Ignoring the question, Cordon deflects, saying, "You two nitwits enjoy watching me towel off?"

"You're lucky we're not jacking off," Gio answers.

"I probably am. And no, there won't be a three-way," Cordon answers, adding, "I could hear everything you two knucklefucks said while I was showering. You need to get that door fixed so it closes."

"I live here alone."

"You gotta have some shorts bigger than this."

"Why would I have shorts bigger than those? I mean seriously. I'm sure you could fit me and Lucious into a pair of your pants."

"Go. Find me something."

Gio grumbles as he goes through his closet, digging. From under a pile of old clothes, he pulls out a pair of battered sweatpants.

"Try these. This guy left them here a while back. He was pretty big," Gio says, tossing them to Cordon.

Cordon eyes the sweats dubiously.

"They don't have crabs or anything. I washed them. He just never came back for them. I think he was semi-straight and came like in two seconds, the moment I touched him. Probably embarrassed."

"What'd he go home in?" Lucious asks.

Gio shrugs. "The whole thing lasted like ten minutes and he was out the door. He paid, though. That's all I worry about. Wish they were all that fast."

Cordon turns and slides them on, both Lucious and Gio staring at Cordon's ass.

As he turns back around, they both applaud.

"Glad you're both having fun. Shirt."

As Gio digs around in his clothes for a shirt that will fit Cordon, Cordon turns to Lucious.

"You okay?"

"For a girl whose father wants her dead. Yeah, exquisite."

"You're still alive," Cordon reminds her.

Lucious smiles sadly. "So far. But my father has money to send more guys and more guys. Eventually, someone will kill you. And then me."

"Here!" Gio pipes up, tossing Cordon a shirt. "I won it in a wet underwear contest."

Opening the shirt, it reads: *BIGGEST DICK*.

Breaking up laughing, Lucious rolls her eyes dramatically. "My God, does that fit!"

Cordon tosses the shirt back to Gio.

"I'm not wearing this."

"You think I got a closet full of extra-large clothes? I can't believe I have anything that fits you. And you should be proud to wear that shirt. Plenty of old men would pay a ton for a monster gym bunny like you, especially if you're advertising a monster cock, too."

"Not looking for a career change."

"Please. Considering how insanely fucked up the one you have is, you should at least entertain options."

As Gio goes back to digging through his closet and then his drawers, trying to find something large enough for Cordon, Cordon's cell phone rings. He retrieves his blood-stained pants and pulls the cell phone from the pocket.

"Annie?"

Annie locks the door to Cordon's spartan apartment, her cell phone pressed against her ear.

"I'm here, Cord. Now, are you going to tell me what this is all about?"

"Go to the safe under my desk."

Even though she doesn't get the answer she wants, Annie bites her tongue. She slips over to his desk and finds a safe she never knew was there, hidden underneath.

"Okay…"

"Seven, nine, six, six, five," instructs Cordon.

Annie presses in the code, and the safe unlocks. Opening the door, there are envelopes stuffed with cash, paperwork, and a half dozen handguns.

"Take a gun," Cordon orders. "I want you to keep it with you. Make sure the safety is off and I want you to keep it off. If something comes down, don't be afraid to use it and use it quickly."

"Okay," Annie gulps.

"Get Dad. Bring him back to my place. Stay there. Doors bolted. Top and bottom."

"Cordon, you know Dad is not about to leave his apartment," Annie protests.

Accepting she's right, Cordon thinks silently for a moment before he sighs. "You're right, you're right," he mutters. "Go into the kitchen. Open the cabinet under the sink and pull everything out."

Annie does as requested.

Hearing everything hitting the floor, Cordon then says, "See the latch, pull up the bottom of the cabinet."

There is a hook bolted to one end of the cabinet floor. Again, Annie does as told, revealing a hiding area under the kitchen cabinet. Inside is a green military duffle bag. She muscles it out and sets it on the floor.

"Okay," she says.

"If he refuses to leave that fucking hovel of his, open the bag and have him take his pick. Then you get back to my place and lock yourself in. Don't go home, don't answer the door, and do not leave until I tell you it's clear."

"Clear?" Annie asks. "What's that mean? Goddamn it, Cordon, tell me what's going on!"

"I've been set up. They know about you and Dad. And I don't want them using you to make sure I do what they ask. I need you safe."

Trying to keep it together, Anne closes her eyes as she asks, "Where are you?"

"Palm Springs. But I'm coming back to Chicago as soon as I can. But, please, Annie, I have to know you're safe. Understand?"

"Yes. I'll get to Dad. Try to get him to come with me. If not, I'll let him pick whatever gun he wants or whatever..."

"Good," Cordon nods with relief. "Be aware of where you are and who is around you. These people...they're deadly."

Annie nods, not even aware she's doing it. "I'm scared," she admits.

"You should be. It means you'll be cautious. I want you to call me every half hour. Let me know you're okay. If I don't answer, leave a message. I'll be checking," Cordon tells her before he adds, "I love you."

Again, she nods. "Love you too, Cordon."

Annie checks the gun and makes sure the safety is off before going back to Cordon's vault and closing it. She slings the heavy military duffle over her shoulder and moves toward the front door.

***

A man in a hoodie bangs on the front door of Annie's home as another man slips off into the darkness toward the back of the house. The continual banging brings Aaron, gun in hand, and he shoves it into the man's face.

"My motherfucking brother-in-law send you? Huh? I don't care how tough he thinks he is, I'll put that homo in the hospital. You tell that big cocksucker that when his sister comes back, and she always comes back, she'll have him to thank for the shit that's going to rain down---"

Aaron doesn't see the other man, who slipped to the back of the house, creep up from the shadows behind him. A flash of a blade slices across Aaron's neck mid-rant. As the blood pours down the front of him, Aaron's eyes widen in shock. The man in front of him pulls the gun from Aaron's hand, shoving Aaron back into the house. As Aaron collapses to the floor, the man behind him steps over him and out the front door, pulling it closed.

***

Gio pulls out an extra-large tank top from his closet and shakes it out. Holding it up, Gio figures it's at least close to being big enough to fit Cordon.

"Here," he says, tossing it to Cordon.

Cordon glances at the front of the shirt, his eyes raising to Gio, as he displays the shirt for Lucious, who chuckles. The shirt reads: Sun's Out, Guns Out, causing Cordon to sigh.

"You don't have just a plain white shirt?"

"Not that will fit you! Damn, you're particular. It's either big cock or big arms. Your pick."

Resigned, Cordon pulls the tank top over his head and wiggles his upper body into it uncomfortably, the shirt clinging to him like neoprene. Refocusing on Gio, Cordon moves closer to him.

"I got a couple other requests…" Cordon announces.

"Can I say no?" Gio asks.

Cordon doesn't crack a smile, which gives Gio his answer.

"We need your car. We need to get to Los Angeles. When we're there, I'll park it somewhere safe and tell you where it is. There's another five grand in it for you."

Gio's eyes light up at that number. "Okay…" he says, retrieving the keys to his Miata. Handing them to Cordon, Gio adds, "Take care of it."

"Yeah. We wouldn't want anything to happen to your sorority girl car."

Lucious groans. "I think it's cute!"

"There's a shock," Cordon snarks.

"What do you drive, Big 'N Dumb? One of those giant trucks with the gigantic wheels, with a gun rack in the back window? Or like a converted ice cream truck loaded with guns and explosives?" Lucious asks.

"Cut me some slack, junior. If it wasn't for you and your fucked-up family, I'd be kicking back right now in front of my flat screen, eating a plate of sushi and having a beer."

"Add a guy bouncing up and down on my dick and that sounds like a date!" Gio giggles.

"Me! Me!" Lucious reacts, her hand waving in the air, causing Gio to laugh even harder. Even Cordon has to crack a slight smile.

"Glad you knucklefucks find this funny. I'm facing at least 40 years for assault, B&E, kidnapping, and gun charges. I'll be in there forever if they tack on murder. That's if your dad's minions don't find us first and chop off my head."

Lucious stands, her mouth turning to a pout. "I didn't ask you to kidnap me. You did that out of greed."

"You got me there," Cordon admits, his demeanor growing more serious by the word. "But you wanna know why I really came after you, kid? I truly thought you were underage and being kept by a pedophile. I get that your home life sucked. But I didn't want to see you abused twice as a kid. The fact you're an adult and chose to live with Lansing, that's on you."

Gio wags his finger in Cordon's face, playfully. "Know what my grandma used to say about people who don't have nothing nice to say?"

Cordon's hand engulfs Gio's hand, moving it out of his face. "You two skinny assholes should hook up. You're ideal mates. Two squirrels with daddy issues whose heads I could rub together and not even get a spark," Cordon sniffs. "Want me to say something nice? How about stop peddling your cock? Finish school. Be something other than a piece of meat. You're worth more."

Reacting sharply to the stinging compliment, Gio sours. He reaches over and yanks open the refrigerator door, displaying the few items inside.

"Worth more? Talk to the refrigerator," Gio fumes.

Accepting that he's overstepped, Cordon takes in Gio's small apartment, nearly a third of it taken over by his mini studio where he performs sex acts on himself to pay his rent, a bed where he entertains strangers to buy food, the music blasting through the walls so loud you might as well be in the club next door. This kid, not even eighteen, does what's needed to survive. Cordon wishes he hadn't judged. What more could he expect this kid to be doing? He's taking care of himself. Gio isn't stupid. He can't afford to be. His future, that's up to him as well, and Cordon lecturing him about it, will not change the present.

Especially with what Cordon needs to ask next.

Cordon's hands go up in defeat. "You're right...sorry. It's your life, and you're doing what you need to, kid," Cordon responds before adding, "But I need one more thing from you..."

"What now?" Gio asks, pursing his lips.

"I need the ten Gs I paid you."

Gio's entire body tenses. He steps around Cordon, forcing Cordon to turn to him.

"You want my car AND my money?" he yelps, sassy in his voice. "Oh, hell to the no! I got you to Lucious, that was the deal. I earned that money! No. Sorry. Not happening."

Cordon takes his wallet and opens it, pulling out the credit card that Fu gave him.

"Take this. Max it out. I don't care. But I need cash."

"Too bad. I'm not giving you the money I earned."

Cordon presses the credit card against Gio's chest.

"Take it. Buy a plane ticket home. Fill your refrigerator with steaks and lobster. Go to college. I don't care. There's a huge limit on it."

Gio walks away, letting the card drop to the floor.

"So her dad can show up at my door?" Gio snaps, pointing at Lucious. "Like he's not following your credit card purchases? Guess what, Big 'N Dumb, I go to the movies too. I know how this all works. Keep your card, you use it."

Lucious steps between them. "Look, Big 'N Dumb, we don't need his money. You use your card---"

"Don't tell *me* how to stay alive! And the next one of you to call me Big 'N Dumb will find my foot up their ass!" Cordon snaps before pointing to the door and telling Lucious, "Go outside!"

Lucious doesn't move, unsure, his eyes bouncing back and forth between Cordon and Gio.

His anger percolating, he shoves Lucious toward the door. "I said wait the fuck outside! You want to stay alive, you better learn to listen!"

Opening her mouth to protest, Lucious says nothing. She slips to the door, giving Gio an apologetic look. "I'll be in the car," she says, giving Gio one more puppy dog glance.

"Remember, kid," Cordon tells Lucious before she exits, "I'm the bigger target."

Understanding what he's inferring, Lucious exits. Cordon turns back to Gio. He doesn't have to say anything; his look tells Gio he's no longer fucking around. But Gio is not about to go down without a fight. He takes the roll of cash and jams it down the front of his shorts into his underwear. The expression on Cordon's face twists from anger to disappointment as Gio crosses his arms over his chest defiantly.

Stepping up to Gio, Cordon presses him back into the apartment-sized stove in the tiny kitchen. Cordon towers over Gio, hoping his looming physicality will prevent Gio from prolonging the inevitable. But Gio remains defiant, not moving, his eyes locked onto Cordon's. Under different circumstances, Cordon would give this kid credit for standing his ground. Not unlike Lucious, Cordon underestimated Gio's fortitude. These kids who grow up abused and ridiculed for their sexuality or sexual preference, called names, beaten up by parents and bullies, ostracized and humiliated, find a resolve so deep, they become desensitized to fear. 'Fuck it, been there, done that, don't have time to be scared,' becomes a mantra. Fighting that hard and that long to survive, to simply be who they are, they evolve into the grittiest and most powerful.

"Sorry, man," Cordon growls with sincerity, as his hand slides down the front of Gio's pants. Gio fights him, trying to pull his hand out, but Cordon isn't leaving without the money.

"Get out! I earned this! God, get your hand out of my pants!"

Gio punches his arm over and over until Cordon grabs Gio by the shirt, lifts him off his feet, and slams Gio into his refrigerator. Fear floods Gio's eyes, as he's now face to face with Cordon.

"Big fucking ape! Soon as you're out that door, I'm calling the police and telling them you stole my car and robbed me!"

Tears fill Gio's eyes as Cordon again slides his hand down the front of Gio's pants into his underwear and comes up with the roll of bills. He sets Gio down to the floor and turns, walking toward the door.

"Enjoy yourself?" Gio spits out.

"I'm not enjoying anything about this. I said I was sorry."

Cordon picks up the credit card from the floor and tosses it on Gio's bed. As he gets to the door, Cordon turns one last time, locking eyes with Gio, who wipes his tears away. Not Cordon's proudest moment, but a result Cordon needed. Which is how Cordon's been programmed to get through life.

***

Annie's battered SUV rattles down the street, pulling into the first parking spot she finds. She parks badly, the backend sticking out, and quickly rushes from her car. Lugging the military bag, she crosses the street, heading towards her father's apartment building as her phone rings.

Checking it, she sees that it's the Chicago Police, which stops her in her tracks.

"Hello…," she says, her eyes holding a mix of emotions as she says, "Yes, he's my husband."

Her bottom lip trembles as she listens.

"Oh, God… He's dead?"

Tears fall down her cheeks as she glances around, now terrified to be out in the open.

"Okay. Yes. But I can't get there right now. I'm…I'm out of town," she rambles. "I'm sorry."

She hangs up. Annie can't be sure that not telling the police what's going on is the smartest move. But not knowing what her brother is involved in leaves her little choice. He's mentioned doing some work for the Chicago Police Department. Someone in the department had to be tied in whatever Cordon's involved in. But Annie doesn't know enough about it to be sure of anything, except that now her husband is dead. That his murder is in retaliation for whatever Cordon's caught up in.

And if she had been home too, she would be dead as well.

With the heels of her boots clacking off the sidewalk, Annie reaches around and feels the gun she has in her jacket pocket, making sure she can get to it quickly. She clomps up the steps to the door of her father's building and puts a key in the lock, her hand trembling. Getting inside, she makes sure it locks behind her.

Hustling down the hallway, Annie finds Nelson's apartment door cracked open. She freezes, her shaky hand reaching into the pocket and slipping out the gun. Pushing open the door, Annie peeks down the long, dim hallway. Seeing no one, she holds the gun out in front of her, making doubly sure the safety is off.

"Dad…" she gulps out, terror preventing her from speaking in a full voice.

Getting no response, Annie slowly steps down the hallway, the sound of a game show coming from the TV room at the end of the slender apartment.

"Dad?" she calls louder.

Still no answer. She moves, step by step, to the TV room. Coming around the wall quickly, gun ready, she finds the TV on and her father in his chair, his eyes closed, his body slumped to the side. Moving to her father, she shakes him but gets no response.

"DAD!" Annie yells. "DAD!!!"

Shaking him harder, he still doesn't come to, but a bottle drops from his hand. That wakes Nelson from his stupor. He bolts upright, his eyes open, hazy.

"What the fuck are you doing?!" he grumbles.

Annie sighs with relief, her shoulders relaxing.

"Your front door was open!" Annie crackles.

Nelson looks at her oddly, pissed off. "I took out the trash. Guess I forgot to close it. Fucking shoot me."

Annie drops the duffle bag at his feet, allowing him to see the gun in her hand.

"I was joking," Nelson adds, surprised.

Annie dashes from the room and back up the hallway, slamming the front door and locking it before storming back to her father, grabbing the remote from his chair, turning down the TV.

Hurriedly, she explains to her father what Cordon relayed to her, and that Aaron has been murdered in their home.

"I want you to grab some clothes and your medications," Annie tells Nelson, who watches the TV as his daughter talks. "We have to go. Now."

Nelson's face screws up. "Piss on that," he says with finality. "I'm not going anywhere."

"Dad, wake up! They murdered Aaron. They'll kill you too! We need to get to Cordon's. It's the safest place."

"There's a hundred assholes that could have offed your husband. He had that effect on people. Hell, sissy boy could have done it. I'm not going anywhere. I'm staying right here," Nelson yaps, rubbing his face. "You go. Get out of my place, little girl. Before I make you sorry you were born."

"I told Cordon you would never leave," Annie says, dejected. "God knows why he would want to make sure you're safe the way you've treated him all his life."

"I don't need nothing from that faggot."

Annie's face grows hard. She squats over the military bag and unzips it, revealing the cache of weapons. Nelson rubs his eyes as they focus in on the variety and number of weapons inside. As Nelson reaches for the G-18 9 mm. on top, Annie swiftly zips the bag closed, almost catching Nelson's fingers.

"I'll tell him you said that."

As she moves to pick up the bag and muscle it back onto her shoulder, Nelson seizes her by the wrist. Annie swings up the .38 in her hand and places it against her father's temple. It takes all the strength she has not to pull the trigger and tell the police she found him that way when she arrived.

"I better hear an apology or you aren't getting shit out of this bag," she snarls, having had her fill of her father's abuse.

Nelson glares up at his daughter but seeing in her eyes that she's not joking as she makes sure he feels the barrel of the gun against his head, he grits his teeth as he drops his head.

"Sorry..."

"That's a little better," Annie states, settling the bag back on the floor.

***

Outside Gio's apartment, the overbearing music is even more intrusive. Feeling shitty about what went down with Gio, especially after the kid did everything Cordon asked, Cordon skulks towards the parking garage, still pissed off at himself. The pulsing music bounces off the concrete walls of the parking garage, making it almost impossible to even hear the music due to the various echoes. Glancing up, he spies one of the security cameras knocked loose from the wall, dangling by its wires. He didn't notice that when they walked to Gio's apartment, and Cordon always notes where the security cameras are mounted in any location he walks through. Stopping, Cordon turns, searching for another security camera. He finds one. On the ground. Someone has also knocked it off the wall.

Picking up his pace, Cordon rounds a support pillar when the sound of a struggle lodges in his ears, mixing with the pounding music. Taking out his gun, Cordon dashes around the concrete wall, spotting Gio's Miata. Lucious is in the passenger seat, and someone is behind him, strangling him with his necklaces as Lucious fights.

Cordon takes aim and blasts two shots, hitting the strangler in the upper torso, dropping him. Lucious pulls away, gasping for solid breath as Cordon rushes up, his gun ready. He checks the man he shot. Dead. Then he turns to Lucious, examining the burns on his neck from the necklaces.

"We got to get something on that," Cordon says as he pats Lucious on her back. "Breathe, kid. Breathe…"

Cordon feels something poke into his back. He recognizes it immediately. The barrel of a gun.

"You had to kill Mickey," says a voice Cordon identifies as Jackie's. "I know you're a good enough shot. You couldn't have just wounded him?"

"Like he was just trying to wound Lucious?" Cordon responds, holding up his gun. Jackie takes it from him, then pulls a second from Cordon's waistband.

"You of all people should know not all things are equal," Jackie comments, moving around so she can face Cordon. "Guess I shouldn't be surprised, considering how you've made your living."

Jackie places herself between Cordon and the car.

"Thank you for giving me your phone the other day," she announces. "Made tracking you much, much easy. Figured I'd like you to do the hard work then just steal the food out of your mouth."

Lucious sits taller in the seat, still coughing, trying to catch a deep breath and control her racing heartbeat as her eyes lock on Jackie, trying to figure out how to grab her gun or knock her over without getting Cordon shot in the chest. Looking up at Cordon's face, Lucious realizes Cordon isn't looking at Jackie. He's staring over Jackie directly at her. Locking eyes with Cordon, Lucious watches as Cordon's eyes signal Lucious to look down just outside the car.

Leaning over the edge of the door, Lucious spies Mickey's gun on the ground. Lucious' hand slides onto the door handle.

"Don't take it personally, Cordon," Jackie continues. "It's just a job. We're alike there."

"There's a difference," Cordon says, taking a slight step back, knowing what Lucious is planning.

"What's that? I have a gun and you're sort of screwed?" Jackie half-jokes.

"I don't yammer as much."

As Cordon finishes his sentence, Lucious shoves the car door open, slamming it into Jackie. Cordon dives onto the Miata's hood as Jackie's gun fires, just missing him. As Cordon slides off the hood, onto the ground on the other side, Jackie fires again, not seeing Lucious grab the gun as she swings around towards him. Enraged, she continues firing, blasting out the front windshield, which shatters all over Lucious.

Cordon stands, drawing focus. Jackie holds her aim right on him. "I hope your hell is women talking, asshole," Jackie snarls.

The first bullet hits her in the shoulder. The next bullet hits her in the chest. As she screams in pain, her aim whipping towards Lucious, Cordon flies over the hood of the Miata, knocking the gun from her hand before tackling her to the ground. Jackie pulls a knife from her boot, but Cordon swats it from her weakened grip and stands over her, staring down as the life oozes from her, spreading across the concrete floor of the parking garage and pooling around her body.

Lucious steps from the car, the gun in her hand. Her entire body trembles as she stares down at Jackie, gurgling as she takes her last breath. Lucious wants to break down and cry, but she can't. Not now. This feeling differs from what she felt earlier when she killed the men her father sent after her. It's not just that Jackie is a woman, though there is that. Taking her life in this garage, knowing she would have killed her or handed her back to her father without batting an eye, shooting her feels more personal. Yet, Lucious can't find the anger, only the sorrow.

Jackie's mouth moves but there's no sound, and Cordon is unable to understand what she's trying to say. Reaching down to the pocket of her jeans, blood on her hand, causing her hand to keep slipping, she tries to reach inside. Finally getting her fingers in the pocket, she slides out a piece of paper but stops, her hand falling away.

Her eyes stare up at Cordon.

"She's dead?" Lucious asks, her voice tight, terrified, as if she needed verification, and vindication, for what she did.

"You saved my life, kid. Probably both our lives." Cordon tells her.

Seeing the conflict in Lucious' eyes, Cordon reaches over and gently takes the gun from her hand, setting it on the hood of the car. Lucious turns away from the body. Leaning over, Cordon extracts the piece of paper Jackie was struggling to pull from her pocket. Opening the paper, there's a drawing of a banded arrowhead. Furrowing his forehead, Cordon can't match it with anything, so he shoves the paper into the pocket of the sweatpants with the roll of cash. He steps to Lucious and squeezes her shoulder awkwardly, trying to comfort her.

"Hey..." Cordon says, but as he's about to continue, both he and Lucious hear a scream overpower the club music. They both immediately recognize the voice.

Gio.

Grabbing the gun off the hood of Gio's car, Cordon races back towards Gio's apartment. Hearing a struggle inside, Cordon lowers a shoulder and crashes through the door, coming up with the gun, his aim steady and deadly.

"Let the boy go," Cordon rumbles.

Lucious appears behind Cordon, and her eyes widen in horror.

In the corner of the kitchen, a knife-wielding man holds Gio by the hair. There are deep, open slashes across Gio's face and torso, the entire front of Gio's shirt sopped with blood.

The man with the knife sneers at Cordon, holding Gio between Cordon and himself. "Give me the slanty-eyed bitch and you can have this one," the knife-wielding man snarls.

"Your friends are both dead. So are you. How excruciating I make it depends on what you do next."

The knife goes to Gio's throat as Gio sobs, softly begging for his life.

"You want him?" the guy with the knife asks as he grins. "Put the gun down and come and get him. I'd enjoy carving on a canvas as large as you."

Lowering his aim, Cordon sets the gun on the floor.

"You, bitch, step in and away from the gun," the knife-wielding man waves at Lucious.

Lucious complies, moving to another corner of the apartment as Cordon steps toward Gio. His eyes implore Gio to stay calm, as Gio continues to sob in an inaudible hush.

"It's going to be okay, kid..." Cordon assures Gio as he takes another step toward him.

"Let the boy go and come for me," Cordon chides the knife-wielding man. "I'm right here. You got the knife, I don't. Let him go."

The man with the knife lets his grin expand to a full smile. "As you wish."

He plunges the tip of the knife into Gio's neck and rips it wide open. Blood gushes from the wound, his eyes frozen in the horror of death as he collapses to the floor. Lucious screams, wanting to rush to Gio but knows she'll never get there without being gutted herself.

The man with the knife leaps at Cordon, ready to do damage as he pulls out a second knife, swinging them with vicious accuracy and driving Cordon backward.

Getting his hands on a cheap bar stool, Cordon comes up with it, blocking the knives as they whoosh through the air in front of him. With his rage seething, Cordon backs up near Gio's small sofa, still blocking the blades. His hand finds a lamp and he brings it down hard on the man's arm, forcing one knife to clatter to the floor as the other blade swipes in front of Cordon's face. nicking his cheek.

Flipping the set chair around, Cordon rips two of the legs off, now having two aluminum rods in his hands. Knowing Lucious' background in martial arts, Cordon flips the chair to her and Lucious does the same, ripping off the other two chair legs, flipping them in her hands like bo staffs. As the man with the knife turns toward Lucious, Cordon rushes him, his meaty hand slamming around the man's hand holding the knife. Cordon squeezes with everything he's got, crushing bones.

The man barks out in pain, and punches Cordon with his free hand, but Cordon doesn't flinch as he continues breaking the bones until the knife clangs to the floor. Lucious sweeps in and knocks the knife across the room with one of the chair legs.

Throwing the man back into the wall, Cordon rams a chair leg into the man's shoulder and drives it through with all his rage, pinning the snarling, screaming man to the wall.

Cordon grabs the other leg off the floor and slowly walks up to the man, who tries to protect himself with his free hand, but Cordon presses the chair leg into his other shoulder, piercing the skin, through the meat, dislodging the bone, all the way through and into the wall behind him, crucifying him.

Lucious steps back, having never witnessed such deep-felt wrath before. The glaze in Cordon's eyes is feral, lethal, as Cordon licks his curled lips, instinctually knowing how to deliver pain.

Dropping to the floor, Lucious releases the chair legs and crawls to Gio. The blood still pumps slowly from the oozing slash in his neck. As Lucious tries to stem the bleeding, Gio's eyes open.

"I got you. I got you," Lucious calls to him softly, reassuringly. But Lucious knows that there's nothing she can do to save Gio. All she can do is hold him in his last moments and let him know someone is with him.

Sweeping a pair of Gio's underwear off the floor, Cordon steps right into the man's face as the man continues screaming.

"I'm going to kill you more painfully than I've ever killed anyone," Cordon says in an almost inaudible growl. Digging his fingers into the sides of his face, Cordon pries open the man's jaws, and stuffs Gio's underwear deep down into the man's throat until he gags, hardly able to breathe. He grabs a pencil and snaps it in half, jamming it into the man's mouth and jacking it open, preventing him from closing it without sending the lead through the roof of his mouth. Cordon then grabs a third chair leg from the floor and bends it into a U, shoving the ends into the wall on either side of the man's head, until it's held in place, and he's unable to look to the side or up and down.

"Look at me!" Cordon demands as the man's eyes turn side to side, not willing to look directly at Cordon. "LOOK AT ME!" Cordon screams at the man, not even an inch from his face, his gray eyes almost black with madness. As the man peers into Cordon's eyes, Cordon stares back silently for a long moment, then screams in the man's face with such savagery, Lucious jumps, clinging to Gio's body protectively.

Cordon backs away a step, and then with venomous fury, slams his forehead off the man's nose. Blood pours from the man's nose like a spigot, and into his open mouth.

"Your own blood will soak that cloth and you will slowly drown. It will take a long, gruesome time. Your mind will fuck with your body as it panics for air, and you feel yourself drowning," Cordon rumbles, his mind crashing back to a time when torture was his entire existence.

As Cordon picks up the last chair leg from the floor, he moves to the stove, turning it on. The terrified man tries to scream but cannot.

Frozen, the ugly maliciousness of what he's witnessing rattles Lucious to her core. She's too horrified and too frightened to do anything to stop Cordon.

"I don't want you to bleed to death before you drown," Cordon spits out through gritted teeth, his nostrils flaring wide as he rotates the end of the chair leg in the orange flames from the gas stove.

As Lucious watches incredulously, Cordon jams the smoking end of the third chair leg into the man's neck, near where Cordon impaled him to the wall, where . The man tries to scream through the soaking underwear, coughing, choking, his head shaking back and forth as no air is getting through, no oxygen going to his brain. He's drowning in his own blood.

Cordon does the same thing to the other side of the man's neck, producing the same reaction. When the man passes out from the pain, slumping, Cordon grabs him by the face and punches him in the nose again, bringing more blood pouring down.

"Wake up, motherfucker. I want you to feel this!" Cordon screams, completely overtaken by a frenzied anger that's erupted inside him. Staring into the man's eyes as they flutter back open. Cordon's gray eyes hold nothing.

Turning to Gio, Cordon shoves Lucious back before gently picking up Gio's lifeless body and carrying him to the bed. Cordon gazes down at him.

He knows this was his fault.

Tears flood Cordon's eyes and he looks up to the ceiling, his guilt excruciating, and screams from the deepest and most tormented caverns in his soul. Lucious turns away, not wanting to witness this sort of raw anguish. Cordon's entire frame shakes with despondency and remorse as he leans over and holds Gio, sobbing as he kisses Gio on the head, muttering how sorry he is, as the man responsible suffers toward death, just feet away.

A gunshot causes Cordon to protect himself, spinning quickly towards the man impaled on the wall. His head is half missing. Blood, skull and brain matter splash across the wall like the spray from a fountain.

Lucious holds the gun.

"Fuck you and fuck my father," Lucious says to the dead man.

Cordon steps up and takes the gun, Lucious' head falling to his chest. As Lucious bawls, Cordon holds her tightly, both wrestling with their overwhelming emotions. Cordon tries to gain control again and bury them back where they've lurked untouched for decades.

"We need to go," Cordon says into Lucious' ear.

His words make Lucious even more despondent, her sobs harder. Cordon tightens his grip on her, clenching her against his chest. Together, they stagger towards the door. Outside, Cordon releases Lucious and staggers away from her, disappearing into the shadows, where he finds a place to be alone. Lucious understands, keeping her distance, allowing Cordon his space, his solitude, his pain.

BLOOD IN THE WATER

The water shimmers in waves of white and red and blue, the lights from the motel fracturing on the surface. The light in the pool is out, which allows Cordon and Lucious to swim nude, the blood washing off their bodies unseen as it snakes into the water.

Cordon climbs out, striding to a stack of guest towels piled up on a lounge chair outside of the older, roadside relic that fills up only a few weeks throughout the year, its laziness invaded this week by gay men and parties. Drying off, Cordon tries to wrap the towel around his waist but it's not big enough, leaving him nothing to tuck in or tie. He holds it over his junk and walks to the edge of the pool where Lucious swims and drops another towel, as Lucious swims over.

Lucious climbs out, unabashed at being nude, even in front of Cordon, and dries off with equal shamelessness. Not unlike Gio, Lucious' body was a trade, a tool to get what she wanted. After tying the towel around her thin waist, she stands in front of Cordon. Cordon reaches out and slips his hand under the necklaces.

"Where did you get all these?"

"Different places," Lucious shrugs.

"What do they mean?"

"Different things. Each one is kind of a memory."

As he lets them go, one charm catches Cordon's eye. An arrowhead that resembles the bloodstained drawing he took from Jackie's pocket.

"Maybe you should take them off while your neck heals," Cordon suggests.

Cordon moves behind her to help Lucious take off the necklaces, but Lucious presses her hand against the necklaces, stopping him.

"I'm good. I don't take these off. They keep me safe," she states.

"Safe?"

Turning to Cordon, eyeing his muscled body, secretly wishing he would drop the towel he's holding at his waist so she could see him in his entirety, Lucious' hand pats the necklaces.

"I know it's not real, not really," she says, "but I feel each one holds something important, something that will protect me."

"How's that worked out in the last six hours?" Cordon asks.

"I'm still alive, right?"

Cordon's mind immediately returns to the images of Gio laying dead on his bed and Lucious can see it in his eyes. "Yeah...we're alive," Cordon agrees uneasily, stepping away from Lucious.

"I'm sorry. I didn't mean it the way it came out," Lucious calls to him.

Cordon nods, his eyes scanning the roadside hotel.

"It's almost dawn. What do we do now?" Lucious asks.

Cordon nods across the pool deck towards one of the hotel rooms. Through the open curtains, two big guys, bears, are stripping out of their clothes after a night of partying.

"Promise me you won't hurt them," Lucious says, the death and damage she's witnessed a few hours earlier having exhausted her down to her bones.

Cordon collects the blood-stained sweatpants and cleans out the pockets including the car keys, the roll of cash, and the drawing of the arrowhead pendant, which he looks at once more before crumpling it and tossing it into the pool, letting it float into a drain.

Cordon watches the two men necking, their hands on each other's bodies as they fall onto the bed. He pads across the parking lot as other men getting back from a night of partying stare at a nude Cordon striding with lionesque confidence up to the door of the room. He flips the towel he's holding in front of him to the ground and beats on the door with his fist.

Lucious watches as the two men jump off the bed to peek out the window at the man standing at their door in the buff. They open it, both taking a step back to view the raw machismo of their mountainous visitor. Cordon speaks to them, talking with them closely. All three laugh, converse a moment more, the two men inside touching Cordon's chest, before stepping back from the door and allowing him inside.

Lucious moves closer to get a better view through the hotel room window. She's having a difficult time reconciling the man who just entered the hotel room with the man who walked out of Gio's apartment a few hours before. The two men slide their hands over Cordon's body as he takes each one and pulls them into a wanton embrace. Cordon's hand travels down their shirtless torsos to their pants, unbuttoning them. As the men slip out of their pants, Cordon struts to the window. He and Lucious stare at one another through the glass. Lucious shivers at the icy expressionless calcified on Cordon's face. Extending his arms, Cordon grabs each curtain and snaps them closed. The show's over for Lucious, and the voyeurs standing in the parking to appreciate Cordon's nude body.

After the gaggle of oglers slip off to their rooms, Lucious waits. In less than two minutes, the door of the hotel room opens, and Cordon stands in the frame, dressed in a sleeveless flannel shirt and jeans. He nods Lucious over.

Jogging in, Lucious sees the two other men, clad only in their underwear, both on the bed, not moving. Lucious takes a hard breath, his eyes squinting with dread.

"Unconscious, nothing more," announces Cordon.

"You sure?" Lucious asks, wanting verification but only gets a callous glare from Cordon.

"Find some clothes, we gotta move," Cordon tells Lucious as he grabs the car keys off the dresser.

Lucious takes much longer than Cordon would like to pick out clothes, unhappy with her choices, since both men are much bigger than her, and dress like urban lumberjacks, even in this heat. But after being chided by Cordon endlessly until she finally selected something, Lucious succumbs to the pressure and throws on a pair of baggy shorts and a button-down shirt that hangs off her. "I look like a Mathlete on spring break," Lucious complains as she kisses the two unconscious men on the forehead, apologizing.

The lights of Palm Springs disappear into the dawn of morning as Cordon drives the Pathfinder west, the town seeming to sleep a few hours before rising to continue the party. Lucious stares out the side window, needing sleep herself but too amped for that ever to happen. The previous night was too bloody to be a blur, still Lucious can only remember events in chunks of violence, fractured pieces of terror. Her mind won't let her replay the entire night.

Still numb, Lucious cannot believe the things she's lived through in the last six hours. Even worse, the things she's done. She's killed people. People who had lives. Loved ones they will never kiss again. Friends they will never again laugh with. Young yet pragmatic about death, Lucious understands that the choices these people made led to their deaths. Just as the choices Lucious made to take their lives allowed her to survive. Not without scars, physical and emotional, but still standing.

Lucious glances at Cordon next to her. If this big man hadn't gotten duped by her father, hadn't come to Palm Springs, none of this would have happened. Nor would this bloody mess exist if she hadn't run away. If religion and the need to control did not twist her vindictive father, if Lucious hadn't been born in the wrong body. So many 'ifs'. They reverberate in ways Lucious could never have expected.

Lucious couldn't fathom her father actually wanting her dead. When she was a child, her father coddled her because she was his only son. Lucious shined, the star in the family, causing her sisters to despise her secretly. Her father would have castigated her sisters if their disdain had been overt. But even as a child, Lucious understood there was something odd about herself, weirdly feeling that her sisters were superior to her being a boy. Lucious craved his sisters' femininity, their coy behaviors, their clothes, their hair, their makeup. She hated that she had a penis, and they didn't. Though Lucious couldn't grasp her feelings intellectually, she felt women were more powerful, beautiful, and innately sexier than boys.

And Lucious loved being sexy. But unlike most boys, she didn't want to make love to that form. She wanted to *be* that form. As Lucious aged, the more her longing to become the butterfly, unfettered by this ugly cocoon, grew.

Which only enraged her father. Fu put extraordinary effort into molding his 'girly' son into a man. Martial arts. Hunting. Church groups. Military school. Not unlike Cordon, Lucious became a black belt, winning fights because she was done being beaten up and pushed around. She became an excellent markswoman. And by fourteen, she compensated sexually by having sex with every man who was willing. She didn't give a fuck if her predilections were 'shameful' to her father. She built herself into a champion because Lucious never liked to lose and she understood that these skills might one day keep her alive. The more her father groomed her to be the man he wanted, the more she rebelled and became the woman she wanted.

Lucious knew one day she would get it. No matter what it took, she would physically become the girl she envisioned. And this was the fight for her life.

Cordon's phone ringing brings Lucious back from her thoughts. Cordon checks his phone, grimness tightening on his face, his jaw clenching as he answers.

"I'm going to kill you," Cordon says into the phone, immediately alerting Lucious that Cordon is speaking with her father. "For Frank. For Lucious. For a kid you don't even know. And I intend to make it excruciating for you."

Fu's bedroom is palatial, roughly the size of most middle-class homes. Most of the furniture is 18th century Queen Anne, a moniker that Fu dislikes, so he refers to it as Early Georgian. Back near the windows is a four-poster bed. A reading nook with floor-to-ceiling bookshelves nestles into a corner. Two tapestries adorn the wall between various paintings. Across the room, Fu sits at his only modern piece. An overly fussy Francesco Molon desk.

"We have your friend, Mr. Finn," Fu says into the phone.

Cordon doesn't speak, only his rhythmic breathing lets Fu know he's still there.

"I believe you may be in love with her. Or him. I'm very confused by what I've seen."

"That's the biggest mistake you've made," Cordon warns.

Fu smiles, feeling a hopeful sense of victory.

"Eliminate Lucas, and we can discuss sparing...it's...life."

His eyes slide to Lucious, who sits up attentively, waiting for clues to the conversation. But Lucious can feel heat radiate off Cordon, allowing him to assume correctly what his father is requesting.

Cordon stays silent, barely breathing, until Fu asks, "Are you still there, Mr. Finn?"

"Yes."

"If I do not receive proof that Lucas is dead by tomorrow morning, your friend will be by the end of the day."

"Make peace with your god, Mr. Fu."

"Don't overestimate your reach, Mr. Finn."

"I'm not."

Cordon hangs up.

"He wants you to kill me," Lucious states rather than asks.

Cordon doesn't respond, his mind in overdrive, trying to figure out his next move.

"Are you going to do it?" Lucious needs to know.

Cordon's hand lands on the back of Lucious' neck. He glances at her as he continues to drive. "My father is the sickest son-of-a-bitch that's ever existed. Horrible man. Despised me all my life. Did awful things to me..."

Pulling his hand off Lucious' neck, Cordon's nostrils flair at his own similar, dark memories. Lucious' eyes never leave him, knowing she's witnessing something rare, a peek under Cordon's thick, scaly armor.

"Only way I survived was to become this...thing. This monster," Cordon says, hitting himself in his chest with his fist. He grows quiet for a long moment before sadly adding, "And for some reason, that little boy locked inside me still wants my piece of shit father to respect me."

"You mean love you?" Lucious quizzes.

"My father can't love. He's incapable of that. I'm not sure I'm capable of it. When you never have it, you never learn it."

Lucious nods with raw understanding. At least she had her mother who loved her unconditionally and buffered at least a portion of her father's resentment that rained down on her.

Cordon allows the silence to settle him before he tells Lucious that her father kidnapped someone he cares about.

Taking in his words, Lucious turns back to Cordon. "And he wants to trade her for me?"

"He wants me to kill you."

Lucious sucks in a breath and holds it.

"That's not gonna happen. I'm not going to hurt you. That's a promise," Cordon assures Lucious, squeezing her shoulder. "But I am going after my friend. And I'm going to kill your father. I'm going to right this. All of it."

"He'll kill you," warns Lucious.

"After I get Natasha, I'll deal with your father," Cordon states, adding, "But right now, I need to get somewhere where I can clear my head and plan my attack."

"There's a really insane club a few miles up. It's not in the city of Palm Springs, so it's totally off the chain. It doesn't even open until three in the morning."

Cordon's head twists in Lucious' direction. "I say I need to think and the first place you think of is a club? Jesus, you *are* a little butt munch."

Lucious laughs. She shrugs again, saying, "Butt Munch. The nasty Muppet."

Cordon cracks a rare smile as Lucious presses her case. "When I want to forget everything, I like to get fucked, do drugs or dance my ass off. Seems the first two aren't on the menu, so.... Look, it's a great place. You can come dance and sweat and let your mind go, or you can stand in the darkness and let the music bounce off your big forehead. It's the best place to forget life and just be in the moment."

"Too many people will see us."

"You think anyone will care? Everybody in the place will be drunk or high or a mix of both. And we'll look like just another muscle daddy and his young, hot, gorgeous Asian trans girlfriend. Trust me on this, music's loud, there's a ton of bodies doing all sorts of things and lots of dark corners for you to hide. Perfect place to lose yourself, focus, and make plans. And I can burn off some memories of tonight."

"I don't know…"

"If I'm going to die, I want to be surrounded by a bunch of beautiful, half-naked men. Then if I'm killed and go to heaven, I won't even notice."

Lucious waits for a response, but Cordon just shakes his head, mumbling, "Butt munch."

***

With the TV blaring, Nelson sleeps in his chair, a ratty Afghan blanket pulled over him. A hand slowly grabs the remote, picking it up only inches off the TV tray next to the chair, and turns up the volume even more. A man steps behind the chair and strings out a garrote which drops to the sleeping Nelson's neck.

As the garrote pierces Nelson's skin, his eyes pop open. Nelson struggles against the wire, blood quickly oozing from where the garrote has cut through the skin. Nelson swings at the person behind him, trapping him in the chair, his arms unable to reach the assailant.

Throwing the blanket off as he struggles, Nelson's hand sweeps up with the 9 mm., firing over and over. Three bullets rip open the man's face from the chin up, killing him instantly.

Nelson bends forward, coughing hard. He pulls the garrote from where it's embedded into his skin and drops it to the floor just as footsteps pound toward the room from down the hallway. Another man storms into the room, a gun in his hand, not seeing that Nelson has pulled a rifle up from under the chair. Nelson fires wildly in the man's direction as the man dives into the room. Nelson blows apart a curio cabinet, his TV, childhood pictures of Annie, and the man, who topples to the floor, dead.

There is silence. Nelson glances at the two dead men and the mess he's made in his TV room.

"Never fuck with an old motherfucker," he grouses, pulling himself from the chair, his hand covering his bleeding neck.

***

The sun is up, the morning already hot and dry, but the club is dark and humid with the smell of poppers and drug sweat. Dim purple and blue lights are the only illumination, making all the glistening muscles in the room take on an alienesque glow, as if no one in this club is human. The dance floor gyrates with shirtless men, many in harnesses, chaps, and leather armbands. Their bodies pulse to the heart-thumping music, some coupled off, most dancing alone or in large groups, almost every one of them stoned but still preening.

Couples edge off into the inky corners to have sex or share hits. The sickly sweet aroma of amyl nitrate attacks Cordon's nostrils, giving him a dull headache. A group of skinny, shirtless club kids, including Lucious, dance with utter abandon, not far from where Cordon stands, against the black wall, looking more like an agitated bouncer than a horny muscle daddy searching for a boy to take home.

Basking in an aura of anonymity allows Cordon to forget the horrors of the past day and reassess how he will handle everything going forward. He prepares himself that he won't come out of this alive. And that Natasha might already be dead. But if she is, Cordon vows to get her away from Fu, and then kill him.

And whatever happens to him from there, so be it. Cordon has always been ready to die. But he never thought it might happen. Until now. As he closes his eyes, he knows he's ready. And that makes him even more dangerous.

Keeping his eyes closed for a moment, allowing the pounding music to crawl inside him and take over, Cordon relaxes. Lucious might be right about the club. The pounding music, the dancing, sweaty, shadowed bodies, and the pulsating echo of the club music allows him to drift deeper into his own thoughts. Even the parade of anonymous hands touching his body as men pass by, their eyes staying on Cordon until they realize he's not interested, all work to put Cordon in a hazy state of rest, his mind somehow clearer than it's been all day.

Opening his eyes, Cordon catches sight of a beautiful Latina, hair down to her mid-back, makeup perfect, tight dress that fits her curves. She smiles at him as she sips what's left of her drink. Sex, as much as he craves it, will only screw up an already screwed-up situation. As long as he still has the kid, he cannot afford any more distractions. When all this shit is over, Cordon vows to himself to deal with who he truly is and what he wants. *Of all people*, he muses, *why the fuck do I give a shit what anyone thinks?* He wants to find a person to love. Who can love him back. Before his demons completely devour him.

Cordon turns away from the woman, taking a couple of deep breaths to refocus. He stares blankly across the dance floor in Lucious' general direction, his thoughts turning back to what is ahead, and how he intends to survive it. Nevertheless, his eyes drift back to the woman for one more look. She smiles at him again. Cordon gives her a bruised smile in return, shaking his head, so she knows not to approach him.

Dancing with a group of young guys, all shirtless and two only their underwear, Lucious moves as if she's trying to shake off the night as well. Taking a sip from the Red Bull in her hand, she glances back at Cordon, seeing him eyeing the beautiful trans woman sipping from her drink. Lucious feels a ping of jealousy. Which freaks her out. Cordon is so not her type. For a one-nighter, sure, who would turn down a man like that? But to feel possessive of Cordon? Stone cold jealousy? Like some woman is moving in on her man? Lucious dances more erratically, trying to shake the feeling. But she can't. This big, brooding man has protected her and promised to take care of her. His damaged beauty is undeniable. But getting involved with a man while at the height of this insanity, Lucious is smart enough to know that it would never amount to anything more. Especially with someone as lethally unbalanced and intimidating as Cordon. Better to admire him from a distance.

Because getting close only escalates the chance of being murdered.

Lucious stops dancing. Now it makes sense why her father sent Cordon Finn to kidnap her. And why he's so cavalier about both of them dying.

Lucious is grabbed by one of the guys she's dancing with. He leans in and shouts over the music, "That mega-hot muscle daddy against the wall keeps staring at you. I think he wants you! Go jump on that mountain!"

"No," Lucious says, shaking her head. "He's...we're...he's my bodyguard."

"Bodyguard?!?!" the other young man exclaims. "Are you famous?"

One of the other guys pipes up. "Make your bodyguard take off his shirt!"

Yet another guy leans in and adds, "Get him out here to dance. I want to touch him! See if he's real!"

The boys cluck with stoned laughter as Lucious smiles, waving in Cordon's direction. "Hey!" Lucious bellows at Cordon, continuing to wave at him until she has Cordon's attention. "Hey! Come dance with us."

As the gaggle of young guys falls all over themselves with anticipation, Cordon waves them off.

"I'll suck your dick!" one of the young guys yells at Cordon, who doesn't crack a smile.

"Damn! He's intense!" this young man says to Lucious.

"You have no idea," Lucious responds before pushing through them, moving to Cordon.

"Come dance," Lucious pleads to Cordon, grabbing hold of his forearm.

"I don't dance."

"Sure you do. Everybody dances."

The young men behind Lucious wave at Cordon, one whistling, trying to coax him onto the dance floor.

"You always look like you're trying to shit bricks of hot magma," teases Lucious, reaching up and squeezing Cordon's bicep.

"Damn!" Lucious crows. "All this muscle shouldn't go to waste. Come on, dance, have some fun. Enjoy the attention."

Lucious twirls around until she's behind Cordon and pushes him toward the group of young men she's been dancing with.

"Get out of your head for a few minutes. It'll do your battered soul some good. And those guys won't bite. Well, a couple of them might, but you might like it," Lucious continues.

As she gets Cordon onto the dance floor, the young men descend on him, their hands caressing his chest and arms, having never been this close with anyone this physically large before. Like a colony of ants on the march, hands slide under Cordon's shirt, trying to lift it over his head, but none of them are tall enough to do it. For a brief moment, Cordon succumbs to the pleasure of being touched. A few of the young people kiss his torso, their mouths latching onto his chest, his arms, and stomach.

Joining in, Lucious settles her ass against Cordon's crotch, grinding. Surrounded by the attention, Cordon grabs Lucious by the waist of the pants and pulls her in even tighter, his hand stretching up her back, much to Lucious' delight. Cordon snaps up another in the group and locks lips with them, his other hand around Lucious' neck as Lucious continues to grind into him. Discarding the first person he's kissing, Cordon grabs up another and kisses them, before spinning Lucious towards him and pressing his lips against hers.

Lucious feels that Cordon has completely relinquished all his fear, the emotional and psychological walls he has erected, the shell which has solidified around him, shattering in a quake of his own need. Cordon owns this moment of uncompromised lasciviousness.

Then, as if he's teased them enough, Cordon shakes off the younger crowd that surrounds him and wrestles his shirt down over his torso. He gives them an apologetic shrug as he backs away to a collective "Awwww..." from the pack of young people, who reassemble blithely, dancing again. Lucious stares at him oddly, unsure what caused the abrupt shift. Seeing the disappointment and question in Lucious' eyes, Cordon gives her a coy wink before turning away. His demeanor grows serious again as he strides through the club toward the back.

Walking out onto the back patio, the daylight blinds Cordon. He bumps past a group of leather-clad men heading back into the club, one of them grabbing Cordon's pec. Cordon pulls the man's hand off his body, squeezing it until the man barks out in pain. He turns to the group of large guys, a frozen seriousness again locked on Cordon's face. "Keep your fucking hands off me," he warns.

The men puff up immediately, but seeing the darkness raging from Cordon, his hands balled into fists, the men think twice about a confrontation and move back into the club.

As Cordon walks further out onto the patio, into the full sunlight, he opens his fist.

Inside is one of Lucious's necklaces. The one with the arrowhead on the end. The same one that resembled the drawing Jackie had in her pocket. It dangles off of Cordon's finger, catching the sunlight as it swings slightly.

BRUTAL TRUTH

Wrestling with the cords that strap her to the headboard, Natasha's continuous struggle causes some slack in the bindings. Laying back, exhausted from the fight, she tries to look at the chain around her neck, the metal irritatingly uncomfortable. Frustrated and scared, not even sure why these men have taken her, Natasha steels herself. She is determined to make it out of this alive. Whatever the cost.

With her head resting on a pillow caked with makeup, blood, and tear stains, she eyes a screw that holds the ornate metal railing to the wood headboard. She has jarred it loose. But the straps prevent her from reaching it. Laying back, Natasha thinks a moment.

"Hello!" she calls out. "Can someone hear me? I need to go to the bathroom. I need a drink of water!"

The door to the room opens and a security man steps in. Behind him, Natasha notes the hallway. She sees the edge of a stairwell, which means she's upstairs in a very large, what looks to be quite expensive, home.

"I need to pee. And I'm thirsty," Natasha announces to the man wearing a suit jacket and tie.

The man makes a call before he unties her from the bed frame. Holding the chain around her neck, he unlocks it from the hook in the wall and allows her to stand. Natasha's entire body aches, her body wobbling as she stands. The man nods towards a door in the room, and Natasha moves in that direction, the man holding the chain attached around her neck, infuriating her as she opens the door and finds a small bathroom. The guard steps inside with her, locking her to a metal U-bolt attached to the back of the door, which allows her to reach the sink and shower.

"You're fucking kidding me," she says as he pulls on the chain that is now attached to the door. "You have a fucking gun and there's no window in here. Where do you think I'm going?"

Without a word, he shuts the door, leaving Natasha inside.

Natasha grabs the door knob to lock it, but there is no lock. She sighs, sitting on the toilet. She scans everything in the small space. Shower. Sink. Toilet. Mirror. Towel rack. Toilet paper holder. That's it. Moving to the sink, she turns on the water. Checking herself out, she cleans the dried blood on her face and examines the bruises on her neck from the chain. After drinking water from the tap, Natasha snaps the towel off the rack to dry her face. Her hands move to replace the towel, but she grabs the towel rack instead with two hands and tries to wrestle it from the wall. It makes a noise, so she turns on the water in the shower full blast and tries again.

But again, pulling on the towel rack clatters, and the bathroom door swings open, the man stepping in. He grabs the chain and yanks Natasha by the neck. But she holds tight to the towel rack, and as her body collapses in his direction, the rack breaks off the wall. The man reaches for his gun as Natasha spins on her toes, slamming the metal rod down on the man's arm. The gun drops to the tile floor at their feet. As the man dives for it, Natasha swings the rod up, the end catching him in the face. She drives the metal rod into his eye as he screams.

He jerks her down to the floor by the chain, both going for the gun as his anguished moans fill her ears. As Natasha's fingertips touch the gun, the man throws himself on top of her, pinning her down. He slowly and painfully extracts the rod from his eye, blood pouring down the right side of his face. Frenzied, he grabs the chain around her neck and twists. As he's about to smash her head into the floor, Natasha flicks the gun closer and wraps her fingers around it, and points it over her head at his face. She fires behind her, emptying the revolver until the man's body drops on top of her back, the chain falling from his dead hands. She rolls over, pushing his body off hers. As she crawls to her knees, fingers wrap into her hair, yanking her up. Natasha clambers for the gun but cannot get it in her hands before she's smashed to the floor. She fights as she is dragged from the room, lifted to her feet by her hair, the barrel of a gun jammed into her jaw before she's thrown onto the bed.

Chen climbs on top of her, gun to her head.

"You sad, fucking whore. Next time, I kill you," he snarls through his clenched teeth.

Natasha can only nod as Chen roughly binds her again to the headboard. Turning to two security men who have entered the room, he nods towards the bathroom, snapping, "Clean that mess up and get rid of the body. This freak doesn't get out of this bed again for any reason. Let her soil herself. She stays here!"

***

The sunlight glints off the arrowhead as Cordon holds it up, his thick fingers examining it until he realizes it's actually two pieces. Pulling it apart, he reveals a flash drive hidden inside. His eyes narrowing, Cordon's mind spins.

"Little bitch," he mutters aloud before jetting back into the darkness of the club. Pushing through the bodies and onto the dance floor, Cordon finds Lucious dancing closely with another shirtless club bunny, Lucious' tongue in the young guy's mouth.

As Lucious spins, she finds Cordon towering over them. Pushing the guy away, she peers up at Cordon with concern.

"What's the matter?" Lucious asks.

Cordon opens his hand and lets the top half of the necklace fall, dangling. Opening his other hand, he reveals the flash drive.

Lucious' hand goes to her neck, feeling the other necklaces and chains. Her eyes lock with Cordon's.

"Outside," Cordon demands, turning again and pushing his way back through the crowd, toward the patio.

"Fuck," Lucious utters under her breath.

Once her eyes have adjusted to the sunlight, Lucious finds Cordon at the end of the outside bar, hunched over a cup of coffee. Lucious moves to the open seat no one else would dare sit in and climbs up.

"Those marks on your neck...they weren't trying to strangle you. They were after this," Cordon growls.

Lucious says nothing, gesturing to the bartender for a cup of coffee as well.

"What's on it?"

Lucious opens two more of the pendants she wears around her neck, displaying the same sort of flash drive hidden in the pendants.

"My father's financial information."

Cordon's face screws up harshly, his jaw tightens, his hands balling into fists as if he's about to attack.

"A kid died because you're blackmailing your father?! None of this has been about you being trans."

As the bartender settles the mug of coffee onto the bar in front of Lucious, she sits up straight, her eyes never leaving Cordon.

"*All* of this has been about me being trans! It's *always* been about me being trans! It's why I left. It was that or I was going to kill myself. Or he was going to kill me. He wants me to be a reflection of him! But I can't be! And he hates me for that! He hates who I am! Beatings, humiliation, therapy camps, drugs. He tried everything to change me. But instead, he created a warrior. Fuck him, I wasn't letting him win! Even when his head of security was raping me, gun to my head, I wouldn't let them win."

Cordon remains silent. Lucious' words are both penetrating and painfully familiar.

"I came all the way out here to get away from him. I didn't want him to find me. Lansing...he had security. I needed to be safe. My father couldn't just let me go, he couldn't live knowing I would become who I wanted to be. He had to win. And to win, I have to be dead. Otherwise, I could reappear. Whatever story he concocted about my whereabouts, what I was doing, who I was, would bite him in the ass. Especially if I had transitioned. But if I was dead, he could mourn Lucas and move on."

Lucious' eyes glare in Cordon's direction, her ire erupting more and more with every word. Lucious holds up one of the other flash drives that hangs around her neck.

"These were my insurance policy," states Lucious.

Cordon takes a harsh breath. "How'd that work out for Gio?"

Her eyes filling with tears, Lucious spins on Cordon, who refuses to look at her. "You got him involved! You're the one who made a deal with the devil. It's because of you he's dead. Not me. You're the reason a lot of people are dead and that we're both being hunted."

Gulping back any show of emotion, Cordon asks, "Have you taken any money from your father? Or should I ask, how *much* have you taken?"

"I spent the last few years plotting my exit, knowing that if I stayed, I wouldn't be alive much longer. Everything my father put me through...including laughing at me when I told him his head of security was raping me over and over," Lucious continues before pausing, finally locking eyes with Cordon. "I didn't *take* anything. I was owed! And I'm owed a lot more."

Cordon's eyes close tightly, nostrils flared, his breathing shallow.

Images explode in his mind: his father, drunk, smashing into walls, the loud, violent argument between Marissa and Nelson. Cordon stands, taller now, in his mid-teens, his size equaling that of his father. Hearing his little sister's tearful screams from down the hallway, Cordon quickly pads in that direction, his bare feet slapping the wood floors, faster and faster, as he comes to the bedroom where Annie sleeps.

Nelson has Annie, nine years old, in his arms. He slaps Marissa away as she tries to rescue her daughter.

"Nelson, give her to me! Please! Let her go!" Marissa pleads.

Again, Nelson knocks Marissa away. "She's my goddamn daughter! I'll do what I want with her!"

Annie fights to pull free of her father's grip as he lifts her up, kissing her face.

"Stop!" Marissa begs, getting her arms around Annie. "Give her to me, Nelson! You're not doing this!"

Furious, Nelson shoves Marissa back into the wall, pinning her there as he again kisses Annie as she squirms to get away.

"Come on. Give your daddy some love," he snarls at Annie, kissing her face again, enjoying holding Marissa at bay, unable to help her daughter.

"Put her down, you drunken piece of shit," Cordon calls as he fills the doorway to Annie's room.

"What, faggot? You jealous I love her and not you?" Nelson laughs.

Buffeted by his father's words, Cordon balls his fists tightly, trying to stay strong. "Let her go, Dad. You're drunk. You need to go to bed."

"Don't tell me what the fuck to do!" Nelson screams, letting go of Annie and Marissa at the same time to face his son across the room.

Marissa grabs up her hysterical daughter, comforting her, rushing her into a corner of the room away from Nelson.

"You fucking cocksucker," Nelson laughs, moving towards Cordon. He goes eye to eye with his son, letting a smile snarl onto his lips. "What are you going to do, homo?"

Nelson's hand goes to his son's face. Cordon knocks it away. This, Nelson enjoys.

"Don't you knock my hand away, sweetheart. If I want to touch my little boy, I'll touch him."

As he reaches up again, Cordon again slaps his hand away from his face.

"Go to bed."

"You want to go to bed? Is that what you want?" Nelson chides his son, continuing to touch Cordon's face, Cordon knocking his hand away each time. "You want your daddy? That what you want, little bitch?"

Nelson goes nose to nose with his son. Cordon doesn't move. He doesn't blink. He stands there, glaring into his father's bloodshot eyes.

"Sad little cocksucker," Nelson crows, his spittle landing on Cordon's cheek.

Nelson's hand goes to the zipper on his blue jeans. He slowly unzips it. Cordon doesn't move. It's almost as if he isn't even breathing. Marissa watches, pressing Annie's face to her chest so she can't see, sensing this is the defining moment between father and son.

Nelson reaches up and puts his hand on his son's head, a cruel smile greasing across his lips as he tries to force his son down towards the floor. "Go ahead, boy. You know that's what you want."

Cordon slaps his father's hand away, the look on Cordon's face never faltering as he glares at his father.

Sweeping in with his other hand, Nelson wraps his fingers around Cordon's neck, his fingers grabbing his son's throat, ready to squeeze the life out of him. Cordon smacks at his father's hand, but Nelson refuses to let go. The more Cordon struggles, the more joy Nelson derives from debasing his son.

Not able to get a breath, his mind swirling, something snaps deep in Cordon. His fists come up in a flurry, punching his father in the chin, jacking his head back. The next punch connects with Nelson's stomach, the breath blown out of Nelson's chest, doubling him over.

As Nelson's hand falls from Cordon's neck, Cordon drives a shoulder into his father, shoving him back. Nelson stumbles, falling back over his daughter's Barbie dream house, the toy crushing under him as he hits the floor.

Silently, Cordon turns and walks out of the room, down the hallway towards the front door. He hears his father's footsteps stumbling down the hallway after him. Before Cordon can turn, Nelson falls into him, tackling his son onto the floor. Grabbing Cordon by the hair, Nelson bashes his son's forehead into the floor, dazing Cordon, and paws at Cordon's pants, trying to pull them down.

"This what you want, pussy boy!?!" Nelson screams, his words slurred, his arms flailing as he continues to grind Cordon's face into the floor, before wrapping his hands around his son's neck, strangling him from behind. When Cordon's finally unconscious, Nelson kneels on his son's back, pulling down Cordon's pants, revealing his ass. As Nelson shoves down his own jeans, Cordon's eyes snap open. With everything he's got, he spins over, knocking his father off him. Cordon staggers to his feet, blood dripping from his head. As Nelson tries to get off the floor, Cordon kicks his father in the face, sending him back into the wall. Nelson sways, fighting consciousness, Cordon charges, booting Nelson in the crotch over and over, causing Nelson to vomit before he slumps on the floor in a pile.

Marissa rushes up to Cordon, a towel in her hand, which she presses against his bleeding head. Stepping over Nelson, she assists Cordon into the kitchen and cleans him up.

"The basement. There's a cot down there. Your father won't know. Stay there. Go in and out the basement door. I'll make sure you have food. Don't let him see you. I'll tell him you ran away."

Abject sadness washes into Cordon's eyes as he looks at the beleaguered Marissa.

"But you and Annie..." Cordon mumbles.

"We'll be fine. I know how to make your father pay," she insists, before taking Cordon's face in her hands. "He hates you. And sooner or later, he's going to do something to you that there's no coming back from. Hide or go. Those are your only choices."

Swallowing hard, Cordon nods with anguished acceptance. Knowing that, whatever his life was, it was over. He wishes he had kept kicking his father until Nelson was dead. Prison couldn't be worse than what would come if he stays.

Cordon has no choice. He's now on his own.

The bartender warming his coffee brings Cordon back to the moment. Turning to Lucious, Cordon asks again, "I need to know. How much have you taken from your father?"

Lucious sips from her mug of coffee, letting the bitter warmth slide down her throat before she responds. "A million for every year of my life."

Cordon's phone buzzes with a text from Annie. Reading it, Cordon's face turns even grimmer than it was.

"My sister's husband is dead. My father is in the hospital."

Lucious doesn't know what to say, staring into the coffee cup, guilt clinched in her eyes. Cordon replaces the arrowhead cover over the flash drive.

Saying nothing, a jumble of thoughts racing through his head, Cordon still isn't sure about his next move. Especially now, with the added layer of money.

Reaching over, Cordon grabs the chains around Lucious' neck. He snaps them off in one solid rip and scoops them up in his hand before Lucious can do anything but grab her neck, wincing in pain, shocked.

Cordon slides off the stool, flips a few dollars onto the bar, and walks away from Lucious, heading back into the club's darkness. He doesn't break stride, morning partiers clearing out of his way as Cordon moves toward the front of the club. Lucious dashes through the bodies trying to catch him. She spies Cordon exit out the front.

As Cordon storms down the sidewalk, he spots two police cars parked by the Pathfinder he stole. Turning back, he runs into Lucious rushing at him.

"Are you going to leave me here?" Lucious questions incredulously, as Cordon continues past her.

"Go back to where you were living. Say whatever you want to say about me taking you, whatever. Blame me. You're safer there than you are with me."

"Where are you going?"

Cordon rounds a corner, onto a dark side street, Lucious following.

"Where I should have gone the moment I realized your father set me up. The moment he killed my friend, Frank. The moment I knew he had Natasha, that he hurt my family. I'm taking this fight to his doorstep."

Cordon stops at an older Toyota pickup. He moves to the driver's window and smashes it in with his elbow. He opens the door and slides under the dash, hot-wiring the truck.

Cordon climbs in. But as he pulls the door shut, Lucious grabs it, stopping him.

"He'll kill you," Lucious pleads.

Cordon pushes her back away from the door, shutting it but Lucious stays at the truck window.

"My father has a small army around him. I don't care how badass you are, you can't beat that. We barely came out of last night alive. Think! Think!" Lucious begs.

Seeing the fear in Lucious' eyes, Cordon takes a few breaths, licking his lips. "I have thought about it, kid. Have a good life. That's your best revenge."

"You're cornered."

"And I only know one way out," Cordon responds directly, "and that's to come out swinging."

"God, I loathe heroes."

"Hero?" Cordon reacts as he throws the truck in gear. "I'm just some queer who has spent his life ashamed. You don't get it. I wanted to be you. Someone strong enough to be who I was. But I wasn't brave enough. Instead, I became the worst possible fucking thing in the world. Me."

Cordon reaches through the window, his hand going to Lucious' face warmly.

"You don't know what I've done in my life. Who I am." Cordon goes silent for a moment, pulling back into the shell he's created for himself before he adds, "I'm going back to Chicago. I'll be there by tomorrow. If I'm successful, you won't be living in fear for the rest of your life. You'll be free to be who you want to be, who you are. If I fail…"

Cordon hands the necklaces back to Lucious.

"Clean out every nickel you can and disappear. Believe me when I say I'm sorry for my part in this."

Pulling Lucious to him, Cordon kisses her on the forehead. Lucious steps back as Cordon guns the engine, pulling away from the curb, driving off.

Fighting her tears, Lucious' hand squeezes the necklaces in her palm as something shifts in her eyes. Something has crystalized for her, a plan of action, a punishment, a connection. Turning, she heads back in the opposite direction.

Her walk turns into a trot, and then into a run.

THE FIGHT AT THE DOOR

Driving to busy John Wayne Airport, Cordon books a flight on a tyro airline to Madison, Wisconsin, for that afternoon. Once there, he intends to hotwire another car and drive to Chicago, knowing Fu is monitoring the O'Hare and Midway. Buying another burner phone and grabbing a shower in a hotel near the airport and a clean change of clothes, Cordon's head is clearer. He knows what he has to do.

Once he's sure Natasha is safe, he is killing Fu.

Checking in with his sister while at the airport, his eyes darting person to person, looking for anyone who might be searching for him, Cordon finds out his father is in Jackson Park Hospital. He's expected to be there a few nights before they release him. Annie tells him she's staying with her father, only slipping off to grab a shower at Cordon's place because she feels safer there.

"You armed?"

"Yes."

"All the time?"

Cordon quiets for a moment, again searching the terminal. His eyes narrow as he says, "I'm sorry about Aaron. It's my fault."

Annie doesn't respond, letting his words linger between them.

"When are you coming home?" Annie asks, exhaustion in her voice.

"I don't know," Cordon lies, rubbing his tired face with his hand. "I just have to know you're safe. Don't be alone if you can avoid it. Don't tell anyone when you're coming or going or where you'll be. Not even the nurses at the hospital."

"Are there people listening to us right now?"

Cordon's silence gives Annie her answer.

"Get home. I need you," she tells him before hanging up.

Fighting tears, Annie slumps into a chair. With her husband's murder and now her father being in this hospital, the emotional fatigue overwhelms her. Crossing her arms over her waist, she leans over and rocks herself. It's what she used to do when she was little and needed to self-soothe. Which, considering the life she had at home with her father, was often.

The unimaginable buried deep in her mind erupts to the forefront, invading her thoughts. Annie fears she's never going to see her brother again. The one person who has loved her unconditionally, who protected her when she was young. Whatever this is, whoever is behind the brutal death of her husband and the attack on her father, is now careening out of control in Cordon's direction. And though he never said it, she could hear in his voice that he was not just accepting the battle, he's preparing for it.

Her tears fall to the floor, puddling on the tile before she looks up at her unconscious father. She knows he created the emotional maelstrom in which both she and her brother have been forced to exist. The prolific damage he inflicted on his two children is something neither of them will ever recover from.

Especially Cordon.

Thanks to her mother's protection, Annie went on to have a life. But a flurry of horrible choices, and the controlling men who came with each one of those choices, rotted any hope that she would escape her past. Only the job at the boatyard, which pays her well, settled into the plus column. But she couldn't break the hold her father has on her. And everything Nelson touches has been poisoned. Still seeking his approval, she never found love, only torment. So much and so often, she confused the two. Even after her mother passed, Annie couldn't cut that cord. The heaping abuse from the devil she knows still feels less toxic than the ones she feared were just outside the circle she never steps beyond. Her father. Aaron. She never felt she deserved better. Annie won't mourn Aaron's demise, but she also knows that she will fall for another man who will disrespect her, treat her badly, and cheat on her. That is the nest she's lived in all her life.

Standing, Annie can't control her sobs, her entire body heaving. She shakes her arms as if trying to scare away her animosity and dissolution, to rid herself of this mantle of torment she's carried since childhood. "This can't be my life," she says aloud, needing to hear the words spoken.

She wants to repeat it, to say it over and over and over until she believes it, but Annie cannot form the words through her painful sobs that start in her gut, fill her chest, and catch in her throat.

But she knows she's done.

***

Across the upstairs hallway from where Natasha is being held, Lucious' older sisters, Janine and Grace, chatter closely, laughing, as they exit a bedroom and trot down the stairwell to the first floor. Crossing through the dining room where their father eats a late breakfast, perusing a stack of documents, the girls kiss him on the cheek.

"Janine and I are driving to the club for brunch with a couple of our friends and then downtown to shop," Grace announces to her father.

"Can't wait to see that bill," Fu responds, only partially joking.

The girls giggle and make a hasty retreat from the dining room, moving past Chen, who stands near the kitchen. It's apparent from their looks that even they don't like him.

Once they're out of earshot, Fu glances back at Chen, who scrolls through his security iPad.

"Mr. Finn never arrived in Chicago overnight?"

"No," Chen responds, still eyeing the device. "We had everyone on alert but..." Chen shakes his head.

"Mr. Finn will do as requested. Ultimately men like that, they are weak. They succumb to save themselves. Even one as hardened as Mr. Finn."

"The detail is tired. I'm going to send some home. We will need them tonight."

Fu smiles to himself, enjoying his perceived taste of victory more than the blueberries on the top of the pancakes his fork cuts into.

Worry lines dig into Chen's forehead as he scrolls faster through the iPad in his hand. His jaw clenches.

"Sir," he says, urgency in his voice, moving up to Fu, setting the iPad down on the table. "We have a problem."

Fu's attention goes to the video on the iPad. Palm Springs Pride. The parade is in full swing, with the colorful floats and semi-naked young men and women, drag queens, dykes on bikes, social groups and businesses throwing beads and other trinkets to the crowds that line the streets. But all of that is the background: the focus of the camera is on a corner of Palm Canyon Drive as parade attendees face the camera yelling, "FU Fu!", one after the other, waving papers at the camera.

"What is this?" Fu questions Chen.

"Palm Springs...the gay parade. But I don't know what they're waving," Chen questions.

He and Fu peer closer, trying to see what papers everyone is waving at the camera.

Fu's eyes widen. "That's my name," he says, pointing to the papers. "Are those...my tax returns? How did they get my tax returns?!?"

Chen leans towards the pad and stares as one parade-goer yells "FU Fu!" and holds the papers right up to the camera lens.

It is not only Fu's tax returns but other financial documents as well.

"How did this happen...??!!!" Fu roars, his fists pounding on the table.

The question is redundant. They both know exactly how this happened. Lucas. But when one of the young men holding up Fu's financial papers bumps the camera, turning it, Fu and Chen see a handmade sign that reads: BE FAMOUS TODAY! Take A Page. Hold It Up. Say F.U., Fu!

"What is this being broadcast on?!" Fu barks.

His fingers punching on the iPad, Chen finds the website this feed is being run through.

"Gio9+.com" Chen says.

"What is that?!"

"A gay web camera site."

"Shut it down! Stop it! Stop it! Find it and shut it down!" Fu demands.

Chen is quickly on his cell phone and as he walks away, he's already trying to contact his people in Palm Springs to get down to the parade and take the camera down.

After twenty minutes, Fu is now fuming intensely. Each person who holds up his financial information infuriates him more as Chen steps back to the table where Fu cannot take his eyes off the iPad. Glancing up at Chen, Fu can see whatever he has to say isn't positive.

"Your financial documents have been distributed up and down the parade route. I have people searching for Lucas now and someone heading to find where this camera is set up. As soon as they find it, it will be taken down. But sir, there's something else...something worse," Chen offers. "Your son is draining your bank accounts."

"*WHAT?!*" Fu screams.

Fu takes out his phone and immediately punches in one of his bank's apps.

"I shut down any more withdrawals from your accounts."

"Accounts?"

"Your personal and business accounts," Chen admits. "I have shut down any withdrawals—"

"*HOW MUCH!?*" demands Fu.

Reluctant to answer, Fu again asks the same question, this time screaming it in Chen's face.

"Over a hundred million dollars," Chen responds.

Fu knew Lucas had drained eighteen million from an account. He was willing to let that slide; since he planned to eliminate his son, the money would come back to him. But this? How could no one have contacted him the moment massive lump sums evaporated from various accounts overnight?

"Goddamn him," Fu utters, his voice low, simmering.

Fu stands. With no warning, he attacks Chen, striking him over and over until he beats Chen to the ground. Chen refuses to fight back, taking the beating. Fu grabs him by the throat and his eyes bulge as he glares at Chen.

"I hired you to take care of my problems! Take care of them! Kill that *thing* upstairs and get it out of my house. Find Cordon Finn and kill him. But when you find Lucas, I want him brought here. I will punish my son for dishonoring me," Fu mutters with disdain. "Then I will kill him myself."

Fu releases his grip on Chen's throat and storms out of the dining room. Dishonored and disrespected, Chen stands, his eyes cast down, particularly embarrassed that his security team witnessed his humiliation. Chen's rage radiates as he cleans himself off. He glances up towards the second floor where the bedrooms are, his eyes narrowing, needing some sort of retribution and knowing who he is going to take it out on.

***

Hearing the doorknob rattle, Natasha shimmies her body so she's sitting up as high as she can in the bed. The door opens and Natasha takes a deep breath, her hands pulling on the bindings.

The chipped paint on the fingernails reveals the person at the door isn't Chen. It's Lucious, holding a pair of soft blue sweats with the word JUICY emblazoned on the backside of the jacket and pants. Lucious signals Natasha to stay quiet as she moves up to her.

***

Cordon flips himself over the back Plexiglas wall of the estate, which separates the property from Lake Michigan. Clad in camo, guns strapped to his torso, knife to his thigh, he stays low against the wall, taking in the remarkably simple property. Patio. Pool. A large utility shed sits off to the side, so it doesn't ruin the view from the house of the lake. There are two men near the multiple sets of French doors leading to the patio, automatic rifles strapped to their bodies. Knowing that approaching from the back would only bring a plethora of security, Cordon's attention shifts to the windows behind the corner hedge in the backyard. Sliding his body along the wall, he makes it behind the hedge and moves up to the windows, viewing the security men on the first floor. He counts four. Pulling out a blade from the sheath strapped to his leg, Cordon runs it along the edge of a pane of glass in the window, loosening it. Tapping it quietly, he uses a piece of chewed gum to pull it towards him. Cordon reaches through the opening and unlocks the window, pushing it open wide as he maneuvers his shoulders through the space and slides in on his belly. Once in the house, Cordon silently shuts the window and replaces the pane of glass, holding it in place with the same piece of gun he used to remove it.

Two of the first-floor security men pass by the front door, manned by another member of the security team. They nod at the guard, who opens the door, allowing them to exit the mansion. As the guard at the door closes it, Cordon stands from behind the open door. Before the guard can raise his gun or say a word, Cordon has the security man's face in his hand and slams it off a stone pillar. The security guard drops to the floor and Cordon's boot connects with his face. Taking the man's automatic rifle, Cordon empties the bullets into a tall, ornate vase near the door and drops the rifle to the floor near the unconscious security man.

***

Upstairs, Chen steps into the bedroom and swiftly moves to Natasha on the bed. He smiles, his hand running up and down the side of her body. Natasha bristles at his touch, which makes Chen more aggressive, leaning his body down to her.

"Killing you won't be difficult," he harasses, his lips sliding to her neck, "but I do wish we had more time,"

Natasha twists her body away, as Chen's lips continue down her neck to her breasts just as her unbound hand slams down on his neck, the screw from the headboard clutched in her fingers. Furiously, she stabs him, diving the screw as deep as she can into Chen's skin. As he tries to pull himself off the bed, she reveals that her other hand is no longer bound to the bed either, and it wraps around his head, wrestling to control him as she continues to drive the nail deep into his neck. Chen can't wrestle himself free of Natasha's grip. He stumbles, fighting, but collapses to one knee next to the bed, Natasha still on top of him.

Feeling him weakening, Natasha releases her hold as Chen bleeds out at her feet. Leaning over to him, Natasha whispers, "Killing you wasn't that hard either, asshole."

Chen tries unsuccessfully to speak, one hand trying to stop the blood pulsing out of his neck with each heartbeat, the other moving for his gun. But before he can reach it, Natasha sits and rolls back on the bed, flying back at him, smashing him in the face with both feet, the gun falling from his grip as she lays him out on the floor. She kneels on his head, pinning him there, until he stops grasping for the gun, just outside his reach, the life draining from his body.

Stepping off of him, she picks the gun up. Grabbing the blue sweats that Lucious left for her, Natasha slips into them before marching to the bedroom door, peeking out.

***

Stalking into his bedroom and slamming the door, Fu's acute anger bubbles through in every jerky move of his body as he talks to himself. But suddenly, as he glances across the room, Fu stops in his tracks.

Perched in the wingback chair in a reading nook is Lucious, her legs crossed tightly, clad in a tight red dress, thigh-high boots with heels, full makeup, and wig. She is striking. Feminine and sultry.

"Am I beautiful, Daddy?" Lucious asks, standing so her father can take her in completely. "Are you proud of the person I have become?"

Lucious picks up a sandstone Uma, an ancient, and very expensive sculpture. As Lucious plays with it, Fu only becomes more incensed.

"Put that down!"

"You always got so angry whenever I came into your bedroom. Much less touched anything," Lucious states, tossing the sculpture from hand to hand. "Your things have always meant so much more to you than I ever did. Even when I was doing exactly what you wanted to make you proud, these things mattered more," she continues, throwing the sculpture into the air and spinning around, catching it behind her back.

Fu freezes, aching to rush over and save his sculpture. But he won't give his child that satisfaction. Having Lucious in his home, Fu knows he can correct the problems in his life that she has created.

"Where is the money you stole from me?" Fu demands.

"My money. It's *mine* now."

"Not for long," Fu says, turning away from Lucious in disgust. He starts for the door. But Lucious cuts him off, getting between her father and the bedroom door.

"What am I worth to you, Dad?" Lucious asks her father.

Fu says nothing, his eyes burning through Lucious.

"*What. Am. I. Worth?!*" Lucious bellows, throwing the sculpture against the wall, shattering it.

Doing everything he can not to lunge at Lucious, Fu sticks his finger into her face.

"I gave you everything, Lucas!"

"Lucious! My name is Lucious!"

"I raised you to be a man! And you disgraced me by turning yourself into...this foolish and disgusting thing standing in front of me. You are not a girl! You're a boy! I don't care what you want to be! What you've turned yourself into is unnatural!"

With blinding swiftness, Lucious spins and kicks her father. Fu blocks the kick but stumbles back. He rushes towards his bedside table, scrambling to open the top drawer. Ripping it open before Lucious attacks, Fu digs in. And digs. And digs.

"Your guns are gone. All of them. Do you think I don't know where you keep your weapons? How many times after you humiliated me, I snuck into your room and thought about taking one of your guns and killing you?" Lucious says, slowly striding to her father. "But now it's just you and me, Dad. You hate me, I disgust you. Now's your chance to do something about it. I'm right here. I've given you a gift. Is that what you wanted? To kill me?"

"I can't stand the sight of you. Pathetic. Repulsive. Faggot."

"I'm not a faggot. I'm your daughter."

Picking up a heavy dragon sculpture from the top of the bedside table, Fu spins on Lucious.

"You are *nothing* to me!"

Fu heaves the sculpture at Lucious. Lucious takes a cool step to the side as the weighty sculpture thuds onto the floor, fracturing into pieces.

"Your fortune is falling to pieces."

Fu grabs the poker from the fireplace and swings it at Lucious as he yells, "Where's my money?!"

Lucious takes a blow to the shoulder but is able to keep her father back. Grabbing the bedside table to take the flurry of swings, Lucious pokes it at her father like a lion tamer with a chair. Fu continues to swing, cracking the legs off the table.

"It's *my* money now, Dad. Retribution for everything I endured in this house!"

Fu stops swinging, catching his breath as he glares at Lucious. "No one ever had an easier life than you," Fu spits at Lucious. "I handed you everything. All I ever required was that my son carry himself like a man. But you couldn't even be what you were born to be! You are not a girl! You'll never be a girl!"

"I will be who I always have been!" Lucious counters.

"A sad freak? An embarrassment? Unnatural? I won't allow that!"

"And that's why you sent the man to kidnap me. From a place I was happy, and people accepted me. So you could eliminate me. What sort of man can kill his own child?"

"You aren't my child. You aren't anything but a thief, a reckless and pathetic disappointment."

"Aww, poor you," Lucious taunts, infuriating her father into swinging at her again with the poker.

Swinging at her again and again, Fu catches Lucious' arm. Lucious drops the fractured night table but as her father brings the poker up over his head to strike her in the face, Lucious dives out of the way, rolling, and kips back to her feet in the heeled boots, the end of the poker embedding in the wood floor.

Lucious kicks her father in the side, knocking him back but he's able to pull the poker with him. Whipping the poker around at Lucious again, she steps into the swing and catches the poker under her arm, her elbow coming up into Fu's nose. Blood sprays from Fu's nose, shocking him, as Lucious wrests the poker from his hand, Fu stumbling back.

"Chen! Chen!" Fu calls as he scrambles for the door. Lucious launches the poker at the door, where it lodges right by Fu's head, shocking her father.

Fu swings open the door and races into the hallway. But as Lucious takes her first step to give chase, her father flies back into the room, his body slapping against the wood floor as he sprawls there, stunned.

Cordon steps in, his eyes landing on Lucious before he shuts the door behind him.

"Nice outfit," Cordon states.

Lucious spins on her heels with a smile. "Thank you! You like?"

Cordon smirks, his eyes going to Fu, who crawls away from him.

"Where you going? You're not leaving here until you understand how much a parent's hate fuels a child's rage," he says to him before his eyes again go to Lucious. "He's yours to deal with."

Lucious nods. "Two doors down," Lucious adds, pointing. "She's beautiful. And she's alive."

Cordon slips out of the bedroom, shutting the door behind him. Quickly, Fu skulks to it on his hands and knees. But as he grabs the handle, a gunshot rings out from the other side of the door, and the doorknob flies out of his hand, clattering across the floor. Fu grabs his hand in pain, realizing Cordon has locked him in the room with Lucious, and there's no way out.

Grabbing the knob from the floor, Fu heaves it at Lucious. Lucious catches it.

"I'm owed. I'm owed so much..." Lucious says, moving up to her father as Fu climbs to his feet. Backhanding her father with the knob in her hand, Lucious knocks Fu back to the floor, the heels of her boots dropping on each side of Fu's head as she stands over him.

***

As security men rush back into the house downstairs, Cordon kicks open the bedroom door and is met with the barrel of Chen's gun. In Natasha's hand. Seeing it's Cordon, her eyes well with tears and she falls into him. Cordon kisses her.

"You okay?" he asks.

Natasha nods, glancing back at Chen laying behind her in a pool of blood.

"You did good," Cordon tells her as he takes the gun from her hand and checks the clip, making sure there's enough ammo. He hands the gun back to Natasha.

"Are you willing to use this?" he asks her.

She nods, reluctant.

"You're going to have to if you want to come out of this alive," Cordon tells Natasha as regret washes over him. "I'm sorry this happened to you because of me."

They move to the door together, Natasha's hands still shaking. Cordon puts his hand over hers, calming her as he carefully opens the door, peeking out into the upstairs walkway. As they move along the wall slowly, the vast foyer below floods with Fu's security detail. Finding the man at the door unconscious, they spread through the house, four of them racing up the stairwell to the second floor.

"Here we go," Cordon says to Natasha as he aims toward the top of the stairwell. Firing, he hits the first man at the top of the steps, sending him flying back into the others. Cordon grabs Natasha and they dash toward Fu's bedroom. Cordon kicks the door open and they rush in, the door slamming behind them.

Racing to a tall armoire, Cordon shoulders it across the room and over in front of the door, tipping it over to lower its center of gravity, just as the men outside try to push in.

Spinning, Natasha spies Fu on the floor, bloodied, Lucious still standing over her father, hands curled into fists. Fu reaches out to Natasha. "Help me. Please," he begs.

Before she can respond, the bureau in front of the door moves, the door opening enough for an arm to jut through, gun in hand. Without thinking, Natasha runs to the door. She bounds over the tipped bureau and smashes into the door with her shoulder, breaking the arm sticking through, the gun dropping.

As bullets eat through the door, Cordon grabs Natasha, covering her body with his as they fall to the floor. Cordon protects Natasha while securing the bureau against the door with his legs, bullets piercing the floor around him. He whips up an automatic, and with guns in both hands, he fires through the door until the clips are empty.

Silence.

Cordon throws himself across the room, grabbing hold of Fu's four-poster bed and wrenches it around, shoving it toward the door, dumping the priceless bed on top of the equally expensive bureau, barricading all of them inside. As Cordon turns to Lucious, his hand slaps across Lucious' wrist, stopping her from delivering another brutal blow to her father's face. Cordon forces Lucious back away from her father.

"Enough now!" Cordon orders, then exhales. "I know what you're feeling and trust me, he's not worth it."

Lucious tries to fight free of Cordon, wanting to end this with her father. But Cordon won't let her go. Leaning up to Lucious' ear, Cordon says, "I won't let him turn you into me."

Lucious locks eyes with Cordon, the two of them connecting, an understanding that goes far deeper than stopping Lucious from beating her father.

"He is already like you," Fu spits out from the floor, his face bloodied. "A worthless pervert."

"Lucious is far braver than you've ever been, Fu. She's never needed anyone else to fight her fights. Take that to your grave," Cordon growls, dropping his knee onto Fu's neck. Fu struggles, pinned to the floor, his air supply cut off. Fu punches, slaps, and scratches at Cordon's leg, trying to push it off him. But he's not moving Cordon, because Cordon doesn't want to be moved.

Fu's terrified eyes go to Lucious. His hands reach out to her, his fingers grabbing hold of her ankle, silently pleading for his life. Lucious glares down at him, nothing but loathing locked in her eyes.

Hallow points rip through the walls and door from the hallway, disintegrating the wood into shards. Cordon leaps over Fu and grabs Lucious and Natasha, rushing them both across the vast bedroom toward Fu's large desk. Holding onto them both, he dives over the desk, taking both with him, as chunks of the desk are chewed away by bullets. Natasha grabs Lucious, protectively holding her, as Cordon rolls from behind the desk, taking aim at the wall across the room. He fires, emptying the clip, each shot two feet apart.

Everything falls eerily silent.

Sliding to the door, Cordon punches a hole in the wall where the hallow points have chewed small holes. Peering through, he sees eight bodies in the hallway, one man still alive, writhing in pain. Seeing Cordon, the man reaches for his weapon. Cordon dispatches the man with two shots.

Moving to the door, Cordon throws the mattress and four-poster bedframe off and then shoves the bureau back. He waves to Lucious and Natasha to follow.

"Stay behind me," he warns, handing them both semi-automatics. "And aim to kill."

Pulling out a cell phone, Cordon punches in a number. "Annie! I need your help. I need a boat," he speaks quickly, giving his sister the address of Fu's mansion. "Get as close as you can, we'll come over the wall," Cordon adds, "And Annie, bring the big guns."

As Cordon goes through the door, followed by Natasha, Lucious stops, looking back at her father on the floor, clutching his throat, his face streaked with blood from the beating she gave him. As Fu tries to climb to his feet, he sneers at Lucious. Stepping back into the room, Lucious spins kicks in the air, bringing her heeled boot across her father's face. Fu flies back, flopping to the floor, unconscious.

Lucious stares down at her father, loss, rage, and pity, waver in her eyes. Lucious knows she could kill her father right now. Break his neck. Crush his skull. Put a bullet in through his heart. But seeing her father broken on the floor, Lucious raises her foot, bringing the heel down to her father's face. She holds it there, right on his nose. With one step, she could end his life.

"You're not him," Lucious hears from behind her.

Turning, Cordon is at the door, deep lines in his forehead.

Lucious pauses. She lifts her heel high over her father's face. Bringing it down with rage, it slams against the wood floor an inch from his head. As Cordon reaches out to her, Lucious rushes in his direction, taking his hand as they enter the hallway.

They race from the room to catch up with Natasha. The three of them move down the walkway, stepping over bodies, toward the grand staircase.

"How did you get back to Chicago before me?" Cordon asks Lucious.

"You flew commercial. I hired a jet."

"Millionaires can do that," Cordon jokes.

"Yes, they can."

As they pass the last of the bodies in the hallway, one sits up behind them, pointing his gun at Lucious' back. Catching this out of the side of her eye, Natasha yanks Lucious out of the way, her gun coming up and firing before the man can get off a shot.

He falls back to the carpet, dead.

"Thank you," Lucious says, giving Natasha's arm a squeeze.

"You save me, I save you," Natasha smiles.

But their smiles are short-lived as the sound of vans screeching to a stop outside echoes into the mansion. Seconds later, more men dive through the open front door, their eyes wide at the carnage. Spotting the three figures on the upstairs walkway, a barrage of gunfire rings out from below. Natasha dives into a vase alcove, firing back, as Cordon pins Lucious against a wall. Bullets devour chunks of Venetian plaster just over their heads.

As three men rush to the staircase, the men downstairs reposition to get a better angle on Lucious and Cordon. Knowing they will die if he doesn't move, Cordon leaves Lucious and runs toward the upstairs railing, and dives over it. His hand locks onto a metal baluster as he fires down, killing two of the men and sending the others racing from the house for cover.

The baluster snaps and bends as the men on the stairwell spin their weapons towards Cordon, suspended in the air over the foyer floor, unprotected. Natasha and Lucious sprint toward the railing, guns blazing. They kill the three men on the stairs before they can settle their aim on Cordon.

Cordon spies another gunman slithering in through the front door on his belly, taking aim at him. As he's about to let himself drop, taking his chances hitting the marble floor below, a vase is launched from over his head and whistles down at the gunman. He can't react fast enough as the vase Natasha has thrown smashes into his head. Before he can recover, Lucious puts a bullet in him.

Another gunman dives into the foyer but before he can come up, Lucious stands right over Cordon and puts two bullets in him.

"Grab my hand!" Cordon calls to Lucious.

Lucious stares over the upstairs railing as Cordon tucks the gun and reaches for him.

"Seriously!? You're like a gorilla!"

"I'm a piñata hanging here! Grab me!"

Seeing more men piling out of the second van, Lucious grabs Cordon and uses everything she's got to pull him up. Natasha rushes to them and helps as well, but as two men rush into the foyer, Lucious lets go of Cordon and fires two shots, taking them both out at the entrance to the house.

"Get me up, NOW," Cordon demands, swinging his body back and then up toward them. Lucious grabs his legs and flips him over the railing as another half-dozen men enter, firing as they do.

Staying low, Cordon shoves Natasha and Lucious down the hallway towards the back of the house, bullets on their heels as they dash to a corner bedroom. Looking back, Cordon can see men ascending to the upstairs walkway. He shoves Natasha and Lucious into the room as bullets embed into the door as Cordon slams it.

Locking it, Lucious grabs a George III corner chair and jams it under the door handle, but Cordon grabs Lucious and flips her behind him, screaming, "Get back!" just as another round of bullets splinters the wood door, the ornate corner chair disintegrating as bullets tear it to shreds.

Cordon, Natasha, and Lucious take shelter near the walk-in closet, guns ready as the door disappears in front of them, crumbling from the automatic weapon fire. Cordon's eyes land on a large, round table with a wooden base and a metal table top. He rolls across the floor, knocking the table onto its side. Kicking, he breaks off the base before glancing back at Natasha and Lucious, pointing to the two French doors behind them.

Lucious quickly grasps what Cordon is planning, fear in her eyes.

"Wig off, heels off!" Cordon barks Lucious, who quickly does as requested. She then pulls off the red dress, stripping down to her underwear.

"What are we doing?" Natasha asks.

"I think we're going swimming," Lucious says to her.

Cordon lifts the metal tabletop, holding it between himself and the door. It takes the gunfire, the bullets denting the thick metal but not piercing it.

"Pool! Go!"

Lucious lifts Natasha to her feet. Cordon protects them with the table as they back to the French doors leading to a balcony while the gunmen obliterate the lock off the bedroom door.

As they kick the door open, guns aiming into the room, the French doors fling open, and Natasha takes Lucious' hand and they jump over the balcony railing. The gunmen run across the room, firing, but Cordon continues to block them with the tabletop. He backs out onto the balcony, each shot that the tabletop takes, jacking his body. Flipping himself over the balcony rail, Cordon falls backward toward the pool as Natasha and Lucious plunge beneath the surface. Bullets hit the table, but none of the gunmen can get a kill shot off.

Cordon takes the tabletop with him into the water, sinking to the bottom of the pool. He signals Natasha and Lucious to stay behind him as bullets whiz into the water around them. Pushing off the bottom, they all swim to the surface, still protected by the tabletop.

As they emerge, Natasha and Lucious have guns in their hands. They come up firing.

Surprised, the two gunmen on the balcony are hit. They collapse to the floor, dead, as the others dive back into the house for cover.

"My sister is in a boat on the other side of that wall! We may have to swim for it. Can you both do that?"

Natasha and Lucious both nod, frightened but ready.

"When I pull gunfire, both of you go," Cordon tells them.

"But—" Natasha starts, but Cordon stops her.

"No questions. Shoot to kill and get over the fucking wall," he says swiftly as they back toward the far edge of the pool, leaving them with fifty yards of open grass to cross to get to the back wall.

Lucious flips herself out of the pool, pulling Natasha with her. They stay tight behind Cordon and the metal tabletop, both firing again, driving the gunmen on the balcony back into the bedroom for cover again.

Seizing the opportunity, Cordon drops the heavy tabletop and lifts himself out of the water, pulling his two guns up as he rolls across the deck, taking cover by a cabana. Two men race from the back doors of the house, Cordon firing before they can get their bearings, dropping them both. Cordon glances back at Lucious and Natasha, pointing to the trimmed hedges behind the pool, signaling them to get over and stay low.

They bolt for the hedges, diving over them in unison, both coming up, firing, Lucious toward the men on the balcony, Natasha toward the men coming out the back doors onto the pool deck.

Cordon runs for the shed on the back of the property, dodging bullets as they eat the turf at his feet. Cordon spins, firing back, as he throws himself toward the shed. He kills a gunman on the balcony, sending him over the railing, as Lucious kills another, firing from the back door.

Diving behind the shed, Cordon reloads quickly. He takes another two clips from his pocket and heaves them at Natasha and Lucious. Natasha quickly snatches them up and she and Lucious reload as well.

Bullets hit around them and chip away at the front of the shed.

"What's in this shed?" Cordon calls to Lucious.

"Lawn equipment, pool stuff," Lucious responds.

Cordon's eyes light up as he balls his fist and punches a hole through the side of the shed, then rips off a few boards, creating an opening.

Crawling in, Cordon quickly takes inventory. Lawn equipment. Jugs of chlorine. Yard chemicals. A gas mask. Five-gallon containers of gasoline. "Fuck, yes," he mutters to himself as he hoists chlorine jugs and gasoline toward the riding mowers.

Outside, two men race from the back of the house, firing toward where Lucious and Natasha hide, pinned down. They fire back, Natasha killing one, but the other leaps over the hedge, only to be met by Lucious, who unleashes a flurry of punches on the guy. The gunman tries to defend himself, but Lucious is too quick, spinning her body into the man, locking his arm, forcing him to drop his automatic weapon. Natasha scoops it up.

"Duck," she yells.

Lucious does, spinning away from the man as Natasha takes him out with two shots before she and Lucious fire again at the house, daring anyone to come at them.

"Lucious, Natasha...when you hear the crash," Cordon calls to them, "get to the wall. Fast."

"What about you?!" Natasha calls back.

Cordon doesn't answer as he shimmies back into the shed. A half-dozen men exit through the patio doors, carrying M4 carbines. They fire at the shed, the pointed, thick bullets shredding the resin exterior as they do.

As the men continue their assault, three riding mowers crash through the bullet-weakened front of the shed, loaded with cans of gasoline, chlorine and yard chemicals. As the men stop in their tracks, Cordon steps out of the collapsing structure, the gas mask on his face, and fires three shots into the large gas cans.

Still motoring forward, they erupt into a toxic fireball of flames and black smoke.

As everyone's attention spins towards the explosion, Lucious grabs Natasha's hand and they bolt as fast as they can across the green lawn for the back wall.

Blown off his feet, Cordon flies back into the flaming shed, which collapses on top of him. The two gunmen closest to the shed are blown to pieces while flames engulf another. The deadly cloud of smoke and gas that wafts at them before they can escape consumes the other three men. All the windows in the house blow into shards, which missile at the men inside, injuring and killing them.

Crawling out from the flaming mess, Cordon comes up firing as men stumble out of the house, bloodied and injured, pieces of glass and wood embedded in their skin.

Lucious leaps and grabs the top of the wall, and muscles her way up. Staying prone, she reaches down. Natasha jumps toward Lucious. Lucious grabs Natasha's hands and pulls her to the top of the wall.

About fifty yards off the back of the property, a speedboat rocks in the small waves offshore. Annie, a high-powered rifle perched on her hip, waves to Lucious and Natasha.

"Jump!!!!" Annie screams to them.

Seeing Natasha and Lucious on top of the wall, Cordon takes off on a full run for them, firing over his shoulder with both hands.

Turning back, Lucious spies her father emerge onto the balcony from the master bedroom, an M-16 strapped to him. Fu fires.

As Lucious is about to jump, a bullet rips into Natasha's arm. Her eyes widen as she wobbles on top of the wall, losing her footing. Lucious grabs for her but the slickness of the blood running down her arm causes Lucious to lose her grip on her. Natasha falls off the wall, landing hard in the grassy yard of Fu's property.

Natasha pulls her body up against the wall, blood seeping from the wound. "Go! Go!" Cordon barks at Lucious, recklessly running toward Natasha before she's killed. He spins quickly to see Fu on his bedroom balcony, turning his aim on Lucious.

"*Jump, goddamn it!*" Cordon screams at Lucious.

Just as Fu fires, Lucious dives out toward the lake, the sound of the bullets cutting the air around her. A horrified Lucious plunges under, disappearing into the darkness of the water. Pulling up the shotgun from her hip, Annie takes aim, firing at the balcony over and over. A bullet splits the wall next to Fu's head, causing him to cower back inside the doorway.

Grabbing the steering wheel, Annie throws the boat into gear. As Lucious emerges from the water, Annie spins the boat towards her, and Lucious swims in her direction.

"Stay down! Come up on the other side of the boat!" Annie warns.

Lucious swallows a breath of air and submerges again, swimming under the boat as Annie blasts shot after shot toward the house, giving Lucious cover.

Allowing the boat to glide over the top of her, Lucious pops up on the other side. Reaching up, she snatches the tow line and pulls herself to the side. Annie steps back to Lucious and hoists her in, then slides a semi-automatic across the seats to Lucious. Checking it quickly, Lucious spins from the floor and takes aim at her father's bedroom balcony just as he comes back out, firing again. Lucious drives her father back inside again, her aim exact.

"I should have killed him," Lucious says with regret, wiping tears from her eyes, the image of Natasha being shot and falling from the wall still fresh. "Please get out of there, please get out of there..." Lucious repeats as she continues firing toward the balcony, hoping to finally kill her father.

In the yard, Cordon fires at anyone still standing until he's out of ammo. It's then two men rush down the patio steps, racing in his direction. Licking his lips, the rage consuming him erupts. Cordon flips off the gas mask and uses it to beat the men, spinning, slapping each of them with it over and over, getting the straps of the mask over the neck of one man, flipping him over his back and yanking, snapping the man's neck.

As the second man attacks, Cordon unleashes a ruthless beatdown before two more security men jump into the fray, both caught up in the maelstrom of Cordon's viciousness. Cordon destroys both men, killing them with brutal efficiency and shocking speed.

Blood covering his body, Cordon stands, his eyes locking with Natasha. Even amid the madness and evil of the last few days, Cordon's feral brutality horrifies Natasha. He steps over the men's broken bodies, stalking toward Natasha. As he reaches her, another shot rings out, a bullet ripping into Cordon's shoulder. The bullet goes all the way through the meat, blood pouring from both sides. This only causes Cordon's rage to explode. He spins towards the house just as Fu steps out onto the patio, M-16 in his hands.

Seeing Cordon wounded delights Fu, who fires again. Cordon dives forward, rolling, staying just in front of Fu's aim. Cordon comes up from the roll with a rock in his hand as he sprints toward Fu. He knows he either ends this now or allows Fu to terrorize his life, as well as Lucious', well into the future. Like he's throwing a fastball in a MLB game, Cordon unleashes the rock, hurling it directly at Fu. It cracks Fu in the head, stunning him, his aim dropping as he fires into the thick Plexiglas wall behind Cordon. Before he can steady himself and his aim, Cordon throws his body at Fu, slamming into him like a train into a compact car caught on the tracks. Cordon's hand wraps around the barrel of the M-16, driving it into the ground as he lands on top of Fu. Cordon grabs Fu's hand, wrenching it off the trigger, squeezing until the bones break.

Fu grabs Cordon's shoulder, digging his finger into the bullet hole. But Cordon is beyond physical pain, zoned in on one thing and one thing only: how much pain he can inflict on this man.

"Abomination! You don't deserve to share this earth with the rest of us!" Fu screams as Cordon punches him in the face.

"Hell is your eternity! Yours and my son's!"

Having heard enough, Cordon's big hand comes around fast, clamping over Fu's nose and mouth. "*Daughter!* She is your daughter, you pathetic piece of sanctimonious shit! Die with that!" Cordon growls. With each word, his fingers clamp tighter and tighter around Fu's face as if he's going to compress rock into dust with his bare hand.

As Fu tries to fight free of Cordon's grip, blood trickles down the side of Cordon's hand as his fingers dig through Fu's skin, crushing Fu's cheekbones and suffocating him.

Pulling a knife from under his shirt, Fu's shaky hand drives it through Cordon's forearm, but Cordon doesn't even wince, his grip only growing stronger as he stands, picking Fu up by his face. Cordon lifts Fu off his feet, holding him in the air, blood rushing down the sides of Fu's face. Fu kicks in the air, trying to twist the knife in Cordon's forearm to make him let go, but Cordon is stone. There's nothing Fu can do to break his grip.

His eyes popping, Fu's body shakes as Cordon holds him. Fu's punches and kicks grow weaker, his hand falling off the hilt of the knife. Blood pools in Fu's eyes, and seeps from his ears as Cordon continues to squeeze the life out of him.

All the fight goes out of Fu, his body spasming until he stops moving. Cordon drops Fu's body to the ground and turns away. Cordon hears Fu gasp a deep breath.

"Faggot," he coughs out, barely audible.

Without turning back to him, Cordon lifts his foot and slams it down on Fu's face, crushing it.

***

Every minute they don't see Cordon or Natasha, Annie, and Lucious wrestle with their ebbing hope. Their eyes are peeled on the wall; they both struggle not to feel the defeat that rocks the boat with every wave. Lucious reaches over and takes Annie's hand for a moment, their eyes still focused on the property and the house, ready to take out anyone. While it's only been minutes since Lucious climbed into the boat, it feels like hours.

Suddenly, they see a hand grip the top of the wall.

Cordon muscles himself up with one hand, holding Natasha in the other. They are both bloody and battered, wobbling on their feet. Seeing them, Annie lets out a relieved breath just as a gunman steps out onto a balcony upstairs, taking aim through his scope. But Annie is faster, blasting from her hip over and over. She hits the man as he fires, his shot sailing past Cordon and Natasha, diving into the water. The man crumbles to the balcony floor.

Cordon lowers himself onto the rocks on the other side of the wall and lifts Natasha down, carrying her in his arms as he walks into the water.

At the helm, Annie steers the boat toward them, getting as close as she can before throttling down. Another crew of gunmen emerges from the house, trying to get shots off. Lucious aims up at the balcony, knowing the only place someone can hit them is from above. As gunmen step out, Lucious fires away, driving them back inside, while Annie helps Natasha into the boat and Cordon hangs onto the side.

The men on the balcony lay on the floor, shooting through the railing, as bullets pelt the boat.

"Get this boat out of here!" Cordon demands of Annie.

"I'm not leaving without you!" she cries.

"GO!!!!" Cordon yells, reaching his arm through a rope on the side.

Annie lunges at the steering wheel, yanking the throttle. The boat plows forward, picking up speed as bullets hit all around. Lucious fires back, trying to keep the gunmen at bay. Annie weaves the boat back and forth until she's far enough out of firing range, as Cordon tries to catch a breath of air, the water flooding into his face as if he's being waterboarded.

"We're sinking!" Lucious shouts, water now filling the hull.

Idling the boat, Annie dashes to the side, Lucious with her. Cordon's arm is still caught in the rope, but he's slumped, unconscious. Lucious dives into the water and holds Cordon's head out of the water.

"No, no, no, no, no, you can't die!" Lucious screams before he checks Cordon's pulse and breathing.

"No pulse! He's not breathing!" Lucious bellows. "We have to get him in the boat!"

Cordon is dead weight as Lucious and Annie struggle to get him in the boat. Holding Cordon's face out of the water, Lucious pulls herself back onboard and grabs Cordon under his shoulders, but they simply aren't strong enough to lift Cordon up more than a few inches. Natasha struggles over to the side.

"Pull him that way, try to get him prone!" she orders.

As Lucious and Annie maneuver Cordon's body down the side of the boat so his legs float towards the surface, Natasha reaches over and grabs hold of one of his thick legs. With a scream, she lifts it up.

"On three!" she orders.

Natasha counts down and the three of them lift Cordon's body out of the water, Natasha getting his leg over, and Annie grabbing hold of Cordon's pants and tugging as hard as she can to flip him over the side. Lucious changes her grip on Cordon and with everything she has, she rocks her own body back, pulling Cordon with her.

They get his body over the lip and all tumble back as Cordon falls into the boat.

Exhausted but having no time to rest, Lucious climbs atop Cordon and starts chest compressions and breaths. Annie steps in, helping with the breaths, as Lucious continues the chest compressions.

"Come on, Cordon, you can't die on me!" Annie begs just before giving him two breaths.

Natasha pulls herself up near his head, whispering in his ear, insisting he come back to her. But Cordon doesn't move, his body tinting blue.

They continue to work on Cordon, Annie exhausted as her tears fall.

"Come on! Don't give up!!!" Lucious calls to Cordon as she continues compressions.

Still nothing.

More compressions. More breaths.

Lucious stops for a moment to catch her breath, dropping her head onto Cordon's chest. "Come on, you will not die on us!" Lucious pleads, fighting tears, before she looks up at the sobbing Annie, trying to find the strength to continue.

"*Breathe!*" Lucious screams, her hands going together as if she's going to pray but instead, bringing them down on Cordon's chest hard, three times. "Goddamn it, Big 'N Dumb! Breathe!!!!!"

Lucious brings her fists down again on Cordon's chest with another mighty blow and this time, a wad of green lake debris erupts with a flow of vomit from Cordon's mouth right into Lucious' face.

"Oh, Ugly Betty!!!" Lucious gags as she climbs off of him, allowing Annie and Natasha to muscle Cordon onto his side so he doesn't choke.

Cordon takes a deep, strained breath, his eyes opening wide. He sees all three faces, Lucious, Annie, and Natasha right in his.

"I told you not to call me that." Cordon croaks out, coughing up more lake water, as the other three collapse around him in tearful relief. "What the fuck happened?"

"You died, I think," Lucious tells him. "Did you see a white light or Jesus or anything?"

Cordon sits up, still coughing up lake water, and fires Lucious a look. "Jesus don't want me," Cordon says. "I saw water. And blood. Then it was lights out."

Finding the first aid kit, Annie covers Natasha's and Cordon's bullet wounds with pads and gauze, taping them as best she can.

"Keep pressure on them," she instructs Lucious.

Cordon signals Lucious to worry about Natasha, grabbing a life vest and placing it over his wound, holding it there as he tells Lucious, "Even in my weakened state, I can put more pressure on my wounds than you can with those skinny, little arms."

"You wouldn't be alive if it weren't for these skinny, little arms," Lucious counters, as she holds pressure on Natasha's bullet wound, trying not to cause her any more pain. Natasha winces as she smiles, sending up a thankful prayer that she's alive as Cordon locks his fingers with hers.

Speeding the sinking boat south down the shoreline, Annie recognizes she only has minutes to dock before they take on too much water. As they pass her father's home, police lights now bouncing off the house, Lucious can see her father's broken body on the lawn through the Plexiglas wall as Annie races past. Locked in Lucious' eyes is pained sadness. She fights her emotions and the 'what-ifs' as Natasha holds her.

Cordon reaches out and squeezes Lucious' shoulder. Their eyes connect. Cordon nods. He doesn't have to say a thing. Lucious understands. Lucious nods back, silently announcing to Cordon that somehow, someway, she will be okay with everything that's happened.

AFTER DEATH

Arriving back at the boatyard, Annie maneuvers the sinking speedboat into a slip. With the hull over half full of water, the bow points upward, like the Titanic before it sank.

This is going to be hard to explain, Annie thinks to herself as she climbs out and ties up the boat, which she knows will be underwater within a few hours.

Having given her his blood-stained shirt to cover herself, Cordon picks up Natasha in his arms, carrying her. "We can't go to the hospital," he announces.

"We have to get you two taken care of," Lucious argues, perfectly comfortable still being in nothing but a pair of bikini briefs. "What about an urgent care?"

"I'm sure the police are looking for us," counters Cordon.

"We need to do something. You both were in the lake with those wounds. God knows what got in them," Lucious continues.

Annie waves them to follow her, adding, "Let me make a call..."

Laying Natasha in the backseat of Annie's SUV, Cordon slides in next to her, laying her head on his lap and holding her hand.

She glances up at him with a weak smile. "We look like we've been to war."

"We have been," Lucious states, slipping into the front passenger seat next to Annie as she starts the engine.

Driving through South Chicago, Annie makes a call as she keeps an eye out for the police. Listening to Annie's phone call, Lucious isn't sure who she's talking to, but when she hears Annie say they will be there in ten minutes, Lucious breathes a sigh of relief as she fixes the jumble of necklaces around her neck.

Turning deeper into South Chicago, the area getting rougher with each block, Annie stops in front of a post-war building with a veterinary clinic sign hanging in front. The building looks closed. Or more accurately, abandoned.

Lucious looks over at Annie, her brow raising.

"She was in the Army," Annie explains. "Afghanistan. She took care of the bomb dogs. Also did emergency surgeries on soldiers when necessary."

As Lucious opens her mouth to protest, she is cut off by Cordon who growls out, "Works for me."

Lucious sighs again, this time with a shrug. "Works for him, it works for me. Not my ass they're sewing up."

Jumping out, Lucious stands back as Cordon lifts Natasha out of the backseat and carries her toward the door, where Annie knocks. After a moment, the door is unlocked and opened. Dr. Laura Finnigan, her Irish-red hair pulled back, holds the door as they all enter. Once they're all in, she locks it, ordering Cordon to carry Natasha to the back.

To the noise of barking dogs, Laura digs the bullet out of unconscious Natasha and repairs the damage to her as best she can. Cordon is a little less stressful to repair; the bullet that hit his shoulder, having gone through, and the knife wound, while deep, somehow didn't damage any major vein or artery. Cordon chose to stay awake through his surgery, talking to Laura about her time in Afghanistan. While having only a few bags of human blood to transfuse, blood she had reserved for a crime lord she takes care of, Laura is grateful that no major organs or arteries were ripped wide open in the gun battle. Just like when she had to work on the fly overseas, she is careful to make sure that they don't bleed out much through the surgery, keenly aware that if either of them loses too much blood, they could die on her table. After she finishes stitching up Cordon's entry and exit wounds, she gives him a smile.

"Am I gonna live?" he asks, admiring the stitches in his forearm.

"You both are. But considering how many scars you have, I imagine that it's not your first lucky break," she tells him, checking on Natasha who is still out of it.

"Don't much believe in luck," Cordon answers.

"You should start," Laura sasses right back.

Cordon jumps off the table as Laura cuts a vet assistant's smock up the middle, allowing Cordon to put it on one arm and pulling the other side over his wounded shoulder like a shawl. He moves out into the lobby to talk closely with Lucious, who listens, nodding. Annie watches as Lucious moves to the phone behind the check-in station and makes a call.

Crossing to his sister, Cordon gives Annie a loving smile.

"Thank you."

"I'm just thankful you're alive. That we're all alive."

"We wouldn't be if you hadn't been there for me," Cordon adds. "I love you."

Annie moves to his unbandaged side and hugs him.

"You're a mess," she tells him.

"Takes one to know one."

Annie chuckles.

"One day," she surmises, "one day we might not be."

"You think that's possible?"

She stares up into his eyes, shaking her head. "No."

Cordon laughs.

An hour and a half later, Natasha awakens, groggy, dull pain throbbing through her body, and finds she's strapped to a gurney. A private ambulance sits out front, lights on. As the two EMTs finish prepping Natasha for transport, she glances side to side, unsure of exactly what is occurring around her.

Cordon steps up, smiling down as he takes her hand.

"What's...what is all this?"

"You're going to the hospital."

"Okay..."

"In New York City," Cordon tells her. "Dr. Elvin Nance is one of the best gender affirmation surgeons in the country. You're going in for your surgery next week."

"What?!" Natasha exclaims, her mind still fuzzy. "How?"

Cordon turns in Lucious' direction, letting her step up. "You're beating me to it," Lucious tells her. "I've done lots and lots of research. Dr. Nance is the best in the country. He's who I'll use. And he used to be a she. Since you're already laid up, and you've had all your preliminary tests and exams, your psych work, blah, blah, blah, Cordon asked me to call and see if they might move you up his list."

Lucious then smiles, adding, "And low and behold, the good doctor was financially persuaded to leave his second home on the coast of Maine and make that happen."

"I'm going now?"

"By ambulance, so they can monitor you the whole way," Cordon tells Natasha.

"Is this real?" she asks.

"As real as everything else you've been through," he tells her before he leans over and kisses her, his lips staying close to hers.

"I wish you the best life," Cordon whispers, looking into Natasha's still confused eyes.

Her hand reaches up and touches his face, her eyes swelling with tears. "You've been the man of my dreams. I wish you could..."

Her voice trails off, Cordon wiping her tears with his thumb. "Knowing you're happy with who you are will make me happy. And if you ever need anything, you'll know how to find me. But go live your life. Make it count, Natasha."

Nodding, Natasha kisses his hands before releasing them.

Their eyes never leave one another as the EMTs roll Natasha out of the clinic and load her into the back of the private ambulance. As she waves at him one last time, Cordon accepts that this will be the last time he sees her.

Because he knows he can't stay in Chicago. He's a wanted man.

"Let me check your dressing before you go," Laura says, leading Cordon into the back once more. He sits on the operating table as she checks the packing she did on the wound.

"It's going to need to be cleaned twice a day," she tells him.

"It's not my first time being shot," Cordon remarks, pulling down the waist of his pants to show her a bullet scar on his hip. "There's still some metal in there."

"Why am I not surprised?" she jokes.

Looking over at a dog in a cage eyeing them morosely, Cordon mugs at the dog but gets no reaction.

"What happened to him?"

"Got fixed this morning."

Cordon nods, saying, "I'd rather take a bullet."

"You were in love with her?" Laura asks as puts his arm in a sling.

Cordon nods. The doctor nods back, lips tight.

"Is that judgment?" Cordon asks.

"God, no," Laura states. "I don't do judgment. My wife would kick my ass."

Cordon chuckles as she leads him back into the lobby. Lucious is trying on decorative dog collars from a stand behind the counter, while Annie is on the phone, trying to explain to her boss what happened to the boat that she sank.

"I'm going to buy this," Lucious says, holding up the rhinestone-laden dog collar before clasping it around her neck. "It juxtaposes my other necklaces."

"Juxtaposes?" Cordon chides.

Lucious waves Cordon off. "I think so, so keep your smartass comments to yourself."

As Cordon pays Laura, she hands him a card and instructs him to call her later, so she can come by wherever he is and check the wound.

"I'll take care of that. I gotta get out of Chicago," Cordon announces, then looks at Lucious. "We both probably should. They're actively searching for us, I'm sure."

"You're a man without a country," Lucious adds.

Cordon nods, recognizing that what Lucious is saying is true. He can't stay in Chicago, he killed a local billionaire. California is out of the question. He fucked up Lansing badly. Another billionaire. Tag on all the other charges from the mayhem he created over the last few days, and the only place Cordon is sure he would be welcomed in America is in Colorado, at the ADX Florence, the most notorious of the supermax prisons.

"I'm sort of fucked, aren't I?" Cordon says, more thinking out loud than to anyone.

Lucious steps up to Cordon, reaching up and taking his face in her hands. She expects Cordon to either back away or flinch, but he does neither.

"Without you, I wouldn't be alive," Lucious tells Cordon.

But as expected, Cordon waves the compliment off. "You're stronger than you think. In many ways, you proved you're stronger than me."

Lucious pulls herself closer to Cordon, hugging him. She stands on her tiptoes and speaks into his ear.

"Chicago Executive Airport. Hanger 16. Four p.m. tomorrow. A jet will be waiting."

Cordon pulls back, looking at Lucious' face. Lucious smiles. Cordon looks concerned.

"Going where?"

Lucious continues to smile as an Uber pulls up outside the vet clinic.

"Maybe one day we'll see each other again. Life can be funny that way. But you need to disappear. I do too. For a while, maybe longer. Make sure you're there on time."

Lucious kisses Cordon on the cheek, then moves up to Annie and hugs her, talking closely with her for a moment. Annie nods, hugging Lucious one more time before Lucious walks out the door and gets into the Uber, waving as it drives away.

Cordon watches the car, making sure no one is following. Old habits. Then, he reaches out and takes Annie, embracing her. She presses her head against his chest.

"I'll surveil my place. If they haven't pinpointed me, I'll get in and get what I need. But I'm going to go away for a while."

Sadness fills Annie's eyes as she takes in her brother.

"Are you going to tell me where?"

Shaking his head, Cordon says, "I'm not sure. At least not yet."

Cordon tells Annie it's best she go about her life as if she knows nothing. He'll get her the money for the boat.

"Not necessary. They're going to use it as a tax write-off and then use the insurance money to buy a new one. You know, the Chicago way..." she half-jokes.

Cordon calls Annie an Uber as well. Putting her in the car, he tells her to find a hotel for the next few weeks and stay there, as he shoves the money he took from Gio into her hand.

"I'll be in touch," he tells her, kissing his sister on the cheek before the car drives off. Unsure if she will ever see her brother again, as soon as the car turns the corner and Cordon is out of sight, she bursts into tears. Annie can't help feel that the demons that have haunted Cordon throughout his life finally won. They finally captured him and now his fate is in the hands of everything he's been fighting all his life. As tears roll down her cheek, with South Chicago passing by the window of the car, even Annie isn't sure where she's going. At least for the moment. While she realizes that with her husband dead, and her father in the hospital, this would be the perfect time to escape Chicago, to leave all of this behind and start over somewhere else, she isn't sure exactly how to do that.

But it's an option. And she hasn't had one of those in a long, long time.

***

Laying in a hospital bed, Nelson sleeps. The marks on his neck are still raw as the monitors he's hooked up to beep softly, not waking him. Quietly, a nurse walks into the room, the Crocs on her feet squeak with newness, not a scuff on them. She moves up to Nelson and slips the call button off his bed, deliberately yanking it from the wall.

Sliding a syringe from her pocket, she pierces the tube that's connected to the drip, injecting a clear, thick liquid. It mixes with the drip and enters Nelson's body.

He stirs, seeing the nurse recap the syringe.

"What...what are you doing?" he dryly asks.

The nurse pats Nelson's arm before unplugging his monitor.

"Returning a favor, sweetie," she says, turning to walk out.

It's Lucious. In an auburn wig and pale pink lipstick, large glasses hiding her face.

As Lucious strides out, Nelson searches for the call button but can't find it. Opening his mouth to call out, his breathing labors almost immediately. He tries to call out again, his hand grabbing the rail on the side of the bed. He winces, his body convulsing. He keeps trying to call for help but cannot as his body is overtaken by whatever was pressed into the drip. Nelson's head drops back to the pillow behind him, his mouth open as he takes his final breath, almost as if he's expelling all the hatred and cruelty that resides in him.

He no longer moves. His mouth and eyes are open. But for the first time, possibly since his childhood, Nelson appears at peace.

***

A battered SUV navigates its way through the large hangars, briefly across the tarmac, and finally parks outside hangar 16, where a sleek jet has taxied out of the hangar and waiting. Annie is behind the wheel of the SUV, Cordon in the passenger seat, his face giving away nothing as he stares at the jet.

"That's pretty sweet," Annie says, admiring the shiny jet.

"Yeah. Never flown on one of those," Cordon responds, then says, "Come with me."

Annie fights tears, making it even harder to smile, but she does. "No," she says. "I have to bury dad. And Aaron."

"I love you," Cordon says almost immediately. "You're the only person I can say that to and mean it."

"It won't always be that way, Cord."

She reaches over and takes his hand as a pilot steps from the plane. Cordon waves with his free hand, the pilot waving back.

Cordon pulls out his key ring and slides two keys off it.

"Keys to my place. It's yours now," Cordon tells her.

"Cordon! No, I can't take---"

He grabs her hand and places the key into her palm and closes it, silencing her.

"These keys," he says, holding up three more keys as he takes them from the ring, "are to my safe deposit boxes. There's over a hundred thousand dollars in each---"

"What?!? Cordon, come on. You're going to need money," Annie insists.

"I got enough to get by. This is money I've been saving for *you*. I got ahold of a friend last night, a lawyer, he's doing me a solid. My place is now in your name, you just need to sign some papers."

Reaching into his pocket, he pulls out a business card. "This is him. Call him today, get it taken care of. He's been paid."

"Cordon, this is crazy! What are you taking with you?"

"I got my computer and some clothes, that's all I need."

"You can't do this, Cordon," protests Annie.

"I'm your big brother. I should have saved you from the men in your life a long time ago. I wasn't there for you like you were for me. Keep the townhouse, sell the townhouse, move if you want. Start over. Annie, it's time. You got the money to do it, and there's nothing holding you here. Go somewhere and find the happiness you deserve instead of settling for the shit that comes along."

Condon kisses her on her cheek and steps out, opening the back door of Annie's SUV. He pulls out an oversized military cargo bag, a large duffle, and a satchel he throws over his shoulder. He walks to the jet, stopping one more time to smile at Annie and give her an easy wave. As she watches her brother stride to the plane, with each step he seems lighter, a bounce in his gait Annie has never witnessed, as if he's walking out of one life and into a better one.

She smiles, waving back, willing herself not to cry until he's gone. After he's been inside for a few minutes, an attendant pulls up the door, sealing the plane. Knowing he's going to be safe, she takes a full breath, letting the tears fall. But without sobbing. She will miss him more than anyone in the world, but knowing he's going to be okay, and maybe have the time to get better and focus inward on himself; that's all she's ever wanted for her brother.

Maybe this time, things will be different for him. For her.

As the plane taxis out onto the runway and rolls to the far end, Annie watches as it picks up speed and lifts off. She stays until the plane is out of sight. Smiling, she throws the SUV into drive and does a sharp, squealing turn, and heads back between the hangars, disappearing.

Cordon can't help but continue to glance around the sharply appointed interior of the jet as it ascends. There are eight seats with a small galley and a bathroom in the back. The seats in the last row stretch out to a bed. Cordon chuckles to himself. He's lived in smaller places. And far, far worse. As he turns the attendant stands over him.

"Is there anything I can get you?" the attendant asks.

"You could tell me where I'm going."

"You don't know?"

Cordon shakes his head.

"We'll be landing in Havana in four and a half hours."

Cordon's eyes widen. "Havana? Wow...okay."

The attendant hands a manila envelope to Cordon.

"Once we're at altitude, I am supposed to give you this."

Cordon takes it, turning it over. It's only sealed by the clasp, and he can feel that there's more than paper inside.

"Thank you," Cordon says dismissively, smart enough to know he shouldn't open it while the attendant is standing over him.

Once the attendant moves back to the galley, Cordon squeezes the metal clasps and opens the envelope, sliding the contents into his lap. The first thing he opens is a passport. It's fake, like the three others he packed, but he's impressed at the quality. Cordon then picks up a letter folded in threes, with a paper clip holding another paper behind it. He opens it. The letterhead is from UBS Bank in Switzerland. The account is set up in the alias on the new passport.

Cordon seldom gasps, but the amount in the account causes him to. Twelve and a half million dollars. Flipping the first letter, he finds a note on the second page, handwritten. From Lucious. It reads:

Cuba hasn't extradited anyone back to the U.S. since they normalized relations, and there's worse people than you living there. Enjoy retirement. Ciao, Lucious.

Cordon laughs. It is a deep, hearty howl, something that Cordon hasn't experienced in ages. He laughs until he's out of breath before signaling the attendant.

"You got champagne?" Cordon asks.

THE END FORWARD

The tank top he wears reveals the scars on the front and back of his shoulder where he was shot. The skin has healed over but the scar expands and contracts as Cordon works his shoulders in the small grunt-and-sweat, open-air, gym in the older section of Havana. Cordon loves the aura of the place, even the rusty weights and machines, mainly because tourists avoid it. Still uncomfortable when he runs into any American, Cordon especially avoids them when he's working out. The gym is his sanctuary, the place he goes to lose himself in the clanging and banging of the weights as well as the harsh aroma of humidity and sweat.

Noting a handsome, well-muscled Cubano who keeps smiling and nodding at him, Cordon isn't sure if it's because he's one of the largest men in this gym and the smiling guy is interested in him, or if he recognizes him from somewhere else. The last possibility worries Cordon. He pulls a weight bench off to a corner where he can work out by himself, needing to get out from in front of the mirrors, people's ability to see his reflection only causes him stress.

After the workout, Cordon strolls down the street in Old Havana, the island air thick, making it impossible not to sweat. Not that the inside of the gym is air-conditioned, but there are fans that circulate the air and dry the sweat on your skin. On the street, walled on either side by the crumbling buildings, the ocean breeze doesn't travel, the humidity hanging like a soaked blanket.

As Cordon continues down the street, a group of older women walking past ogle the sweating, mountainous American striding by...and the handsome, muscled Cubano following him a few yards behind.

Once past the women, the Cuban man, Rafael, jogs closer to Cordon.

"*Asere...*" Rafael calls to Cordon, causing him to turn.

Even though Rafael is muscular, his size doesn't compare to Cordon's. Rafael smiles, and puts his hands up, signaling he comes in peace. Rafael smiles wider, disarming Cordon, as Rafael grabs Cordon's bicep and whistles, impressed.

"*Sigueme*," Rafael says, waving Cordon to walk with him down a side street. Concern crosses Cordon's face, but Rafael playfully waves Cordon in his direction.

"Come," Rafael says, his English minimal but his warmth apparent.

Cordon relents, walking with Rafael. They say nothing as Rafael leads him through the streets of Old Havana, which after seven months, Cordon has gotten a handle on. He knows where his favorite stores are. He knows where the internet café is, where he contacted Annie from before he found his apartment which has wifi. He found a great tailor who makes clothes that fit Cordon perfectly. Something he's rarely had in his life. And in Cuba for a fraction of what he would pay in the States.

Leading him toward a small hotel, Rafael points to a table in the far corner of the outdoor patio, where a woman sits, sipping an espresso. Rafael moves up to her, kissing the woman before he points behind him. The woman turns, causing Cordon's eyes to narrow and a smile to wash onto his lips.

It's Lucious. Her hair has grown out, and she now has a substantial rack, which she proudly displays in a low-cut blouse, with a loose skirt displaying her long, shapely legs. Lucious is more feminine and beautiful than the last time Cordon saw her. But when she smiles, even with bright lipstick surrounding it, it's the same smile Cordon remembers.

"You don't write, you don't call..." Cordon jokes as Lucious stands, giving Cordon a tight hug before she displays her new body.

"I've been busy."

"I can see that. You're beautiful."

"Thank you," Lucious coos, as her smile widens. She flips her hair and sits back down, pointing to a chair across from her as Rafael slides into the seat next to her.

"Rafie kept telling me about a giant muscled American at the gym. I knew it had to be you."

Cordon glances at Rafael who gives Cordon a wink and a smile. "You happy, Lucious? You look happy," Cordon responds.

Lucious' eyes trail over to Rafael and shrugs dramatically with a big smile.

"Gloriously! He's Cuban. And look at the size of his hands," she answers Cordon, causing Cordon to laugh.

"I can only guess what that means," Cordon smiles back.

"It means exactly what you think it means, which is exactly how I meant it," Lucious cackles. "And even better, he loves me the way I am but will be just fine with me finishing things. Which I've already scheduled. I hit the jackpot."

"Yeah, I'd say you did..." says Cordon.

"And of course, look at him. Face, body, and a heart. Who knew men like that even existed?" Lucious says, taking Rafael's hand and kissing it.

Rafael leans over and kisses Lucious on the lips, revealing their chemistry. Cordon's face can't hide his mixed feelings about Lucious' last statement, but he's not about to ruin the mood.

"You didn't have to do what you did for me," Cordon changes the subject.

"Yes. I did," Lucious nods. "You were the first person that didn't think I was just some sort of sissy. Which I am, but I'm a badass sissy."

"Yes, you are. And far more."

"I'm free to be myself. I never thought I would have a man who would love me for me. I never had it growing up," Lucious says, causing Cordon to nod, both in agreement and understanding.

"He's a lucky guy."

"How's your sister?"

Cordon glances around, figuring out directions before pointing north. "Lives ninety miles that direction. Key West. Had her move closer. It was good for her to start over. And she loves it."

Lucious reaches across the table, touching Cordon warmly. "You asked me if I was happy. What about you?"

Unprepared for the question, Cordon hems, shrugging, not speaking for a moment. A waiter comes and takes his and Rafael's orders. Cordon just points to what Lucious is drinking, wishing he could get a large glass of ice water, but ice is not something you ask for in Cuba, because unless it's made with purified water, it's easy to get sick.

"Happiness…" Cordon says, licking his lips, "is not natural to me."

Smiling sadly, Lucious again reaches across and touches Cordon again. "You deserve it more than anyone. Even more than me."

"One day…one day," Cordon responds, trying to turn the conversation by nodding at Rafael and saying, "Et veo en el gimnasio."

"Si," Rafael responds with a nod.

Cordon gives him a smile, turning back to Lucious. Lucious can see that whatever Cordon is about to say it's going to surprise him.

"Invite me over to that beautiful home of yours in Miramar. I like my steak rare. Crab rather than lobster. And 'Isla del Tesoro' Extra Anejo rum."

Lucious laughs. She shouldn't be surprised that Cordon figured out that she lived on the island as well and even knows exactly where she lives, but still she is.

"I should have known. And duly noted," Lucious continues, laughing. "I've made the acquaintance of many beautiful girls here in Havana who you might find captivating. Mind if I invite them as well?"

Cordon studies Lucious' beautiful face for a quick second before nodding. "I don't get invited to many parties."

"Well, you'll be the special guest."

Cordon downs his espresso in a speedy gulp, standing. He hands Lucious his phone so Lucious can put her phone number in. Lucious hands Cordon her phone and he does the same.

"I look forward to it, my friend. You got my number and Rafael knows where to find me. And now I know someone who can give me a spot at the gym when I need it. Win-win."

Lucious stands and embraces Cordon, patting his chest. Rafael shakes Cordon's hand heartily, again squeezing Cordon's thick bicep, impressed.

After Cordon says goodbye, he holds Lucious a moment longer. Everything they went through, together and since, has bonded them for life. Cordon gives one last wave before he exits the patio, leaving Lucious with her new love.

Instead of walking home, Cordon turns north on Crespo, heading down to where he can stare across the Straits of Florida as well as view the Castillo De Los Tres Reyes Del Marro in the distance. Cordon holds an affinity for the structure. There is something spiritual for him about a 16th century fortress, sun-bleached, eroded by salt water and storms, yet still standing tall. Still feels strong. Mighty and solid. A building that has withstood everything that has been thrown at it. Even revolution. Cordon would never say it out loud, but he felt that was him.

Turning his attention back to the vast expanse of the open water that separates Cuba from the United States, the only thing Cordon really misses about his life in America is Annie. It gives him some peace knowing she is only a boat ride across this beautiful, exceptionally calm blue water. Though he wishes he could see her whenever he wanted, he considers it a victory that he was able to talk her into leaving Chicago and moving down to Key West. He got her this close. And while Cordon is still reluctant to step foot on U.S. soil, knowing that he's wanted by the FBI, among others, he's made arrangements for her to slip into Cuba by boat to visit. Annie declined moving to Cuba, so this was the next best situation.

Filling his lungs with the salt air, Cordon takes pause. At this moment, it crystalizes for him that everything in his world is settled. It's a foreign feeling. Almost jarring. Six months ago, it would have scared the shit out of him. But here today, having seen Lucious, and knowing his sister is in a good place, Cordon is okay with that.

But he knows it won't last. Not for him. Chaos finds him. It just does, and always has.

Taking another deep breath of the damp salt air, with its hints of decay and hope, Cordon forces himself to accept this moment of serenity, alien as it is.

"Change doesn't mean it'll be bad," he says aloud as if to tamp down the insecurity that comes with simply enjoying the moment.

But deep down, Cordon knows that for a man like him, those words aren't usually true. For a man like him, change is ominous and inevitable. Damaging and dangerous. For a man like him, change amounts to pain.

And for a man like Cordon Finn, he's required to be the one delivering it.

THE END

THANK YOUS AND DEDICATIONS

Firstly – Pre-orders of Book Two in the CORDON FINN VENGEANCE SERIES: A BRUTAL MIX OF BLOOD AND GOLD is now available. A BRUTAL MIX OF BLOOD AND GOLD: CORDON FINN VENGEANCE SERIES: Book Two - Kindle edition by Baker, Bart. Literature & Fiction Kindle eBooks @ Amazon.com. The book will be released on August 1st! After Annie is kidnapped by a white supremacist group, Cordon is pulled back into a life of vengeance.

***

As always, thank you to my family. Joe, Isaiah, and Emmanuel, as well as my sister, in-laws, cousins, nieces, and nephews. And to my friends who also support my writing journey. I love you all and your support means the world to me. I have been blessed that for most of my adult life I've been able to pursue an occupation that I truly enjoy. I am so grateful for all the wonderful experiences and opportunities that writing has provided me throughout my life. And that this is a journey I can pursue for the rest of my life.

And thank you to all of you who read. For everyone who picks up one of my books, who will follow this series, I am humbled and appreciative. Because I'm a writer who surfs a lot of genres and likes to write from dark to light, I know not every book will be someone's cup of tea. But I am thrilled to have readers who have followed me all the way along and readers who find me along the way. It's wonderful when people come up to me and tell me they read one of my books.

In that vein, I am excited to bring the CORDON FINN VENGEANCE SERIES to life. I love writing Cordon. He's a great character. Flawed, damaged, violent, and aggressive, yet loyal, loving, with a sly sense of humor and of self. It's a joy to write in the action genre, and try and twist it a little bit, bringing this fresh character to life. I hope it's jarring and yet, oddly comfortable. I know this series will not be for everyone, so the readers that love it, I hope you'll stick with it. I promise that the journey with Cordon will be fascinating and exciting. And with Lucious and Annie continuing on in the books, there are plenty of great stories ahead. I'm also planning a spin-off with another really messed-up, damaged character, Vivian Tremaine. I think you'll find her and her son equally as interesting and fresh.

And while the CORDON FINN books are as dark and edgy as I can make them, I haven't abandoned writing more heartfelt stories filled with wonderful, funny characters and big emotions. My next on that list is WHEN THE RAIN FALLS. This book will touch your heart and there will be lots of laughter and plenty of tears.

Do me a favor, check out my website, www.bartvbaker.com, and add your name there (you don't need to put an address...just an email address there or at the bottom of the page where it says subscribe). I'm trying (trying being the prime word...) to put together a newsletter list, so I can contact readers when I have a new book or film project. Also, you can now follow me on Amazon. Go to one of my books, look for my photo and the box that says FOLLOW, and click it. Amazon will contact you when I have a new book release or new preorder! You can also follow me on Facebook. I have a page there as well, and CORDON FINN has its own Facebook page. Leave me contact information there, and I'll make sure you are on the mailing list, and know when new books are being released.

And PLEASE, if you read a book you like, SHARE the book on social media, talk about it, WRITE A REVIEW on Amazon or wherever you purchase the book. Especially for indie authors, this is how we build our audience and new readers find us. Join in and help your favorite authors get their books discovered by more and more readers.

Thanks so much! And keep reading!